The Temptation of Aaron Campbell

LISA SAMSON

D1125798

HARVEST HOUSE PUBLISHERS
Eugene, Oregon 97402

THE TEMPTATION OF AARON CAMPBELL

Copyright © 1996 by Lisa M.E. Samson
Published by Harvest House Publishers
Eugene, Oregon 97402

Library of Congress Cataloging-in-Publication Data
ISBN 1-56507-390-8

Samson, Lisa, 1964–
  The temptation of Aaron Campbell / Lisa Samson.
    p. cm.00. – (The highlanders series ; 3)
  ISBN 1-56507-390-8 (alk. paper)
  I. Title. II. Series.
PS3569.A46673T46 1996   95-31306
813'.54–dc20   CIP

Printed in the United States of America.

96 97 98 99 00 01 02 03 – 10 9 8 7 6 5 4 3 2 1

For my husband, Will.
You make me happy
When skies are gray.

Acknowledgments

To Bill Jensen of Harvest House, thanks upon thanks are due and respectfully given for hours of editing, burning up the phone lines from coast to coast, and plot-enhancing conversations over chips and salsa. "A faithful friend is the medicine of life."

I would like to extend my deepest thanks to Margie Brown of Harvest House for her wonderful job in the final stages of editorial, not just on this book but on the first two as well.

And to my friends and family I would like to give my sincere appreciation: Joy Ebauer, Lori Chesser, Gloria Danaher, Maria Danaher, Jennifer Hagerty, Chris Burkette, and Heather Gillot who, two years ago, all read this little book I then called *Honour*.

And, of course, to my husband, Will, who imagined with me the plot of this book as we traveled up Falls Road on a dark, windy September night. Thank you for giving to me tirelessly from the vast resources of your creativity. "I do love nothing in the world as well as you; is not that strange?"

Blessed be God forever.

Before the very forecourt and in the opening of the jaws of hell, Grief and avenging Cares have placed their beds, and wan Diseases and sad Old Age live there, and Fear and Hunger that urgest wrongdoing, and shaming Destitution, figures terrible to see, and Death and Toil.

–Virgil

Prologue

England, the plains of Salisbury
Winter Solstice, 1832

The hooded figures moved noiselessly over the misty plain. From their final destination a faint hum blackly emanated, intensifying with each step forward. It vibrated through the arcane congregation as the full moon shone in frigid strands over the mammoth stones laid ages ago by an obscure people. In the dense chill of the early morning a figure paused to pull his shroud more tightly about his shoulders. His breath stole in steamy clouds from beneath the hood. Now was the time for the ceremony... quickly, before the sun once again claimed victory over the deep night world.

The moon, large and low in the western night, soon would set.

In single file, they advanced to the center of the mystic circle. Stonehenge had been luring strange practitioners for a host of centuries, its original purpose now lost in the mists of time. But these came not to worship, offer sacrifice, or pray to a druid god that never was. They came to make a vow. A secret vow of honor. A vow sealed in blood.

Now in a circle, the hoods were pushed back. The leader, singularly robed in a crimson hue, lit a solitary candle. The dim light from the black taper eerily lit his patrician features from underneath, making him a skull-like wraith, a gruesome apparition.

"Gentlemen of the Brimstone, Brothers of Blood, reveal the implements of honor." The voice rasped hollowly, waiting to be someday filled with hell's final, eternal scream.

Whispers of sound floated up into the humid darkness as dirks hidden in the sinuses of the robes were drawn.

"Formation," he instructed. In immediate compliance, the black-shrouded figures formed two parallel lines, each man facing another. Some moved in eager compliance, others in mechanical obedience. One's steps sprung ardently into position.

"Draw blood."

Silence, as each drew back the fold of a sleeve and slashed his dirk diagonally across his right palm. There were no gasps, no quick inhalations as the blades sliced flesh.

"Display homage to Brimstone." Each figure raised the incised hand, palm facing the brother before him. Blood rolled down forearms in scarlet rivulets to drip slowly off their elbows.

"Upon your honor, Gentlemen of Brimstone, vow to your Brother of Blood that most secret promise."

One figure grabbed his partner's hand, eager to make contact. What an opportunity this might turn out to be!

Palm to palm the pledge was sealed in blood as well as honor, each man whispering to the man whose blood mingled with his own, "To thee I vow in secret, my Brother, that should you need one favor, I will do your bidding with no questions. My word of honor stands secure as now your blood flows within me. If I should fail, may Brimstone take my life, and may Satan, the master of Brimstone, doom my soul eternally."

Palm to palm the figures swayed as the leader chanted eerily in a tongue mankind had ceased to understand ages ago.

"Cease the flow!" Palms parted, sticking slightly as fresh blood had begun to dry.

"Present the sign." Each handed the other a playing card. The queen of spades. Upon it they had smeared their blood.

"Shrouds restored!" Hoods went over heads once again.

"Gentlemen of the Brimstone, proceed." Single file, they marched around the massive monoliths 13 times, the figure in red at the rear of the procession. The silence grew denser with each step, each crisp snap of the frozen, brown winter grass felt not heard. The wounds became slow and thick, pulling down the right side of their bodies with throbbing weight. Their booted feet grew heavier as each step led them further into a world of Stygian secrets and darkened nights black enough, long enough to last an entire lifetime. Questions filled their brains as the heavy, solemn covenant made their stomachs involuntarily recoil from its numberless possibilities.

The moon deserted Britain completely as the figures walked back over the plain. The first beam of light appeared on the horizon, and they shed their shrouds and donned their coats.

"Come on, chaps," said the leader, a perfectly normal-looking young man. "Let's go find something to eat. I'm starving."

The rest began to remove their shrouds.

"Terrible, wasn't it, what happened to Professor Mac-Leod?" a sturdy young man said to his compatriot, the eager participant.

"What?" The other young man tucked his garment into an unkempt ball.

"Didn't you hear? His house burned to the ground two nights ago with him inside."

"What of his daughter, Jane? Pretty little bit of a thing. Did she die as well?"

The other shook his head and swung himself up into his saddle. "They only found the remains of the professor. Jane MacLeod obviously escaped, but no one can find her anywhere."

With everyone mounted, they rode for the town of Salisbury. Now, with their shrouds tucked away in their saddlebags, they were just hungry college students in search of a good breakfast.

CHAPTER

1

Scotland
July 1842

Men and women were herded into the salon like a flock of overdressed poultry. The females clucked about their hair. The males strutted to and fro, showing off their finery in front of the hens. Every chair in the center was filled. Gentry from miles around had been invited to Mr. J. Hanawalt's grand new mansion for the much-talked-about private concert which was about to begin. Finally, just as the room began to grow uncomfortably warm, a violin's thin tone lay down upon the heavy air.

Another note harmonized with the stringed pitch, this one fuller and more clear than an instrument made by the hand of man could ever produce. It was the voice of a soprano, and all those present ceased to breathe for just a moment as it washed over them. It calmed some and caused others to yearn.

Looking down as she sang, Maria Rosetti wondered why she hadn't fallen in love with the man who sat directly in front of her. He was extremely handsome, fine of figure, and a powerful force in the House of Lords. Colin Campbell, the Duke of Argyll, was the most eligible man in Scotland—and in all of Britain, for that matter. He was also a widower, still grieving the loss of his wife, Anne, three years earlier.

A faint smile lifted the corners of his eyes as she glanced down at him. The eyes were an extraordinary greenish-blue that melted women and menaced enemies. Yet he was her friend. A male companion to dine with and worry over when the occasion warranted it. They had only one another when it came to close friendships, and each wanted nothing more than the platonic love they had shared so comfortably for so long.

The soiree was progressing smoothly, which was no more than she expected. Maria was pleased to have accepted the invitation of the wealthy textile manufacturer to sing this evening. London was so fetid in the summer that breathing in the crystalline air of the Lothian Hills of Scotland seemed a touch hedonistic when she thought of the singers back in the city. And Mr. Hanawalt was effusively grateful and most pleased that Britain's premier soprano had deigned to entertain those who had congregated in their silks and satins in his sumptuous salon. The fact that the Duke of Argyll, one of Scotland's powerful few, accepted his invitation was another feather in his cap. The corpulent man was fairly bursting with pride. "Not bad for the son of a tailor," he would say later as he kissed his wife good night.

The last note on the harpsichord floated off into wherever it is that musical notes hang for eternity, and the applause erupted. Maria smiled and swept a deep, airy curtsey before taking her seat next to Colin.

Mr. Hanawalt cleared his throat. "Thank you, Mrs. Rosetti, for the fine concert. Thank you, everyone else, for sharing in this auspicious occasion...."

"Goodness, one would think I was the queen or something!" Maria leaned over to whisper to Colin.

His singular chuckle, with one raise of his broad shoulders, told her the conspicuous spectacle of such a gathering was amusing to a simple man such as himself.

"... and refreshments will now be served in the garden where Mrs. Rosetti has graciously agreed to join us before going on to Edinburgh. She will be performing selections from 'The Marriage of Figaro' at the university on Sunday."

The crowd began to rise from their seats and vacate the overheated room for the coolness of the garden. Colin turned to Maria. "It was lovely, as is customary with you, Maria. And it is particularly wonderful to have you here in Scotland. Finally. About coming to mother's house party at Inveraray Castle the weekend after next, you haven't altered your decision, have you?"

"No. In fact, I am most looking forward to it." Her gray eyes lifted mischievously. "Will I finally meet your brother, the infamous Aaron Campbell?" In all actuality, Maria knew what problems Colin's twin brother never ceased to cause.

He ran a hand through his light-blond hair and spoke dryly. "I believe fortune has smiled upon your wish ... if you can call it that. It so happens that Mother's birthday is that Friday evening. Aaron hasn't neglected one yet. I'd wager my fortune that Aaron's body contained no heart at all if it wasn't for Mother. Still, she loves the rogue, and he's as fond of her as ever."

Maria rose from her chair, and Colin followed suit immediately, offering his arm. "Fortunately, everyone has a side to their personality that doesn't match the rest," she observed.

A man's voice vigorously interrupted them in ringing echoes. He slapped Colin heartily between the shoulder blades, startling both he and Maria. "Aaron Campbell! After all these years!"

Colin laughed with unexpected pleasure at the only friend of Aaron's that he cared for—an ordinary-looking man with extraordinary green eyes. His black hair curled in anarchy above his eyebrows. "Wrong again, Robert... after all these years! It's good to see you round about!"

Robert heartily shook Colin's hand. "It's been three years since I've last been home, and you two Campbells are still identical. I was hoping one of you would age more quickly." He winked conspiratorially at Maria. "This used to happen at least once a week at Oxford."

"Robert, I'd like you to meet my good friend, Mrs. Maria Rosetti. Maria, this is Robert Mayfield, an old Oxford chum of Aaron's. He's been sojourning in India for quite some time."

Robert lifted Maria's hand to his lips. "A pleasure to meet you, Mrs. Rosetti. Two weeks ago I was at the opera, and all I've heard about you is true. Your performance was *au fait.*"

"Thank you, Mr. Mayfield. Was it your first time at Covent Garden since you've returned?"

Robert slipped his hand into the pocket of his evening coat and pulled out a season pass, an oval carved out of ivory bearing the words *Royal Italian Opera at Covent Garden* in heavy black script.

"Yes, madam. But it certainly won't be my last."

"Good. I hope you'll join Colin sometime in his box."

Colin nodded in agreement. "Certainly, Robert. Just do not bring along that scoundrel brother of mine with you! By the way, have you discovered where he is staying? I had heard he left London for a while." Colin remembered with an inner wince the check he had signed with his own hand three months ago bailing his brother out of debt once again.

"Word has it in London he's summering somewhere around Edinburgh with the rest of our little crowd. I thought maybe he would be here."

"Now, Robert, what would a knave like my brother be doing at a soiree? Come to think of it, what are *you* doing here?" Colin asked without malice. "This surely is not your kind of party."

Robert Mayfield smiled charmingly at Maria. "He's right, you know. It's not. I just came to hear you sing and to taste some of Mr. Hanawalt's claret. I have heard he has one of the finest cellars in Scotland." His eyes sparkled with mischief, and he bowed without apology. "I am what I am, m'lord. I'd better go look for Aaron down at the Pigeon."

"Yes, do that. Where else would he be but entertaining devils unaware at one of Edinburgh's most disreputable establishments?"

"And with *your* money!" Robert laughed.

"Aye, with my money. But frankly, Robert, I feel rather sorry for him. He is a mere ten minutes younger than I and is compelled to perform a subjective role. Who is to say whether or not I would be the same way had I not been prepared to inherit the title my entire life?"

"He's still a rogue, no matter how graciously you try and explain his tendencies away, and he'll always be a rogue! But it's big of you to look at it that way, m'lord. I'd better find him before he finds himself in too much trouble." Robert bowed to Maria, then Colin. "A pleasure seeing you after all these years, Colin. Mrs. Rosetti, I trust we shall meet again."

The gardens beckoned and, when a crowd gathered around Maria, Colin sat on a wooden bench, hidden by a rose arbor, to watch her in anonymity. He wondered why, in the three years since Anne's death, he had never fallen in love with Maria.

She was the possessor of a feline beauty, with gray eyes that slanted like a cat's. Small white teeth were framed by full, smiling lips, and her skin was so fair and clear that powder would have only masked nature's perfection. True, she was intriguing with that raven hair with its one thick streak of white that began at her right temple. Add that to the fact that she never wore anything but blue, and she seemed quite mysterious to those who knew not her heart. And not many knew her heart.

Tiny she was, yet her figure was that of a woman. Colin's eyes crinkled nostalgically as he thought of Maria and Anne together. The young duchess had befriended the opera singer on the opening night of her debut in England five years ago. Anne had been so sweet and open, Maria seemingly worldly-wise and slightly hardened, but the two had found a soul mate in one another. He never forgot the time he found them sitting in the drawing room stuffing chocolate truffles into their mouths one after the other.

"We couldn't resist any longer, my love," Anne, as small as Maria, had chimed. Both had sworn off sweets together only the day before.

Perhaps in some way Maria kept Anne alive for him. And as long as she did that, he could never love her in the same way he had loved Anne, could he? He couldn't imagine defiling Anne's memory by loving another. Besides, Maria had made it perfectly clear as soon as Anne began to get matchmaking ideas that she would never marry again.

Maria was disarmingly matter-of-fact about it. "The first time was simply deplorable. I have no wish to tempt the fates and end up with another artist like Leo Rosetti to sober up every night."

"But, Maria," Anne had pleaded, "not all men are like that."

"No, you're right. But you found the only exception, Anne."

Anne had hugged her closely then. "You are a dear. I just want you to be as happy as I am, that's all."

Colin shook his head as the thought of his wife transitioned from happy to painful. He sipped half-heartedly on his claret and enjoyed the breeze, hoping that no one would find him in the rose arbor until it was time to go.

"Colin, wake up!"

Maria stood above him, laughing quietly. He immediately rose to his feet.

"Don't inform me I actually was sitting here asleep!"

"Yes, you were. Your mouth was wide open, and your snore could be heard all over the garden!"

"No."

"You're right. No, I don't think anybody even knew you were here. You'll be pleased to know you escaped the entire evening without having to make one ounce of small talk. It's time to go already."

Colin sighed with relief. "Good. I only accepted the invitation because I had not seen you for a month, Maria. Would you permit me to drive you to your hotel in Edinburgh?"

"Permit you? I was counting on it. A thatcher said he would give me a ride in his straw wagon, but I told him I could find transportation elsewhere. We'd better hurry, unless you want to sit talking with Mr. Hanawalt until 2 A.M. I've already had my trunks loaded into your carriage."

He suddenly recalled Maria's addiction to fashion. "Will there be room for us?"

"Of course, darling. You sit on the trunks, and I'll perch on the hatboxes."

Within minutes they were on their way to Edinburgh. The Lothian Hills undulated before them, the work of ancient subterranean giants turning in their sleep. Maria leaned back into the comfortable cushions, laid her head upon Colin's shoulder, and dozed off. Then she suddenly lifted her head.

"You know," she said as if she had been thinking about it all evening, "I'll wager I could tell Aaron and you apart."

He looked very doubtful. "I do not imagine so. There were times that even my father could not tell the difference."

"What about your mother?"

"Yes. But she is the only one. In any case, Mother is a bit batty, Maria. I would not take that as encouragement, if I were you. You will see—you will not be able to find a distinction."

"It will be in the eyes, Colin. You can't live a life such as the one Aaron is living without it showing up somewhere. It will be in the eyes, mark my words."

• • •

The pub was dim and dusty. Glasses clinked together almost rhythmically as each man worked his way steadily to blanket inebriation. With each tick of the pendulum on the mantel clock, the din grew greater. The innkeeper and his wenches became busier, almost running from bar to table. Behind a partition near the back of the room, a table of gentlemen sat quietly, intent on the hand before them.

A handsome blond man unexpectedly slammed his cards

on the table and uttered an expletive. "George Lindsay, may your fingers go to rot with the devil and his angels! One more hand like this one, and I'll know you've stacked the deck against me. I fold, gentlemen." He placed his cigar back between his teeth.

The other men shook their heads humorously and continued. It was the first time Aaron Campbell folded that evening. He was infamous for his tenacity, if not his wisdom. Just then another man appeared from behind the divider.

"Robert Mayfield!" Aaron yelled, alarming no one. "Come over here, you worthless blackguard!"

Robert smoothly pulled up a chair as if he had seen his friends only moments before. "Flattery will get you nowhere, Aaron. Deal me in. We'll reminisce later."

The cards swashed onto the table, each man picking them up as the deal progressed. After a while Robert put down his cards and stared at Aaron. "You've folded three times in the last hour, Aaron. Your brother's preaching sessions must finally be working on you. The groveling is surely getting hard."

"Ha! All in a day's work. Colin doesn't bother me, my friend. The only time I think about my brother is when I'm in trouble."

"I see. So he's on your mind a lot?" Robert replied with a smirk.

"Just deal the cards, you lout."

CHAPTER

2

Inveraray, Scotland
Nine days later

Colin conquered the front steps of Inveraray Castle in threes. Bareheaded and coatless, he looked far younger than his 32 years as he ran through the double doors that were left open to catch the Highland breezes. He felt the years brought on by political gaming and all the stress that went with the life he had chosen drain away. Lady Margaret Campbell stood at the foot of the stairway directly in front of him.

He swung her up into his arms. "Mother! I'm home. And the city is hours behind me!" Gently putting her down, he eyed her with loving skepticism. "You look unique as always."

Margaret Campbell, a woman of unconventional ways, had always been the talk of the clan. An attentive lady of the manor, the people of Argyllshire and its many villages viewed her as more than a little peculiar—downright eccentric, in fact. Her flaming red hair, laced with white, frizzed frantically about her face and shoulders. The rounded face with the large green eyes was quietly beautiful, but the way she looked upon the world with raised eyebrows made her appear in a constant state of mild alarm. Average in height, her slim figure was squarishly boyish, so much so that she took to wearing men's clothes when no visitors were present. She rode in breeches also, much to the utter dismay of the village women and the open amusement of the men.

Lady Margaret spoke in a high, musical voice—a bird-like singsong that neither assaulted nor soothed. "Thank you, Colin, my love. I was just this moment having a talk with Dorian, and he tells me it would be quite impossible to make a life-size topiary out of the boxwood in the garden."

"Of what, Mother?"

"Why, Henry VIII, of course."

Colin winced. "For once I agree with the man. What in heaven's name do you want with a topiary of Henry VIII?"

She tapped her fingers on her chin in time with the foot that seemed to move every time her brain had something worth considering. "I'm not sure. He was just so big and round, I thought he would lend himself well to that huge boxwood out by the pavilion."

"Mother! I've been attending to that old bush since I was eight years old. How could you even consider transforming it into Henry VIII? Our ancestors would be quite indignant if they knew we were paying homage to a Tudor, of all people!"

"Yes, yes, quite right, dear. As usual. Now, let's see, I must attend to the food for the masquerade ball Saturday night. You run along, love. I'm sure you'll find somewhere to play about." And she was off in the direction of the great kitchens, scurrying in her tan riding breeches, snowy shirt, and polished black boots.

Margaret Campbell had never really taken heed to the fact that her children had grown up. She had told them innumerable times that she refused to relinquish her full role as their mother, and doting on them was an indulgence with which she would never cease to please herself. Colin hurried up the stairs to his room where his valet, Jamie, was laying out his clothes. Jamie MacKenzie had been with him ever since he left for Oxford.

"Are ya goin' to garden a bit, m'lord?" Jamie asked in his broad Scottish brogue.

"Yes, Jamie, I believe I shall. I want to feel the cool soil under my fingers and try to disregard all thoughts of London, Edinburgh, and every other place I'd rather not be but all too frequently seem to find myself."

Jamie bent down in front of Colin's leather trunk, threw back the heavy lid, and began to unpack. "I dinna blame ya there, m'lord. There's nothin' so good as gettin' out with the essentials God gave us: the soil, the sun, the rain. I'd love to be outside m'self."

"You go on then, Jamie. I am certainly capable of dressing by myself. I'd rather, actually, but then you know that. I have an idea. Go down to the kitchens and ask Mrs. Grey to pack a picnic for you and Bonnie. I'll tell Mrs. Rider that Bonnie is free for the remainder of the afternoon, as are you." Colin knew Jamie and Bonnie, a parlor maid, had taken notice of each other last year.

Jamie bowed and hurried for the door. "Thank ya, m'lord. Thank ya!"

Shortly thereafter the duke was out in the sun, digging and pulling at tender green plants and tenacious weeds. He loved the garden, the feel of the earth under his hands teeming with life he couldn't see. The heat of the sun on the top of his head burned into his brain a clearer, more natural picture of the way the world was created to be.

He glanced up toward the castle. What a thrill it was to see it each time he came home! A castle of large proportions, its symmetry was pleasing and carefully planned. Built by his famous ancestor Archibald Campbell in the 1700s, Colin loved its four turrets and beautiful Gothic windows. In the back courtyard garden he could see the fountain, sunlight playing in dappled flares off the water. Roses, lilies, and clematis were blooming, and the fragrant perfume wafted lightly over to his plot of garden on the other side of the formal brick wall. Ivy grew up its sides, providing a haven for various humming insects. Sight... sound... smell... temperature. Right then all four were at their zenith. And Maria would be arriving tomorrow.

As would Aaron.

His stomach became heavy at the thought of seeing his brother again. Colin thrust his trowel into the moistened soil, hacking a weed neatly and thoroughly in two.

• • •

The closed carriage drove slowly up Inveraray Castle's long drive. The lush green lawns soaked in the noontime sunshine, and Maria drew in her breath as she stared out of the small window at the picturesque, fairy-tale castle. It was her first trip to Colin's duchy. And Argyllshire was far more beautiful in the summer than anything London could have afforded just then.

Her eye caught the brightness of his hair as the sun bounced off each golden strand. He waited on the steps until the carriage came to a halt. Attending to her himself, he helped her down with a firm ease and ushered her into the magnificent entry hall. Floored in green marble, the cherry wainscoted hall was spectacular. The stone stairs, ornately carved in an ivy motif, curved up the right side to the castle's upper floors.

The gray eyes grew round. "Why, it's beautiful, Colin,"

Maria whispered, staring around her. "What a wonderful place to have grown up."

A high, quaky voice shrilly made its way across to her. "Thank you, my dear." Maria looked in its direction and took in Colin's mother. "So this is your new friend, Colin?" Maria looked at him, eyes amused and questioning.

"Uh, yes, Mother. I'd like you to meet Maria Rosetti. My good friend. You remember, don't you? The diva?"

"Why, certainly. Please forgive me. I haven't been down to London in years. It's a pleasure to know you, Mrs. Rosetti."

She tried not to laugh. "Please, call me Maria."

"Fine, Maria. You must come with me sometime for a walk in the garden. There's a beautiful boxwood that's just dying to become Henry VIII. Colin just doesn't see the true inspiration of such a noble idea. Maybe we could convince him of it." She turned to go back in the direction of the library. "It was a pleasure meeting you, Maria. Make yourself at home. I'm sure you and Colin will find plenty of things with which to amuse yourselves!"

When the door clicked shut, Colin and Maria burst into laughter.

"I told you she was unique."

"That was an understatement. And I believe 'batty' was the phrase you used, sir."

"Well, yes, I did. Let me show you to your room. I chose a special one for you. It was originally decorated by the wife of my ancestor who built this house. It's in one of the turrets, and the view is quite spectacular. She had it done for herself. Probably to get away from him. He could be most overbearing, according to family history."

They walked up the grand staircase, down a long hall, and up a spiraled second flight.

Colin proudly flung open the door. The room was wonderful, done completely in shades of blue. "It's perfect, don't you think? It will match everything you brought to wear!"

"Oh yes, darling." Her eyes scanned the large curved room, taking in the great canopied bed hung in blue drapery embroidered with birds. A chaise looked out over the garden, and there were doors with glass panes leading out onto a balcony—a recent addition to the room, Colin said. Over the fireplace hung a portrait of a lovely woman. She was smiling gently, her dark-blue eyes amused. Honeyed-brown curls hung down to the back of her knees. In her left hand was a bouquet of wildflowers. She wore a navy-blue gown decorated with tartan. Maria was entranced by the peaceful beauty of the Highland woman.

"Who was she?" she asked, not able to take her eyes off the portrait.

"She was Anne's great-great-grandmother. Her name was Jenny. She was the lady of the chieftain of the Maclachlans, who fought under Bonnie Prince Charlie."

"She looks like Anne. Didn't they want the portrait back once Anne passed away?"

"They said I could keep it for as long as I needed it."

"Well, they certainly are a nice family. I remember well when Anne's parents visited London the year before she passed away."

"Yes. We are still in close contact. There is much I want to show you, though," he said, changing the subject of necessity. "Why don't you get freshened up and come down for lunch?"

Three footmen entered the room with Martha, Maria's personal maid, clucking disapprovingly behind them. "Do be careful. That box contains Mrs. Rosetti's favorite hat."

She pushed a stray lock of black back into her severe bun. "Watch that trunk there, mister, or her ointments will spill all over her linens! Honestly!" For times such as this, Martha had been born.

The men, clad in deep-red livery, looked up at the ceiling in exasperation, but did as they were bid. The duke smiled. "Well, I see that you are definitely taken care of here. Are you sure you brought enough clothes?"

"I must keep my standards up. So run along, Colin Campbell, before I assign you to the ranks of most men who wouldn't know a well-cut gown from a pastry bag. I *knew* there was a reason I wanted to keep my widowhood intact!" She gave a wave of her hand, dismissing him, to the shock of his servants. He laughed in their direction. "You'd better stay out of her way, men. I hear Mrs. Rosetti can be a bit of a tartar."

"Women," a young man named Joe muttered as he walked into the hallway. "They're *all* tartars if ya ask me."

It felt good to Colin to be home among real folks once again, and he laughed to himself as he hurried down the steps to his study.

· · ·

"How about a tour of the garden?" the duke queried Maria as he laid down his napkin. They were just finishing a light luncheon of Scotch broth and homemade bread. The other guests would be arriving in a few hours.

"That would be lovely, darling. I'll get my parasol."

Soon they were ambulating lazily around the formal gardens. Colin stayed full in the sun, while Maria peered out at the collection of riotous hues from beneath the shade of her umbrella.

He pointed at the other side of the wall. "I would take you over to my wee bit of earth, but corn and tomatoes aren't very interesting, I'm afraid."

"You grow vegetables? I always thought you grew roses or flowers. Not vegetables!"

"I only grow what I can eat. Except for that boxwood, of course, who's simply dying to become Henry VIII!"

"I'd love to see your garden, Colin. I don't know, just thinking about beans and parsnips puts me in the mood to sing." She glanced at him sideways, smiling like a tart, and began to sing a popular little tune in a dance-hall voice.

"I should get you there promptly before MacCall–he's our head gardener–hears you. He's the most devout Presbyterian you've ever seen!" Colin offered her his arm and led her outside. They made their way slowly over to his garden. Along the way he answered all her questions about the flowers and shrubbery they passed. (Yes, that plant with the smoky-pink flower blooming underneath the white oak was called astilbe, and those bluish flowers were campanula, commonly known as bluebells.) Maria could see that Colin was in touch with the earth, willing nature to take him away from the responsibilities his life as one of Scotland's 16 members of the House of Lords demanded. By the time they reached his plot outside the garden wall, she was carrying a large, colorful bouquet.

"What do you think of when you come to work here, darling?" Maria asked lightheartedly as she fiddled with the long leaf of a daylily.

"This may sound foolish, Maria. But sometimes I think about children when I am out here. I always thought I would bring a son or daughter here with me and teach them about God's handiwork. It is nice, the solace my hobby brings. Yet it was meant to be shared."

"One cannot always tell, Colin. Perhaps someday you will find another wife."

Her tone had softened, and his eyes searched hers.

Maria continued. "The season is almost finished in London. You'd better get a move on, my friend. There are lots of sweet young things just dying for a duke."

He almost felt disappointed at her words. But he shot her a sideways glance of friendly exasperation as he handed her a butter bean.

"So, when does your brother arrive?"

Colin shook his head. "We just received word that he is not coming. I suppose Mother does not even make it onto his list of things worthy anymore."

"Oh.dear," Maria pouted, "and I was so looking forward to meeting him."

"For the life of me, I do not know why, Maria. He looks exactly like me and acts completely opposite. Just let your imagination wander a bit, and you will know all there is to know."

"If all I hear is true, I'm sure you are right," she said wryly.

Colin ran a hand through his hair. "What have you heard now?"

"Nothing new," she said quickly, reassuring him. "The story of his latest escapade has finally circulated around London. You know, his refusal to pay off his debt to the dowager duchess of Winston."

"Of course I remember. How could I possibly forget? It cost me a thousand pounds! A woman that old should not be allowed to gamble." He was a bit irritated. "There is too much of a pity factor on the part of the younger player!"

They sat together on the bank. Colin looked thoughtfully into the distance. He thought back to Aaron as a lad.

Riding alone over the hills. Always running away. Things hadn't changed.

"Tell me I am not crazy, Maria. Tell me he has not made me the biggest fool in London and Scotland as well. Am I wrong to sweep up after him the way I do?"

"That's a question only you can answer, darling."

He nodded. "On the one hand, if I continue paying, he will continue living after the same fashion. On the other, if I quit aiding him, in what state will he eventually find himself? He would be hunted down by some cutthroat, no doubt. My brother does not know the Savior, Maria. How can I leave him desolate, knowing all the while what death will bring to him?"

Maria put her arms around him. She soothed him by humming softly, beautifully, as he looked over the deep water of the loch.

"I love my brother more than anyone else on earth. We're from the same womb, the same seed. We used to read each other's minds, enjoy the same things, love each other wholeheartedly. We always knew when the other had been hurt. I now wonder if he even thinks about me at all."

The left half of his face was shadowed as he continued; the right half was in full sunlight, and his eye squinted against the luminary onslaught. "Aaron saved my life when we were nine. He was always physically stronger and more reckless than I was, and we had a contest to see who could swim the farthest. We swam out about 20 yards from shore, then worked our way down the loch. He was a hundred feet ahead of me when a cramp overtook me. I tried desperately to rub it out, but could not. Finally I cried out, knowing it was just a matter of moments before I went under. Aaron was only a few feet away. He instinctively had known something was wrong, and had turned back. It did not take him long to swim me to the shore. After the cramp subsided, we walked back to the castle with our arms over each other's shoulders. He hugged me that night saying, 'Losing you would be like cutting away half of all that makes me who I am.'"

"What happened that Aaron was driven so completely away?"

"My father passed away our last year at Oxford. As soon as the title was mine, Aaron changed. It was as if he had never really prepared himself for the inevitable."

Maria tried to be encouraging. "I know several young men who went off to Oxford and abandoned the beliefs of their families for those of their teachers and their friends. It happens all the time. They come back eventually."

"Well, those who are impressionable to begin with are doubly so when they are set loose for the first time. But it was more than that. We were too close for him to have drifted away for no real reason other than the wrong set of friends."

"Keep praying for him, darling, like you did for me. Your brother sounds so hardened, but if he is one of the flock, he will turn to the Shepherd."

"Sometimes—usually when I'm walking late at night—I'll pass by a group of men, like Aaron, bent on living life on their own terms. They're laughing and smiling, sometimes even singing. But when they look up at me, their eyes play traitor to their merriment."

"It was not different for me. We must pray for your brother, Colin."

"Aye, Maria, we must. We must ask God to do whatever it takes to bring Aaron to Himself."

As the blue waters shifted before their eyes, Colin and Maria poured out their petition before the Savior. Maria knew what God could do. Colin and Anne had begun praying for her when she met them during her first run at Covent Garden. It was only last year that she had taken the final step and had claimed the Savior for her own.

"I suppose we should be getting back," Colin said quietly. A feeling of heavy importance, of prayer meant to be before the world's beginning, permeated them.

"I feel as if I could stay here forever." Maria's eyes shone with the love she bore for Colin. Strong Colin. Honorable Colin. Patient Colin. A man, surely, after God's own heart. A youthful warrior. And he needed her just then. Not as a man needed a woman, but as one troubled human needs another. She was happy to be his confidante, the only person with whom he let his mask of firm power slip.

They stayed seated for another hour, enjoying the simple fact that they inhabited each other's world.

• • •

The houseguests, nearly 50 of them, began arriving late that afternoon. Colin, a seasoned host, was at his best: witty, intelligent, and charming. Maria was proud to be by his side.

Dinner was an elegant affair. The gentlemen were dressed in evening suits, all looking remarkably similar. The women shone on the arms of their mates in true Victorian fashion, the physical manifestations of their husbands' wealth and position. A glittering, festive air circulated from the animated conversations and reunions of those who had not seen one another for quite some time. Laughter flowed as freely as the wine, and Maria sparkled in the midst of it all in her evening regalia, complete with the magnificent set of sapphires she had purchased only a month before. She eyed the women around her and suddenly became aware that she had more in common, as a lady of self-means, with the men. It pleased her.

The food received praise from even the most difficult gourmands present. Twelve courses made their way in front of the guests before the ladies left the men to their port. Eel soup, sole, dressed crab, Davenport fowl, and roast duck were among the offerings, as well as dressed beetroot, stewed celery, asparagus, and other fresh vegetables. Colin was quite pleased at the compliments he heard concerning the food he had grown, although he didn't say where it had come from until Maria praised his gardening prowess en masse. After the port had been drunk, the group filed together into the salon. Maria was delighted to give a small concert. Lady Margaret accompanied her proficiently on the harpsichord.

The next morning a hunting party embarked. Maria, not much of a horsewoman and always one to feel sorry for the fox, opted to stay at the house with some of the other ladies. They joined her around the piano and sang.

"Sometimes I do believe it's so much more fun without the men around," one local baroness sighed knowingly. Afterward they drank tea in the garden, feeling their youth slip easily back in place as they chatted and spoke of childbirth, children, and living with a man. Soon, however, the party returned, and a large breakfast awaited them.

They whiled away the day in smaller parties. Some played tennis, some chess, others declared a walk over the heathered hills would suit them perfectly. All too soon it was time to get ready for the masquerade ball.

CHAPTER

3

The gown flamed with life. A captivating masterpiece of needlework and craftsmanship, it seemed to float out of the wardrobe by its own volition. Martha merely guided its burning flight by the padded hanger.

"Oh, ma'am," she said in awe, "it's bewitching. Utterly bewitching. A phoenix! You'll be a beautiful phoenix. And I do say it'll seem strange to see you in another color beside blue."

"When it comes to finding beautiful costumes, Martha, I definitely work in the right place. The seamstresses at the opera are amazing!"

Maria examined the dazzling orange-red gown, and it thrilled her afresh. Trimmed in red, orange, and gold feathers, it blazed with a definable heat. A shallow triangle of feathers formed the wings, the apex attached to the small of her back, the side points coming forward to jeweled wristlets where feathers cascaded onto the backs of her hand. Rubies and feathers adorned the scooped neckline and the small cap sleeves which stopped just over the edge of her shoulders. Around her throat and at her ears was a breathtaking set of ruby jewelry. Flaming feathers cascaded in her black hair. The crimson satin half mask was adorned with ruby and topaz rhinestones and feathers.

Once ready, Maria started for the door. "Did you find out what the duke would be wearing, Martha?"

"Yes, miss. Jamie said he would be dressed as a cossack."

"Good. Our costumes will complement one another nicely. And . . . I shall know who he is immediately."

Martha waved the comment away. "As if you wouldn't anyway, ma'am. He'll be the tallest man there. These Campbells really seem to grow them big!"

"That's true, Martha. Well, thank you for finding out for me, all the same."

Martha's dark eyes lit up in a rare smile. "Anytime, ma'am. I do enjoy a bit of subterfuge every now and again."

Maria worked her way down several staircases to the ballroom. Lady Margaret stopped her at the bottom of the stairs. She was an enchanting Marie Antoinette, complete with a guillotine mark—a blood-red ribbon tied around her neck. Her white skirts were so wide and her silver, intricately coiffed wig so tall that Maria wondered whether or not she would make it through the ballroom doors. But knowing Lady Margaret, she would manage somehow.

"Colin had to see to an emergency in the village. He's just like his father!" She seemed a bit more normal tonight, even in that wild getup. "He said he'll return as quickly as he can and that you should just enjoy yourself until he gets back."

Margaret scurried off toward the direction of the kitchens, obviously with a mission in mind. The weekend so far had proceeded without a hitch, thanks to her brilliant powers of organization. Maria shrugged her shoulders and walked toward the party, almost surprised that Colin's mother hadn't shown up as Napoleon, or—heaven help them all—Robert the Bruce.

The ballroom was surrounded by a multitude of glass-paned doors, leading both to the outside gardens and to the inside hallways. Candlelight and violin music spilled forth. Laughter mingled therewith, creating an unreal atmosphere of carefree gaiety and easy wealth. Maria sauntered in, comfortable with her surroundings. She had been to more parties in her lifetime than she would care to count. They were all alike, she had decided long ago. And when each man and woman present returned to their everyday life and all its disappointments, they would forget about what it had been like to be someone else for a night. Perhaps it was why the masquerade was so popular. It gave one entertainment, anonymity... the chance to throw off self. And one could do it without the aid of liquor or casual affairs. It was a guilt-free, lucid oblivion.

The black-and-white-squared marble floor shone with fresh wax. Candle-lit chandeliers blazed amidst the oil-lit sconces on the walls. Everything glittered and shone as the numerous mirrors reflected the thousands of flickering flames. Jewelry sparkled, crystal shimmered. Bouquets of gardenias were in manifest abundance, perfuming the room from their Chinese lacquered vases perched atop small Doric and Corinthian columns. The dancing had already begun.

The costumes varied widely. Only one Cleopatra could be seen among the guests. There were several Marc Antonys swishing their togas around the perimeter of the floor. Many women took on historical persona. Catherine the Great, Queen Elizabeth, and Helen of Troy were laughing by the punch bowl, presumably discussing queenly matters. Some women were flowers or animals. A beautiful orchid waltzed by in the arms of a Greek philosopher. One lady was dressed as a hawk, the blue-black of her smooth tresses matching her simple, yet extraordinarily cut black gown. Paris, no doubt.

The music lilted in her direction, adhering first to her heart where it had always been felt more strongly than anyplace else. Her brain then siphoned from her heart a goodly portion of the waltz's rhythms, melody, and harmonies, and she began to sway in three-quarter time. *One-two-three, one-two-three*, the tempo vibrated through her. Seconds later her body took over the bounties of Strauss' genius that her brain had garnered from her soul. Her feet demanded the strong rhythm pattern. Her vocal chords stole the melody. And the harmony, each part, soothed her inner ear—that portion which seems connected directly to the brain.

A handsome cossack entered the ballroom through the garden door.

Maria sauntered in his direction, her hips swaying gently in time to the music. He was looking about him.

She tucked her arm through his and squeezed playfully. "Darling! You've returned. I'm positively dying to get out on the dance floor." Her eyes were feverish, heady with the mood of the ball, as they looked up at him.

Returning her mood measure for measure, his eyes lit up with a spark, and he spoke in a voice that would soften the hardest of hearts. "Then, may I have the pleasure of a dance with a true bird of paradise?"

"First let me have a look at you." Both of his hands she took and pulled away to examine him in his fancy cossack outfit. The flowing white shirt he wore under a beautifully embroidered vest. The red pants which cinched his small waist made him seem a little larger than usual. The pant legs were tucked into polished black boots. A black half mask covered the upper portion of his face.

"You look wonderful, darling," Maria said mildly as she stared up at the smiling mouth. He suddenly put his arms around her waist, pulling her closer than he had ever done.

"And you are stunning, my little phoenix. Absolutely beautiful. You couldn't possibly realize what your beauty is doing to me right now."

Maria looked at him, more than a little shocked. Colin never spoke thus. Had never even hinted at such emotions lying underneath his normally placid exterior. She suddenly laughed, realizing he was joking. And glad of it.

"Colin Campbell, no pretense with me, please. I know it's you underneath that mask. Those passionate words are wasted."

"I hope not." He smiled, and she realized for the first time what a beautiful mouth he had.

"Then maybe it's the outfit that's making you feel hot-blooded. You know what they say about the Russians!"

"They have nothing on the Scots, fair lady. We Celts have always hungered for more than just delicacies of the palate."

She laughed. "Ha, m'lord. You should go to Italy sometime. Don't forget I was married to an Italian. The first three months of my marriage were about all the fire one small person like myself can handle for a lifetime. So," she changed the subject as he whirled her onto the floor, almost lifting her off her feet, "your business in the village didn't take as long as you expected?"

He looked away as she sought his eyes. "No. It was quickly handled."

Maria didn't much care about his business; she just wanted things back to normal. This didn't seem to be Colin's usual idea of a joke. And she was more than a little uncomfortable at being held so close.

They joined the waltz. Colin's hand spread upon the small of her back, his fingers curling around the side of her waist. They moved lightly over the silky satin, drawing her ever closer. Slower, slower they danced, as the music kept up its lively pace. Something strange was happening to Maria as she felt Colin's thighs moving against her own. The feathers of her costume, along her cheek and neckline, caressed her softly with each exhalation that whispered from his lips.

She looked up at him, but his eyes were closed, his face affected, yet calm. *What is happening?* she thought as they danced slower still. Indeed, the rest of the room seemed to have faded into oblivion. Her mind clouded with feeling, physical passion, heat. But the confusion remained. She wasn't supposed to feel this way. And about Colin? Certainly not!

The music stopped, finally, after they did. They simply stood, Colin with his eyes closed, holding her close. Maria, head against his chest, was breathing heavily, her feelings physically pleasing but emotionally disturbing. When at last he spoke, she glanced up quickly, coming out of her stupor.

The blue eyes glowed beneath the black mask with a fire she had never seen in them before. "Come," he said huskily, "I have a mind to take some air out in the garden."

Maria agreed, glad to get out of the room, away from so many strangers. And yet, more than flowers had gotten their start in a garden.

Sitting next to an arbor blooming with climbing red roses, well out of view of the ballroom, Colin took her hand and pressed it to his lips. Turning it over, he kissed her palm.

"Colin?" She pulled off her mask. "Are you all right?" This burning feeling in her stomach was disconcerting.

"No, Maria, I'm not," he said forcefully, removing his as well. "It's been three years since Anne died. I thought, truly, that there could be no other woman for me. And now that you've taken a decided place in my life, have shared my fears and my hopes, I've finally come to realize that I do want to love again. I want to love you, Maria. I want to kiss you, Maria. To feel you tremble at the craving I can diffuse through your body when my lips caress yours. I want to show you what loving a man can be."

He took her chin in one hand, the other curved around the side of her throat, his thumb resting against her slamming pulse. And he bent his head toward her mouth.

She pushed against his loving advances. "No, Colin." Pleading with him not to kiss her, she felt like crying out. The strange fires long ago extinguished were flaring to life with a vengeance. She had no idea what to do, how to respond. It had been so long. And yet she couldn't seem to take her eyes off his mouth, the sensual curve to his bottom lip.

"No, Colin," she said again. "Not like this. Not here."

Jarring her back to the temporal, the blue-green eyes scanned her face, relishing in her sweet discomfort.

"Yes, Maria. It's time for us to awaken. It's time we love each other."

His head descended and his lips found hers. The heat of his mouth made her whimper. In spite of the fact that her heart was turning within, her hands found their way to his blond hair, grabbing soft handfuls as she kissed him back with a passionate vengeance—a vengeance at herself for being so foolish right now. And yet she felt powerless to stop. He intoxicated her. Left her wanting more and wanting nothing. Confusion reigned. Why now? Why this way? And what had taken him so long?

"Maria!"

Through the haze of desire her name was called. It sounded familiar, haunting almost, and so distant. Impossible it was to pull herself from the two-dimensional world of passion, the feverish drunkenness caused by the continued pressure of his mouth as he deepened the kiss, the trails of heat his fingers were leaving on her neck.

"Maria!"

Again it was called, closer now. Her eyes opened, trying to bring the light of complete consciousness into the foggy world to which she had succumbed with delicious ease. She could feel the warmth of him, smell the sweetness of his breath as he crushed her to him even more closely, and slanted his mouth across hers. But the voice came again, and she heard the intruder brush against a hedge, and a footstep on the path next to her.

"Maria." It came again. And she recognized the voice now as she pulled away. But it was too late.

He had seen them.

"Aaron!" Colin said, voice angry as he placed a protective hand on Maria's elbow. "What do you think you're doing?"

Aaron Campbell smiled broadly and shrugged. "Just thought I'd see if I could play my brother the duke convincingly. She fell for it." His words were so matter-of-fact, Maria felt the icy hand of betrayal mercilessly squeeze her innards. Her cheeks flushed a deeper crimson, reddened with mortification at having been so easily carried into a world of pleasure she had shunned for years. And pleasurable it was—that was the most detrimental part about the passionate exchange. The reality of what had happened sounded throughout her entire being like a high note. Aaron winked and smiled with a self-indulged amusement. Ever the actress, Maria hid her feelings.

"Colin, I'm sorry. I thought he was . . ." her voice filtered off. *You*, she was about to say.

Colin drew himself up tall and strong. "Aaron, I will see you in my study. *Now.*"

"*That* sounds like an order," he said dryly. Yet the amusement he felt at the situation was evident in the grin he didn't bother suppressing. "Well, I suppose my brother the *duke* has spoken." He bowed in mockery and pushed by Colin as his feet led him back to the castle. With each thump of his retreating boots on the pathway, Maria felt herself returning to normal. Whatever normal was now.

"Well, my dear Maria, you have finally met the darker side of the Campbell twins. I am sorry he put you through that. There is nothing I can say to excuse what he has done."

"Oh, Colin, I don't know what to say. . . ."

"You do not have to say a thing. I'm sorry I overreacted. I didn't expect to see you with him. Of course, you're a grown woman, and who you choose to kiss in gardens..."

"I really thought he was you." Maria decided honesty was best, considering the delicate nature of the circumstances. "And I am truly sorry. I suppose my response was purely to your brother's animal magnetism."

"Aaron does have that effect. Think no more about it, Maria. We'll forget my brother's foolishness. He doesn't mean to cause the harm he does with these practical jokes of his."

Maria lifted her eyebrows and crossed her arms in front of her. "I thought you said you'd make no excuses."

Colin bowed. "As ever, you are correct. Now, if you'll excuse me, I shall repair to my study and try and make sure this never happens again."

"It will take more than a speech, no matter how eloquent, to tame your brother, m'lord. Much more than a speech."

Colin nodded and was gone.

On the way to his study, confusion set in. *I thought he was you.* Her words ricocheted through him. Maria hadn't kissed Aaron; she had kissed *him*. Had love for her not flowered because hope failed to water it in its dry soil? He didn't know. What he *did* know, however, was that seeing her in the arms of his brother had made his blood boil.

• • •

Colin's study was lit by only two candles. The strains of music seeped quietly into the dim room, reminding the occupant that a party was going on without him, however dull and stuffy it was.

Several portraits stared down into the gloomy darkness. Aaron slumped in an armchair, glass in one hand, cigar in another. The decanter was placed close by. Colin stormed in. He wasn't a duke any longer. He was an angry brother.

His voice was quiet, yet filled with rage. "What brought you back?"

"Cigar, brother?" Aaron offered with a smirk.

"Did you enjoy it?"

"What? The kiss? Oh yes. Very much so."

"You know what I'm talking about, Aaron! Was your fun worth it?"

"Oh, come now, brother, what did it hurt? Maria looked like a woman in desperate need of an awakening. Certainly, if you were man enough, you would have done the job long ago."

He drawled. He stared his brother down. Colin would have none of it.

"Do you know *anything* about Maria, Aaron? Did you know her first husband was a heavy-handed man? She's wounded deeply, although she hides it well behind a hardened facade. How could you be so careless, so irresponsible?"

Aaron examined his cigar, then spoke. "She didn't seem wounded when I held her in my arms, brother duke. One dance with me, and your little statuette became flesh and blood once again. One kiss, and I tore through her defenses like a Highland charge. There wasn't a chance of refusal."

"Naturally not. But then, Aaron, men have been forcing themselves on women for ages, have they not?"

"Please, Colin, that accusation has been used time out of mind by men who haven't the courage to follow their passions. As soon as my lips touched hers, she began to drive the moment with her own passion. A passion, I must admit, a man even of my experience, has only come upon once before." He drew in on the cigar, and his head was enclouded for several seconds as he exhaled.

"Aaron, Maria is not one of your barroom flopsies, existing only for your sickening juvenile amusements. She is a lady, a treasure beyond words."

"If my travels have brought me only to 'barroom flopsies,' as you so poetically put it, brother, how did I hold such sway over a woman like Maria? No. My tastes run much more sophisticated than barmaids and dancehall girls."

"You are a pathetic excuse of a man."

"At least I am true to my nature. You're a hypocrite, brother." He ground his cigar into an ashtray. "This isn't about my behavior at all. It's about Maria, isn't it? You're angry simply because I've done what you've been dying to do for God knows how long. Admit it, brother. You've wanted Maria all along. Even before Anne died I could see it in your eyes when you spoke of her."

Colin's eyes bore into Aaron's as he rose to the challenge.

"Get out."

His voice was soft, calm, clinical. His eyes were blue steel. "Get out of this house. Do not come here again. If you need anything further, we will arrange it through my secretary. I shall do my best to avoid you, and I would appreciate it greatly if you would extend the same courtesy to me."

Aaron started to say something, but instead he turned to go, realizing that after years of abuse, his brother had finally had enough. He had known he was going too far when he brought up Anne. Colin turned his back to look out the window. When the door clicked shut, he marched over and locked it securely. Two seconds later the decanter lay in splinters on the marble hearth.

Aaron saddled his horse. Stone-faced and angry, he rode away from Inveraray Castle.

• • •

Maria pleaded sick and retired to her room immediately.

"I am sick," she said to herself sarcastically, "to have fallen for a schoolboy prank like the one Aaron Campbell just pulled. I'm more than sick—I'm out of my mind!" It wasn't amusing. Not at all.

Martha, knowing her mistress was in a temper, speedily helped her out of the costume and into her nightclothes. She was gone in no time, glad to be back in her small chamber with her latest romantic novel.

Maria sat at the mirrored dressing table, pulling hairpins out of the elaborate coiffure. She picked up a silver brush and dragged it violently through her long hair. Embarrassment had metamorphosed into anger.

"Fool! Fool! Fool!" she hissed, shaking the brush at the visage before her. "You should have known better. Oh yes, you were so strong, so sure old wounds were forever closed. And all it took was one kiss. One kiss from a rogue like Aaron Campbell, and you lost your head!"

She threw the hairbrush down on the small carpet under her chair, stifling the urge to scream in rage, whispering savagely, angrily instead. "How could you have been such an idiot?" Suddenly she got up from her chair and put on a light wrap. Finding the back stairs, she let herself outside and made her way to the lawn beyond the gardens. The cool night air felt good upon her clean skin as she sat with her back against the wall and looked out over Colin's garden. It was easier to think clearly out here in the night air.

Yes, she thought tenderly, briefly letting herself relive the days of her youth, the first months of her marriage, *it had been good to feel again.* But Aaron Campbell was not someone to whom she would ever choose to endear herself. It had been purely physical attraction. A momentary awakening of old impulses. Heat.

"No," she said aloud. Firmly and purposefully she made a vow. "I will not let Aaron Campbell's charade hurt me in any way. It is as if that kiss never happened."

Again the battlements built up around her heart.

"I'm getting too old for all of this," she said with bemusement, glad she had come to a decision. She arose from the grass with a sigh, wrapping her robe tightly around her body. As she walked past Colin's garden, she bent to pick a beautiful red strawberry, so lovingly tended by the duke himself. It was just what she felt like eating.

· · ·

Lady Margaret breathed the sweet air deeply into her lungs the following morning. "Someone's practicing the pipes down by the loch."

Maria shuddered involuntarily.

Margaret laughed. "They seem to get that reaction from anyone without Highland blood burning soundly through their veins. Naturally, I love them."

"I suppose they are like Scotch—an acquired taste."

"Aye. Much of what makes Scotland so unique is an acquired taste for others. To me there's nothing to be compared to a Scottish regiment, in full Highland dress, marching to the bagpipes. Makes me proud."

They walked in peaceful harmony toward the village of Inveraray. Colin's mother had some business to attend to with the minister's wife. "What clan are you from, Lady Margaret?"

"I'm a Drummond. We're from around Perth."

"No wonder you're so lovely." Maria complimented her easily. "I've heard that beauty has been a hallmark of the Drummond women for centuries."

"So you know your history, eh? Yes, it has. And it has been their downfall as well. But look, here is the parsonage. Would you like to come in? I won't be but a minute."

"Thank you, no. I shall enjoy the scenery. It's quite a quaint little village."

"Aye. That inn over there has been here for centuries." She stepped inside the open door of the small, but well-maintained home before them. Maria looked over in the direction of the inn. A familiar figure stepped out of its door and began to make his way around to the stable at the side.

"Mr. Campbell!" Maria called. And the scoundrel looked up with a disarming smile.

CHAPTER

4

The sight of Aaron Campbell kindled her stomach anew. Seeing him in the morning sun, his golden hair shone as bright as a newly minted coin. Clad in riding clothes, the slim fit of his pants showed off the well-muscled thighs. She remembered their hardness against her own. And the deep red velvet jacket covered the wide expanse between his broad shoulders. But the smile with which he sought to charm himself into her good graces almost took her breath away. Goodness, but she hated for a man like him to have such an effect on a woman such as herself. She deserved infinitely better, she knew, but men with that kind of passionate persuasion came along only once, maybe twice in a century. No matter. Women like her came along even less frequently.

He bowed and walked quickly to where she stood waiting. "Mrs. Rosetti, I suppose I should apologize about last night."

"You give yourself too much credit, Mr. Campbell."

His brows arched, and he smiled appreciatively. "Do I, pretty phoenix?"

"Yes, most certainly. I never thought a man of your experience would be so easily fooled by a costume. You failed to discern rightly between reality and the masquerade."

"No, no. I believe *you* reversed the rules of the masquerade ball last night."

"What do you mean by that?"

"Supposedly one comes in disguise. You, however, shed your chilling persona and came as who you really are. Perhaps I *do* give myself too much credit, but then again, I was the only one to see the real Maria Rosetti, wasn't I? I saw the firebird rise from the ashes. I felt it come near to being consumed by its own flame. And I was the wind that fanned its fire."

"You do think highly of yourself, Mr. Campbell. I'm surprised you were so easily fooled, poor man. To be so deceived... well... I naturally thought a man of your experience would be more perceptive. Perhaps your ego has clouded your vision. For I was most certainly in disguise the entire time."

He was not to be convinced. "No, you wore your true nature. It cannot be denied that what stands before me now was the phoenix I held in my arms last night."

"So you believe I am that bird of flame, incapable of destroying itself by its own passion, rising again and again to burn forever brightly?"

"You know you are."

"Then what of you, Mr. Campbell?"

"What of me?"

"Doth a moth not seek the flame to his own destruction? Can a man take fire into his bosom and not be burned?"

"If he is made of the same element as the woman who holds him to her breast, no. He will not be burned."

"I could take that as a challenge, Mr. Campbell. However," she fingered the ice-blue fabric of her morning gown, "the woman who stands before you is merely Maria Rosetti. I am no myth or mysterious being and, unlike the phoenix, I do not rise from the ashes a great flaming bird, nor shall I ever."

His blue-green eyes lit up with a spark. "I could take *that* as a challenge, Maria."

"You'd be wasting your time. Last night I was caught off guard. I assure you, that will not happen again. Not with you, at any rate."

"I don't believe you. I felt you quiver in my arms. I felt the heat of your lips as your mouth responded to mine."

She looked away, embarrassed.

"Well, I am a woman, Aaron, and you have," she cleared her throat, turning back to face him, "certain charms, shall we say? But that has no bearing on the matter at hand. Besides, you have nothing to offer me. And I certainly do not intend to spend my life covering your gambling debts."

"If I had you I wouldn't need to gamble again!" Aaron said instinctively.

After a brief pause, they both laughed, finding the humor in the absurd. He was not put off in the least.

"Go back to London, Aaron Campbell," Maria said as his horse was brought around.

With a sly smile and a quick raise of his eyebrows, he lifted her hand to his lips. "I will for now. But I'll be back." After a promising kiss on her hand, Aaron mounted the feisty black stallion and galloped forcefully from sight.

Maria didn't know whether she was happy or sad. So she simply decided instead to forget him.

• • •

London
Early November

The pleasing mixture of a rain-scented breeze, roasting

chestnuts, apples, and fallen leaves anointed the streets with its late-autumn fragrance. A storm had just abated, leaving the rays of the morning sun to slightly warm the chilly atmosphere and pave Queen Victoria's way in a swath of crystalline light. Old stones glistened with new rain.

The state opening of Parliament was about to begin.

Maria stood on tiptoe as the procession wended its way to the Palace of Westminster. Just four years into her monarchy, the young queen with raven hair and porcelain skin rode in a grand black state coach. Before her, the procession began with an empty coach bearing the imperial state crown, made especially for Victoria for her coronation. Weighing three pounds, the crown would have been too heavy to wear for so long, even by so noble a young woman as Victoria.

Her carriage was accompanied by 109 troopers and seven officers of the household cavalry in their polished steel breastplates. Maria pointed at the two men bringing up the rear of the procession, each carrying an ax with a sharp-pointed handle. "Who are those men, Martha?"

Martha, a native Londoner and employed by Maria since she arrived from Italy, was only too happy to answer. Like all Englishwomen, she loved a ceremony. "They are the farriers."

"Those axes look horrible! What are they used for?"

"It was their job to kill any lame horse in their regiment with the point, and then chop off the hooves to prove to their commander that they didn't sell the beast to some horse trader."

"They don't do that now, do they?"

"Nah, ma'am. It's just a lot of military hullabaloo. They never can seem to lay down their traditions, even at the point of being ridiculous. Still and all, they look wonderful, don't they? Like any woman, I suppose, my heart skips a beat at a man in uniform!"

"What will happen when they arrive at Westminster?" Maria and her maid stood on the parade ground of the horse guards. The wet turf soaked through the leather soles of their shoes, but neither minded for now. Parliament was opening, the world was moving along like it should. That meant they were free to complain about their soggy stockings all the way home.

"When they get to Westminster, she'll don the crown and mount the throne in the House of Lords, then she'll summon the members of the House of Commons to enter for her speech."

"I wish I could see Colin sitting there in such pomp and circumstance. I imagine he's loving it and hating it, all at the same time! Which reminds me, Martha. I'm meeting him for supper tonight at Mivert's after my performance. I'll need you to prepare the navy taffeta gown delivered from Worth's last week."

"Aye, ma'am. Certainly. Will you be breezing in at your usual time?"

"Yes," Maria sighed, looking down at her slightly expanding waistline, "another late supper."

"Well, it will be wonderful to hear about the day's events from an insider's point of view." To Martha, an insider's view was everything.

• • •

"Mrs. Rosetti has already been seated, m'lord." The maître d' bowed as he snapped his fingers. Immediately, someone came for the Duke of Argyll's cape and hat.

"Thank you, Milton," the duke said nonchalantly, used to the attentiveness his title and money commanded. "Please show me to her table."

"Certainly, m'lord."

As they walked through the crowded, elegantly furnished restaurant, Colin Campbell smiled and nodded to his peers with a seeming brightness. As much as he loved being a legislator, at making a difference in the twists and turns of a nation, he hated the prolonged stay in London. Many of his peers disdained their hereditary seat in the House of Lords, showing up infrequently or not at all. Colin, however, would not–no, *could not*–do that. His heart burned with the opportunity to change Britain for the better. It was all he ever really wanted as a man. It wasn't just voting, showing up. It was bringing visions to the table, twisting arms, and changing men's minds. He had been swallowed whole by the political behemoth, and he found that being its dinner was a heady experience.

"Darling!" Maria's eyes lit up. "Just when I was about to order without you. Or better than that, sit myself down with Ben Disraeli over there!" She nodded in the direction of the dark-haired man two tables over in the midst of a serious discussion.

Colin looked over and said dryly, "He looks like he'd want the company of an opera singer right now."

Maria pouted dramatically. "It may be true, but you didn't have to say so!"

"Why not?" he pulled out his chair and sat down. "It simply means that I shall have you all to myself this evening. It's quite an experience for a man to be the dinner companion of the loveliest woman in the room."

"Oh, Colin, you babble so!"

But Colin was right. She *was* lovely. Her dark taffeta gown with its off-the-shoulder neckline and short puff sleeves was enchanting against her pale skin. The sleeves were decorated with silk gardenias, and in her hair a band of gardenias held up the heavy mass of black ringlets.

"You are beautiful as always, Maria. Did your performance go well?"

She nodded. "I could sing 'Rigoletto' in my sleep. I watched the procession today."

His brows arched in surprise. "You? And after a rain? I can hardly believe it. What did you think?"

"It was quite thrilling. But I wished I had been inside the House of Lords with you."

"With the House of Commons in there for the ceremony, there was barely room for anyone!"

"I could have sat on your lap."

"At least that would have made it memorable. It is the same thing, year after year. Now comes the real excitement. Lord Ashley met with me today. It is going to be a busy session. However, our opposition is getting stronger as well. It's sure to be a clash of the titans this year."

He picked up his menu with a sigh, his fingers restless on the fine vellum. "I do believe I am getting old before my time. Everything on here looks disagreeable!"

Maria laughed. "Just ask for a sauce on it!"

"Wasn't it one of your countrymen who said, 'In England there are 60 different religions, and only one sauce?'"

"He *did* have a point, didn't he?"

"Yes. But perhaps he had little to think about except for the food his palate would enjoy. I, on the other hand, have much too much to ponder." He gave another sigh, forceful this time.

"What has happened?"

"The opposition is at it again."

"What opposition? It seems you always have so many battles to fight. And none of them small engagements." Maria's voice became serious. For years Colin had been fighting zealously alongside Lord Ashley–a man committed to bringing about laws forbidding women and children under ten from working in the terrible conditions of the coal mines. Children in factories and textile production had already been limited to a six-and-a-half-hour workday. Colin's father had fought for such legislation years before. The mine owners who would be affected by Lord Ashley's act could be a rough passel. They were not above bullying their agenda through Parliament with threats, slurs, and bribery.

"What happened?"

"Are you sure you want to hear this, Maria? It might upset you."

Maria nodded.

He shrugged. "All right. As I was walking home from the ceremony, I felt this jerk on my arm and I was pulled into an alleyway."

Maria gasped.

"Not to worry–they did not harm me. Not this time, anyway. But some thug held a knife under my chin and whispered that I had better watch my step on the labor reforms this year. He nicked me with the point of the knife." He held up his chin, and Maria could see the thin slash. "Then he said if I did not stop my crusading there would be much more where that came from. He didn't wait for an answer–simply pushed me against the wall and ran off before I could seize him. When I got back to the street, he had faded into the crowd."

"What are you going to do about this?"

"I do not know, Maria. Part of me wants to investigate. But if it comes up hollow, I shall look like a desperate schemer, and it may end up damaging the cause."

"Still, you should do something."

"Well, I cannot think of anything, so I shall just hope in vain it will never happen again. Over and above all that, getting these reforms pushed through is something on which I must keep concentrating. England has no occasion for cruel taskmasters such as these men. I trust we are more civilized than that!" He shook his head in disgust. "However, they do stand to forfeit a great deal of money. But an empire that escalates upon the backs of its women and children—exploiting, even killing them in the process—has no foundation for the future." His voice became determined, the voice of one of the most powerful debaters in Parliament.

"Is it worth this kind of danger, Colin?"

The waiter interrupted them and departed once he took the order. Colin sat back after taking a sip of water.

"When I was eight I began to join my father once a month when he would visit the tenant farmers and villagers to see how they were faring. He always tried to keep up good relations. He never mollycoddled them, but he was a great humanitarian. If there was truly a need among them, he would do his best to provide help. He was greatly loved, my father, and he was such an example to me. I remember standing beside him, feeling so proud to be his son. He had been fighting for factory reforms for years. People thought he was a radical, and I guess he was at the time. Yet I knew I would one day follow in his footsteps."

"Well, certainly you must take precautions for your safety."

"How so?"

"You have a pistol, don't you?"

"Of course."

"Can't you carry one with you? You've certainly got good reason."

Colin laughed. "My dearest Maria, if I armed myself for every threat, hidden or open, that I have received, I should be a walking arsenal. Do not worry yourself about this. I'm certainly not going to lose any sleep. Besides, I doubt if the threat is a lethal one."

"How can you be so sure?"

He laughed easily with a wink. "I haven't had my arms or legs broken yet. They do these things in stages, you know."

Maria looked up at him through her lashes. Perhaps he was right. But she wasn't so sure.

CHAPTER
5

London

A nine o'clock moon shone overhead. A half-moon constantly battling with the clouds. Four new moons had passed since Aaron had walked out of Inveraray Castle. He had yet to lay eyes on Colin. *And I've never been happier,* Aaron thought as he sprang up the front steps of Foxhall, a marble villa built on the outskirts of Regent's Park. A liveried footman dressed in white trimmed with sumptuous golden braid opened the door.

Aaron was shown in quickly and respectfully. Dispatching his hat and coat to the lackey, he waited but a moment in the grand entry hall before the man he had come to see walked swiftly down the cantilevered, curving staircase.

"Aaron, old man! Wonderful to see you!"

Lucius Carlyle, fellow Oxford chum and sometime gambler, shook his hand.

"Thank you for the invitation, Brother," Aaron replied in kind, yet he couldn't help but wonder why he was called to the home of one of England's oldest, most noble families. Lucius' father, Julian Carlyle, the Earl of Beresford, had been in the process of grooming his son to assume the title for years now. The family was known for their wealth and their contribution to the cultural

well-being of the nation since the Middle Ages. Their
social standing was high and much coveted. Lucius made
it to their club at St. James occasionally when he was not
at court. But then he took his leave usually after about
an hour. For the rest of the evening the others were left
feeling rather purposeless in the small pursuits in which
they were engaged.

He was charming and gracious, intellectually stimu-
lating and socially skilled. Lucius was a man who knew
the right words to say, the perfect wine to order. But sup-
porting his charming, smoothly civilized exterior was an
infrastructure wrought of iron. And the features of his
face attested to his ruthlessness. His nose was strong and
powerful, his jaw was bold and much too large for his
face. The deep-set, burnt-umber eyes shone almost black.
And his slight, slender physique completely contrasted
with the power of his mind. Though the controlled young
man had never been heard to raise his voice, even im-
pudent Aaron would never dream of crossing him. No
one crossed the Carlyles. The fact that they consistently
christened their children with Roman names added to
their aura of power and influence.

Aaron scrutinized the home. The decor was even more
fine than that of Inveraray Castle. Precious furniture—
Chippendale, Sheraton, and Louis XIV—could be seen
through the doorways of the rooms which opened from
the hall. For the first time in months, he yearned to see
the beauty of Inveraray Castle and all its treasures once
again. But he squelched the feeling. It was Colin's now.
Everything was Colin's.

"Lovely place your father has here," he complimented.

"We needed something new several years back. Our

old townhouse was renovated and turned into an embassy." He put a strong, square hand on Aaron's shoulder. "Father's waiting in the library. He has a proposition for you—something in which I think you will be most interested."

"Well, old sport, let's see what he has to say."

Lucius led Aaron down a hallway to a room at the back corner of the house. He walked quickly, head held high. Pushing open the door slightly, he peered around it, knocking softly at the same time. He opened it fully upon receiving a nod of approval from the earl.

The library was a massive room lined completely with mahogany bookcases. Persian rugs partially concealed the highly polished hardwood floors, scarlet draperies hung in thick luxury, and comfortable leather chairs littered the room here and there. It was a learned man's paradise. A fire crackled beneath an intricately carved mantel.

Aaron hid his shock at the appearance of the man seated before him and held out his hand. He hadn't seen Julian Carlyle in three years. The earl's mouth was a mere slash, colorless and hard, lips peeling slightly. His cheekbones stood out in sharp relief to the hollows underneath them. His bald head was covered with a scarf, and before he could take Aaron's proffered hand, he was seized in a spasm of coughing. Lucius rushed to a cabinet near his father's chair and poured a glass of water into a goblet. The earl drank gratefully.

He held out his hand to grasp Aaron's. The grip, once firm, was that no more.

"Your grace, it's good to see you again after so long a time."

"Thank you, Aaron. I'm not the same man I was then, unfortunately. But my joy at seeing one of Lucius' friends has not dwindled. Please, bring that chair closer to me and sit down."

"Yes sir," Aaron smiled warmly, "with pleasure."

Lucius offered port. His pinkie ring—a golden lion's head—brushed against the glasses as he poured the ruby liquid. Aaron remembered that ring well from university days. Given to Lucius by his grandfather, Marcus Carlyle, he hadn't removed it from his finger since he was 16 years old when it was handed down to him at the old earl's deathbed.

Julian spoke. "I suppose Lucius failed to tell you of my illness. I could see the surprise on your face when you walked in," he said, exhibiting the uncanny insight the dying have when it comes to the living.

"Forgive me, m'lord. But you know Lucius." He turned to his friend. "We don't see him much anymore with all his politicking."

Lucius smiled, haughty with young health.

Aaron turned back to the earl. "I'm sorry to see you so ill, m'lord."

"Yes, but none is more sorry than myself. And yet, death comes to us all, does it not?"

"It is as you say."

"I'm sure you're wondering why Lucius sent for you."

"Yes." Aaron took a sip of port as the earl succumbed to another spasm. Lucius wiped the blood from his father's lips.

"Forgive me," Julian apologized. "Where were we?" he asked Lucius, still in a bit of a haze.

"The proposition, Father."

"Ah, yes. The proposition. This may all come as a bit of a shock to you, Aaron. And I must apologize beforehand for asking you to do what surely may seem an insurmountable task."

Aaron experienced a rare moment of compassion. "Naturally, if there's anything I can do to help you, m'lord..."

The earl held up a skeletal hand. "Wait until you hear what we have to say."

Lucius interrupted. "Father, perhaps there's another way."

"No, no, my son. We've discussed this at length for months. There can be no other way. I'll come straight to the point. My son tells me that you have run up some more gambling debts, Aaron."

"Yes, I have," Aaron admitted freely.

He leaned forward in his chair. "And that you and your brother have had somewhat of a falling out?"

"Yes. I suppose you could call it that."

"Would you be interested in wiping the slate clean yet again—getting rid of your obligations?"

"I'm all ears, your grace."

"Good. Good." Julian Carlyle sat back once again. "I suppose you've heard of that dreadful Lord Ashley's Act?"

"Of course."

"As you know, our family has heavily invested in the coal industry for some time."

"No. I didn't know of that."

"Well, that is the case, I assure you. If Lord Ashley's Act passes, our family will be left with almost nothing, I fear."

"How can that be? The Carlyles are one of the most well-heeled families in Britain."

The earl shook his head. "Do you remember the hurricane that raged off Portugal several years ago? It destroyed many ships, if you recall. Their cargo was destroyed as well. And most unfortunately, one ship was carrying a fortune in diamonds I had purchased on loan in South Africa. I lost half of my fortune between that and other calamities."

"What about your land?"

"I've been selling it off to invest in coal, Aaron. It is the wave of the future. Soon everything will be run by coal. And the Carlyles will be ahead of the game, cashing in on the progress of industry."

"The old townhouse? Did you invest the funds from the proceeds of that as well?"

"Yes."

Aaron looked about him. "Well what about this house?"

"A favor owed to Lucius brought this about. Although it seems grand, it's not nearly as large as the other."

"So you're afraid that if Lord Ashley's Act passes your family will suffer?"

"I'm certain it will. Aaron, I'm dying. Lucius will inherit all that I have . . . and that includes the decision I made to throw our funds into the coal industry. The last thing I wish is for Lucius to suffer because of it. Perhaps it was foolish to put all of my eggs into one basket, but I don't think so. Even though the country house is stripped of all of its fancies and the vast acreage around it has dwindled significantly, I believe we can get it back once our investments start paying off. What you see here is all we have. Except for our investments in coal. The coal industry is booming now. It is our only hope. Without the labor of women and children, the mines' output would be significantly reduced. Which leads me to your brother."

"I should think Lord Ashley would be the man you should be concerned about, not Colin. Have you tried giving him a friendly warning?" Aaron inquired. "That always works for me."

"Yes, but he keeps crusading. What makes Colin so dangerous is not just his activities in Parliament, Aaron. It is his dealing with the people. The articles he faithfully submits in the *Times* are horribly damaging. And the pamphlets he sends out make me fear greatly. When the masses are incited, there is nothing the rulers can do. I fear for the future, Aaron. Your brother is a dangerous man as far as my family is concerned."

"I've heard many people say that of him, your grace. It is his religion that drives him, and when a man is responding to what he feels is God's will, heaven help us all! I'd give anything to get him back up to Scotland for good. Among my circle it's purely an embarrassment to be his brother. But tell me, what do I have to do with my brother?"

"I need you to help me get Colin out of the way."

"What? Back to Scotland? As much as he loves it there, he has been infected completely by his love of politics. You couldn't tear him away from London during the session."

"No, no, Aaron. You misunderstand me. And again, I must apologize for what I'm about to say. Even from Scotland, he wouldn't stop. We both know that. I've never seen someone as committed as the Duke of Argyll."

"What then, sir, would you have me do?"

"I want you to have him killed."

The blood drained out of Aaron's face, and his hands turned to ice. He couldn't speak.

The earl cut through the silence.

"Of course, although this would benefit us greatly as I explained, you would stand to gain even more wealth than we would. The dukedom of Argyll and all its riches would be at your disposal."

Lucius pulled his chair closer to Aaron's. "That's right. I remember all our conversations at Oxford, Aaron." He put his hand on the arm of Aaron's chair. "Your brother was a millstone about your neck then, and he is now. It was bad luck that you were born only ten minutes behind him. He sits there with everything, and you have nothing but a life of gambling and a mountain of debt. Compared to the vast riches he holds, he has thrown only a pittance your way. And now he has cut you off completely, that vile man. If he really cared about fairness and righteousness like he ceaselessly claims he does, he would have started it with you. He would have given you half of the estates when your father died."

"My son speaks the truth," the earl said. His eyes looked compassionately into Aaron's. "Your brother—the man who should stand closer to you than all others—has turned his heel against you. He doesn't love you, does he? Has he ever bothered to seek you out? Has he ever offered even a portion of his wealth freely?"

Lucius answered. "No. In all the years I've known you, you've been forced to grovel before him, the poor man begging needed funds from his wealthy brother. I don't know how you've managed. You're a better man than me to have put up with it for so long—isn't he, Father?"

"He most certainly is, my son. I've often wondered why you didn't think of this yourself years ago. And the fact that you've sat quietly by and let him greedily keep to himself all that you grew up having attests to your generosity of goodwill. He could learn some things from you, Aaron."

Finally Aaron spoke.

"But why me? Couldn't a common henchman do the job better than I?"

"No. They are not reliable. And if they were caught by Scotland Yard, they would have no qualms in making a confession to save their own skin. With our interests in the mines, they would see clearly we have a motive. It would ruin us even further. As I reminded Lucius just minutes ago, we have thought this through. You are in such debt no one would believe you had the wherewithal to hire anyone to do the job. No one would suspect your participation. What man would murder his own brother? And the fact that you are an identical twin gives more credence to the theory."

Aaron heard every word they said as if coming through water, and yet they seeped into his understanding with a reasonable clarity he found frightening. He shook himself and stood to his feet.

"Your grace, I may be a scoundrel in many ways, but I could never imagine myself a murderer. Especially of my own brother. It is all entirely as you say, and each man in this room has reason to want Colin dead. We are all driven in a desperate strait and cannot steer a middle course. But there must be another way."

"'Diseases desperate grown, by desperate appliances are reliev'd or not at all,'" Lucius quoted from Hamlet. "It is the way of things, Aaron. The natural recourse."

"Tempt not a desperate man," Aaron replied. "Surely no good can come of this plot. Is your fortune worth the life of another? Shall I live with wealth and position only to despise myself?"

"No!" Julian Carlyle cried. "You shall not despise yourself. And if we tempt you, and tempt you we must, we do so out of the common good for all involved."

Aaron shook his head. "How can I do as you ask?"

"You don't have to do it by your own hand! Oh never, Aaron, would we ask that of you. Hire someone to do it for you. Find a good man you can trust."

Aaron got to his feet and shook his still-bowed head. "No. No. I cannot. I cannot do as you ask."

Lucius reached into his inner coat pocket and pulled out an envelope. "Sit down, Aaron." He handed it to him. "You will want to see what I've placed inside."

Aaron opened the white envelope and spilled its contents. Into his scarred palm fell a bloody queen of spades. Redeemable for a promise. The words spoken so many years ago rang through his brain with the deep, painful tones of a gong: "... Should you need one favor, I will do your bidding with no questions. My word of honor stands secure. ... May Brimstone take my life ... may Satan doom my soul."

Lucius spoke quietly. "Do you remember the promise made to your blood Brother so long ago, Aaron? Can you recall the consequences if you do not follow through?"

Aaron nodded, then spoke so softly they could barely make out the words. "Who could have dreamed a frozen night on the flat plain of Salisbury and a solemn promise would turn into a path more dark and perilous than any I have trodden?"

CHAPTER

6

Maria picked up a muffin, fresh and toasted to a golden brown, from the corner muffin man. She split it open with a dainty silver knife, and the warm, doughy steam which escaped ensured a hunger far deeper than she was aware she had felt before. Breakfast was always her most cherished time of the day, always taken in her parlor. A cloth-covered tray sat on the table in front of her. A lovely porcelain teapot held India's finest. Homemade raspberry jam from the country and freshly churned butter completed the luscious spread. In a small vase stood a single white orchid sent by Colin the previous evening. He hadn't been able to make it to her performance as promised, said he had pressing business with his legislative compatriots. Yesterday she had slipped over to sit in the House of Lords. A heated debate began. Colin sprang to his feet, ready to defend his position on labor reform. He spoke authoritatively, with impassioned conviction and flawless reason.

"Gentlemen, gentleman. How many times must these reports be read until compassion ignites within you? The atrocities Britain's innocents have been forced to bear are clear and abundant." He lifted a report, his fingers bent into the sheets at the top of the page as he moved it in a semicircle for all to see. "You've read yourself the Children's Employment Commission report. What has

become of us when children four years old are working
our mines? And most of them start between the ages of
seven and nine! Is this what Britain, the crown prince of
the industrial revolution, has reduced itself to? I pray not,
gentlemen.

"And here," he picked up another bundle of papers,
exhibiting it likewise, "in the Coal Commission report
we find the same heinous treatment of our countrymen.
In extreme cases workers were denied food and rest for as
long as 39 hours. A day and a half they worked, m'lords.
A day and a half in dank and oppressive darkness without so much as a crust of bread. It was 39 hours in an
abysmal pit that would make summer in London seem
like a holiday in the Alps!"

"Sit down, Campbell," someone yelled. "We've heard
all of this before!"

"And you shall hear it again, Sheffield!" Colin responded with a royal wrath and the rush of a bear. "I shall
not stop until all citizens of Britain are treated fairly and
with compassion. You treat your animals with greater respect. According to the same report, women were found
dragging coal carts up to the surface. Incredibly, one ob-
server did not even know they were women until he noticed their earrings. The mine owners have stooped to
using our women as beasts of burden, and we sit idly by
and do nothing. Is this what you want Britain to be,
m'lords? We have always fancied ourselves an enlightened people, a civilized race. But now I wonder. The
people are uneasy. Reforms must be made."

He cleared his throat and spoke in a softer tone. "I went
down into the mines last summer, gentlemen. And if you
saw them as I did, you would not regard our reforms as

radical, but merely ones of compassionate humanitarian-ism. Think of the tiny children I saw crouched by the doorways shedding thin light with one pathetic little candle. Think of them, lords, when you look upon your own children tonight after they have gone to sleep. They will awake to their dolls and their childish, wonderful games. What of the mine children? They knead at my heart, m'lords. Let them do the same to yours. A change is in order. A change must come, and it must come soon."

Colin turned to pick up his papers.

"All this love of England and compassion of the people is easy enough for you to adhere to, Campbell!" Lord Carsdale, a red-nosed, paunchy sot who had squandered his fortune away years ago, chided Colin. It was common knowledge that he was receiving monetary compensation to fight against Lord Ashley and the others, although none could prove it. "You're one of the richest men in Britain. If you care so much about the common man, why don't you open up your own pocketbook? The only charity work I see you doing is bailing out, time after time, that no-good brother of yours!"

There were a great many guffaws and snorts.

"I'd love to debate things on a personal level, Carsdale. Especially with you."

The House laughed again. Carsdale's financial status and consumptive habits were well known. "And as to my charity work, as you put it, I'd be happy to provide you with a list of my estate's charitable giving. Can I count on you to do the same? Why, we'll read them right here tomorrow if that would make you feel better."

Carsdale, affecting moral outrage, harrumphed and sat back down in his chair.

"Let us not forget why we are here, m'lords!" Colin seized the moment. "If we did nothing more than pick fights of a personal nature, Britain would go nowhere. We are here to discourse on the rights of women and children. To be sidetracked by other means of insignificant argument would prove dangerous and, quite frankly, wasteful of time much too precious."

Many agreed. "Here, here!"

And the House of Lords got back down to business.

Colin was magnificent. Maria had felt like cheering. She was so proud of him. Truly, men like him had been found in the House of Lords for centuries, but they were few and far between. Yes, Colin was the true offspring of a firm-hearted people. He would die a noble death someday, for he knew wisdom and the power of the tomb.

Stopping her musings, she poured another cup of tea and sipped slowly. She looked lovely in a light-blue morning gown. The heavy silk was decorated with white fleurs-de-lis. Her hair frizzed around her pretty face; the back fell down in black ringlets. She had a smug look on her face as she thought of Colin.

He strode into the room. "I would give more than a penny for those thoughts."

She started to rise.

"Darling!"

"No, Maria, please do not get up. I just couldn't bear the fact that I canceled last evening, so I decided to drop by for a few minutes on my way in and ask if we could make those arrangements for this evening."

"Of course, my gladiator."

"What are you talking about?"

"I was a bit devious yesterday."

He smiled, wanting only to be privy to her conspiracy. "And tell me what you did, Mrs. Rosetti."

"I snuck into the House of Lords. And I heard your speech and the subsequent dispute with Carsdale." She took both of his hands in hers as he sat down next to her.

"Did you now? And obviously you thought something was funny?"

"Oh, darling, of course. Lord Carsdale should never have spoken in the first place. I wouldn't be surprised if he was already top-heavy, even at that hour of the morning! He is a first-rate example of fallen man."

Colin laughed. "Carsdale doesn't worry me in the least, Maria. If anything, he helps us by being against us. No one takes him seriously, if you must know."

"But they all laughed...." She couldn't help but feel indignant.

"Of course they did. It was funny. Everyone knows what Aaron is."

"And you didn't mind?"

"Deep inside, yes. On the surface, it's only politics. Aaron only deceives himself if he thinks I am thought the bigger fool by paying off his debts." His face hardened slightly. Only in the eyes.

"Many would do the same for their brother, Colin. And they do not understand what it is like to be a twin. I'm sure if anything ever happened to the other, it would feel as if half of you had died."

"Let us talk of other matters, shall we, Maria? Those muffins look delicious, and I have not yet breakfasted. Talk of Aaron can only hinder my appetite, and I have a big day ahead of me."

"Help yourself."

Colin reached for the little silver knife and split open the muffin, disdaining the use of butter, but spreading it with two spoonfuls of jam.

His eyes crinkled at the corners thoughtfully. "Maria, are you happy?"

"What do you mean, Colin? Don't I seem happy?"

"I suppose. Do you ever feel lonely?"

"Do you?"

He hesitated briefly. "No. Not usually."

"Then neither do I."

CHAPTER

7

"Aaron! Aaron Campbell!" Maria called to the opposite side of the street just after Aaron rounded the corner on his horse. "Wait!"

Aaron shielded his eyes against the rain, and they came to rest upon the tiny form weaving her way through carts and people to cross the street. "Hello, Maria." He looked up the street toward his bachelor apartment. He wished to heaven he was still there.

She smiled under her large white umbrella. "You seem in a hurry. Off to meet a lady friend this early?"

Aaron nodded, dismounted, and threw on a charming smile. "I am in somewhat of a hurry. But there's nothing that is as important as seeing you, little phoenix."

Maria twisted her hands on the umbrella handle, the friction warming her palms. "Still singing that tune, are we? One thing I will say about you Campbell men: You are tenacious. But since you are pressed for time, I'll be quick and state my business right away. Your brother is coming to the opera tonight, and we're going out to dinner afterward. Why don't you join us? Mend the tear between you? I know he would forgive you in a trice, Aaron. In fact, he already has. He's just waiting for you to make the first move. He knows you'll come by when you're ready, and not before."

"He's right. I appreciate your invitation, Maria, but it's too late. Simply too late. If he cared so much about me, he would have contacted me months ago. Colin and I have no relationship, nor shall we ever."

Maria's eyes flashed. "Well, I'm certainly not going to be the one to tell him that. You're a fool, Aaron Campbell. You're throwing away the only relationship you've ever had that really means anything."

Aaron sighed in a theatrical manner. "No, Maria, it was thrown on the rubbish heap long ago. But I'd rather not discuss our problems with you. What do you say, shall we meet for lunch tomorrow?" The transition was so smooth that even worldly Maria was shocked.

She looked up at him, disdain branded on her brow. "No, thank you. I cannot spare the cash."

Aaron was left standing in the rain.

. . .

The tavern sign squeaked gratingly, rust on rust, as the wind swung it to and fro. *The Apple and Serpent. The Apple and Serpent.* Aaron read the name each time it swung toward him. *Ironic isn't it?* he thought. Last night he truly believed he had borne the greatest temptation of his life and had successfully thrown it from his shoulders. But an old card was dealt and here he was succumbing through fear and greed, though he didn't care to admit the latter just then.

Aaron had known exactly where to come upon receiving the card. After bumping into Maria he had ridden straight for the inn, tucked back in the windy alleyways of London's notorious East End. This section of the city sheltered more dubious deals than the entire remainder of London. And this tavern had long been known to the underworld as a meeting place for thieves and cutthroats. Thunder suddenly cracked open the clouds even farther, and the rain pelted down in the rapidly strengthening wind. The weary tenements and dark slums around him looked ill-prepared for such an attack.

He opened the door and walked inside.

The interior appeared much like any other tavern. The stale air stank of whiskey, old ale, and the memory of the men who had consumed them. A massive fireplace sheltered the fire, its flames galloping before a charred-brick backwall, and the cookpots bubbling within. What they held was left up to anyone's guess, before *or* after tasting their contents. Long, scarred tables filled the room. The benches that ran alongside each table were not tucked neatly under but remained in the exact places to which they had been pushed the night before when the last of the group of mobsmen, shofulmen, ringers, moochers, and skittle sharps had deserted the evening's activities, which consisted mostly of drinking, fights, more drinking, and more fights. It was a sorry establishment.

Aaron eyed his surroundings and took a scarred Windsor chair near the hearth.

A large, noble-looking man came down the stairs. He was dressed in the subdued manner so common to the gentry. His legs, clad in tan riding breeches, moved in perfect harmony, easily sliding one foot after the other as he negotiated the steps. The polished black boots made no sound upon the boards underneath his feet. Sure-footed as a panther, he never looked down, but gazed in Aaron's direction. The shirt he wore was white and starchy, the cravat tied around his neck in perfection. And Aaron noticed as he came closer that he hadn't fallen into the trap that so many who impersonate gentry fall into. He was not overdone. No rings, no jewelry other than a small golden pin that held his cravat down.

So much for his clothes. It was his face that arrested the attention of any who saw him and left them wondering. His mouth was set not so much in a hard line as a mysterious one. And if his eyes followed that theme, they were even better at wearing the enigmatic guise of an assassin. They were so pale they appeared almost colorless. They were not hardened steel or darkened ice but cold, impersonal snow, void of want, passion, and conviction, yet bade to go on whirling in the wilderness.

"Good morning, sir," he said, standing directly in front of Aaron, legs shoulder-width apart.

"Good morning, Mr. ..."

"Beck," the man supplied. "Just Beck. What brings you here? This tavern is no place for a gambler of your station. State your business and be quick about it." His speech was cultivated and well-modulated. This man did nothing through anger.

Aaron eyed the handsome stranger. Yes, he would certainly do. The chestnut hair, the long and thin nose, the beautiful garments. He would fit in at Covent Garden perfectly.

"You know who I am then." Aaron stated the question. Beck nodded. "Then you must know of my brother as well?" He was trying to say as few words as possible. Beck nodded again.

"I need the services of someone who will remove my brother."

Beck raised his eyebrows and crossed his arms. "I believe that can be arranged. Such services do not come cheaply."

Aaron raised his hand and nodded. He knew that already.

"When and where? Or is it up to your hire's discretion?"

"Tonight. Covent Garden. Second-floor balcony, third box from the right as you face the stage. Final scene."

Beck held out a well-groomed hand. "Any preferences regarding method?" he asked as Aaron put a small bag of money into his hand. Carlyle money.

"Just make it quick and quiet."

Beck stood to his feet and without a word walked back to the stairs. The innkeeper scuttled over to the fireplace and threw some turnips into one of the pots.

"Barney," Beck said quietly, "I should like some tea now. And I do not wish to be disturbed by anyone this afternoon. I have much to do."

Barney knew. "Aye, Jacob," he said with a bow born of habit.

Aaron walked outside and looked up at the sky still filled with rain and grained with lightning. The deed was done. And the storm was thick enough, black enough to last a lifetime.

• • •

Maria gasped at the beautiful bolt of material the company's most accomplished seamstress unrolled before her. "It's perfect, Molly."

The breathtaking sky-blue silk taffeta was shot through with gold thread. It was iridescent, teeming aquatically with a life of its own. "What do you think, Molly?" Maria questioned concerning the styling of the gown. "The simpler the better?"

"Aye, Mrs. Rosetti. Fabric like this stands up better on its own, if you ask me."

"I agree with you, although my opinion isn't quite as valuable as your own," she complimented the woman.

"Thank you, ma'am. Shall I begin cutting? A square neckline, perhaps? Full-length skintight sleeves? A bit of gold piping around the waist and the neck?"

"Wonderful, Molly. It's still early. Can it be ready by tonight? I'd love to take it home with me."

"The girls and I have been itching for real work to do. We're tired of just doing repairs. Believe me, miss. They'll all want to get their hands on this one. You'll easily have it by tonight," she clucked.

Maria wanted a new dress for the evening with Colin. The conversation of that morning haunted her. She could have sworn he was testing the waters. Was the Duke of Argyll becoming enamored with her?

Looking at herself in the mirror, black hair pulled back in a severe bun, her brows furrowed. They seemed so right for one another. No arguments. Ideas which complemented the other's. And they made a dashing couple—she so tiny and he so tall. These past few months . . . She thought and wondered. Colin Campbell had been coming to call a bit more often. Maybe she would give it a chance. After all, she could pull back at any time.

"No."

She said the word to her reflection, mind finally made up once and for all, after many weeks of silent deliberation. Certainly Colin was worthy of her love, and she knew he loved her. She saw that now. And she wanted to love him back. But, in truth, she couldn't. She wouldn't.

Her lips burned once again with the kisses of Aaron Campbell, and she suddenly knew why.

• • •

Aaron arrived back at his room in a soggy state. Although he was soaked clean through, the skin beneath the chilly garments was unusually warm as a heated fear stole through him. Anticipating his master's needs, Bob, Aaron's manservant, hastened to draw a hot bath as Aaron peeled off the sodden garments he had donned earlier that morning.

"I didn't really have a choice, did I?" he mumbled to himself.

"Sir?" Bob looked puzzled.

"Never mind, just hand me the decanter."

Brandy, he thought. *Just give me lots of brandy and I can forget about all this*. At least for a little while. He took a large gulp directly from the container, wincing slightly as the alcohol set his palate afire—a superficial tourniquet, intended to bind his heart's damning regrets from seeping upward to his brain.

Lowering himself into the steaming tub, Aaron fully planned to send himself into a drunken void until the sun rose the next morning and the matter was forever closed.

• • •

That evening, the Duke of Argyll sat quietly in his dressing room allowing Jamie to attend to his every need. Jamie knew something had changed, owning to the fact that Colin usually preferred to dress himself.

He handed Colin his cuff links. "Sir, if ya dinna mind me askin', is there somethin' amiss?"

Colin's eyes twinkled as he heard the question. He had decided it was time to woo Maria. He would not go through life alone any longer. Their conversation that morning, her evasiveness at his question, the warmth in her eyes, her coming to watch him at the House of Lords, well, it told him everything he needed to know. And even before all that, when she kissed his brother in the garden, hadn't she said she only did so because she thought Aaron was him? It was plain, the entire matter. He should proceed. And he would.

"No, Jamie, my life has not been this hopeful in three years."

Already a plan of conquest formulated itself. *I shall, however, take my time.* Colin knew if anyone would be frightened at the prospect, it would be his Maria.

• • •

That afternoon a messenger delivered the note to Foxhall. It was borne immediately to the library. Julian Carlyle picked it off the tray and read it aloud to Lucius.

"Tonight. At Covent Garden. It shall be done."

Lucius sat forward in his chair. "He's really going to do it?"

The earl nodded and faintly breathed a sigh of relief. "It appears so."

A horrible spasm caught his lungs again, and Julian Carlyle gasped for air. Blood spewed forth, and Lucius attended to the old man gently. After it ended, he looked through pained eyes at his only son.

Lucius put his arms underneath the old man and gently carried him up the steps to his bed. "No, Father. You still have much time left."

But the earl was already asleep.
Lucius gently closed the door.

. . .

"Three minutes!"
A sharp rap vibrated the door of the dressing room.

Maria checked her appearance in the mirror one last time. Heavy cosmetics masked her plagued emotions, and her heart hung heavy in the cavern of her chest. She would let him down easy. She would take an offer from a friend to sing in Italy. Winter would be so much easier, and Colin would understand her feelings without her having to utter a word. It would save his pride and keep him feeling as strong a man as he ever did. She owed him that.

. . .

The graceful brougham, washed and buffed to a high luster, slowly made its way through the streets of London. Inside, its owner looked out of the windows seeing nothing but the face of Maria. Tonight he would start down the road to a new life.

And Anne was nodding her blessing from heaven. He knew it.

Not able to get the wide grin off his face, the great debater, the champion of the common man, suddenly felt somewhat foolish. Pulling the curtains, he allowed himself to pleasure in these newly emerging emotions in private.

Covent Garden stood before him several minutes later, and Colin sprang from the vehicle and had to hold himself back from bounding up the steps like a schoolboy.

Politics took second place in his mind that night. He wanted only to see her face. Savor each expression, remember each tone. Maybe that would keep him from standing on the edge of his box and shouting out that he loved her.

Now in his box, he sat fidgeting with his walking stick. When she breezed onstage, the magnificent train of her costume billowing behind her, he was oblivious to all else.

• • •

Aaron jolted out of a tortured sleep, buried in the darkness of the late-autumn evening. The water was cold, the decanter empty, and he still was unable to drive out the voice of conscience now screaming within his brain. All afternoon he had lain in the tub, refusing to move, refusing his mind's eye the right to see a sight so hideous he could not bear it. The mental energy he had expended, not to mention the large quantity of brandy he had consumed, finally took its toll. But not for as long as he had hoped. He should have still been sleeping. Instead, he was wide-eyed and tense, tormented and ravaged. He glared at the empty decanter, muttering a curse.

"Lot of good you've done, old friend."

His tormented mind galvanized his body into action. He spoke angrily.

"So what!" he questioned the bloody card lying on the table beside him. "What could they possibly do to me that would be worse than the eternal agony to which I will have doomed myself if Colin dies? Would Satan take my soul any less if I kept my vow? Would a life lived in self-despisal and utter grief be better than death?"

He jumped out of the tub bellowing for Bob.

"Yes, sir?" Bob waddled in as quickly as his stumpy legs would allow.

"My evening clothes! And be quick about it!"

Bob, used to Aaron's spontaneous commands, efficiently laid out the black pants and tailcoat, white shirt, waistcoat, and cravat. Drying off with a vengeance, his skin smarting from the rough pressure of the towel, Aaron hurried to get dressed.

"Have my horse made ready," he barked as he buttoned his shirt. "I'm leaving at once."

"Your horse, sir? In those clothes?"

"Do as I say, you miserable little man!"

He drank another glass of brandy. "And fetch me pen and paper and procure a messenger right away!"

• • •

The road to the Apple and Serpent was slippery and hazardous. But Aaron pushed the horse forward through the frigid wind and driving rain. He ran into the inn as one possessed.

"Hey, you!" shouted Barney, running forward. "What do ya mean by..."

Aaron grabbed him by his collar. "Where is he? Where's Beck?"

"He's gone, sir," the wide-eyed man stammered. "Left 15 minutes ago!"

• • •

How glorious she is, Colin thought much later as, almost in a daze, he stared down at the stage. Just then

Maria looked his way, her gaze locking into his. They smiled. And the show continued on.

• • •

"Here!" The sopping messenger thrust the note into the footman's hand. "For the earl. It's urgent."

A shilling was placed into his hand, and the Carlyle's servant walked quickly into the library where Lucius sat by himself. His glass of port was still full, and he stared expressionless into the fire.

"Pardon me, sir. A note . . . for your father."

"Give it to me."

When alone, he opened the envelope.

I cannot do it. The message had been scrawled in haste. And Father lay dying.

• • •

Jacob Beck took each step slowly, head bowed, mind set to the task. He checked his hat. "Another topper lost in the line of duty," he muttered to himself as he made his way to the second floor. Like so many before, there would be no time for retrieval.

Looking at the sleek blond head in front of him as he slid behind the drapery to wait, Beck felt a rare tinge of regret as he rehearsed what he would do to the Duke of Argyll. But that would be gone by morning, he well knew.

Regret never lasted through the night. If that long.

• • •

Aaron, racing his horse over the cobblestone streets, spurred the great black beast thundering beneath him to greater speeds. Sweat ran down his face. His eyes blazed feverishly. He had to make it in time. He had to. All the mistakes he had made in his lifetime culminated in this one. His depravity had even shocked himself. Why hadn't he seen sooner the potential dangers of a soul as blackened as his?

"Please, oh please," he whispered over and over again. "Just a little more time. Oh, God," he prayed for the first time in years, "let me make it in time."

Covent Garden veered into view. Reining the horse in violently, he jumped off and ran, taking the steps of the opera house three at a time. He felt as if he were in a dream, running, bolting as fast as he could, his legs seeming to respond as limbs submerged in water. Many such dreams he had dreamed to be sure, but no nightmare had mirrored the horrific event he was living now.

Through the lobby and up the steps he ran. He could hear Maria singing, a pure note, higher than he could imagine someone reaching. It turned into a scream. A man quickly brushed by him, pushing him into the railing. Hoping against hope, Aaron ran faster up the steps. Passing the other boxes, he could see Maria, lying on the stage in a dead faint.

"Oh, God, no!" he screamed as he made it into the box. Colin was slumped in his chair, blood soaking through his shirt. "Oh no," Aaron cried loudly. "Oh no...oh, Colin...no." He stood up, looking at the thousands of faces staring at him.

"Stop staring and get him help! Get his carriage! My brother has been stabbed!"

Colin reached up and grabbed Aaron by the lapels. "Help...me," he pleaded, eyes imploring his brother, as he fell forward out of the chair and into his brother's arms. Aaron's worst nightmares were realized. He had felt a tingling in his abdomen; he had known it happened. It was a feeling he would remember for the rest of his life.

As he cradled his brother in his lap, he was oblivious to the scarlet blood soaking into his own clothes. "I'm here, Colin."

Colin tried to smile. "I always knew you would be here when I needed you most."

Suddenly all was bustling about them. Someone cleared a path through the ogling crowd as Aaron lifted Colin in his arms and carried him outside to the carriage. They settled him on the seat, and Aaron sat beside him, laying his brother's head on his thigh. "Saint Bartholomew's hospital!" he yelled out the window at the driver.

Colin looked up, the light in his beautiful, innocent eyes fading quickly. "Aaron, I'm dying." Incredibly, there was no fear in his gaze. The world was rapidly becoming unreal as time sped up or slowed down—it was impossible to tell. The only proof that it hadn't stopped at all was the sound of the driver's whip, the horses' hooves against the cobblestones, and the wild swaying of the brougham.

"No, Colin, you're not dying. We'll get you to saint Bart's." He silently willed his brother to live. "Just hold on, please. Hold on until we get there."

Colin grabbed his hand, more for Aaron's benefit than his own. "Tell Mother I love her. You were always her favorite, Aaron."

"You were the son she could count on, Colin. Father, too."

"Never mind about that. And please, tell Maria . . . I love her. Aaron, tell . . . her that I'm sorry. Tell her I'm . . . sorry I left her." Colin smiled a little, gathering up what strength he had left. "Do you know, brother, just . . . this . . . morning she told me she watched me yesterday . . . saw me debating that fat cow Carsdale in . . . the House of Lords. I think . . . she loves me."

"You've done much to help England, Colin. And you will continue to do so." *Please,* he prayed, *please live. Live! Live!*

"Look where it got me. I'd be . . . a fool . . . not to know who's behind this." He coughed, blood spewing from his mouth. "Aaron, I . . . am dying. You will . . . be the next duke. And yet I am not . . . dying alone. I always . . . feared I might." His voice was fading, and his eyes closed. Aaron wiped the sweat and blood off his brother's face with a handkerchief, and they rode on. Where was that blasted hospital?

Colin's eyes opened again. "One last . . . time, Aaron. I must plead for your soul. Look . . . to the Savior. Give . . . yourself to Him."

"Colin, I can't. God will never forgive me for all I've done."

"Yes, He will. He forgives all . . . those who love Him. And when death comes upon them, their final hour is one of peace . . . everlasting. Aaron . . . for me . . . to die is gain."

"You don't understand, you can't die. You *can't.*"

Aaron looked down into his brother's face. Truthfully, he could not look away. Could not lose one precious moment of Colin's fading life and the end of what innocence he had left.

Colin gasped, trying to breathe. "Find the Savior, Aaron." He cried out in pain, squeezing Aaron's hand, seeking strength that could not be enough to save him, but might ease him through the final journey.

"Take care of Maria," he rasped. "She needs someone."

"Yes, I will. You know I will."

The life in his eyes had almost faded. With one last burst of strength found deep within, Colin grabbed Aaron by the shoulders. "No matter what happened between us, I always loved you, brother. I love you more than anyone."

"I love you, Colin. I'm sorry... sorry." Aaron bent his head, kissed his brother on the cheek as the light went out. "No!" he cried. "No! No! No!" Aaron Campbell sobbed uncontrollably, clumsily stroking the hair of his lifeless brother. His twin.

In the darkened streets of London, the brougham pressed on in a now-futile race. Inside a title was gained, a fortune won, and a legacy passed down, brother to brother. Colin Archibald Campbell, the Duke of Argyll, was pronounced dead when the coach arrived.

• • •

The funeral procession migrated slowly to the small church in the village of Inveraray. The death bell tolled in dreary gongs against the cold sky. There Colin would be laid in state, next to his father. Two great men. So alike. So driven. So devoted to their Lord. Aaron's legacy lay cold within him. As cold and stiff as the bodies of the men he had despised so foolishly for so long.

A throng of people, commoners and nobility alike, journeyed to grieve their champion. Lord Ashley, distinguished and reverent, along with the other leaders of the reforms movement, paid their last respects to their martyr. He had fought valiantly, had wielded his sword of power with a dignity and grace uncommon. The House of Lords would not be the same again without the virile champion of justice seated at the front bench. All of Scotland mourned.

Maria stood by the tomb as the coffin was lowered. With a face of stone, she closely resembled the carved effigies around her. She would not allow herself to look at Aaron, fearing the pain from the memories his face would bring. For his part, Aaron stood with his mother, holding her up with the arm he had placed around her tiny frame. "He was such a good boy" was all she could say through her tears. Even death itself would not be allowed to relinquish Colin's place as her child.

Aaron stared into the open tomb. Tears would not come. They were a luxury for those who deserved them.

The Scriptures were read, prayers were offered heavenward, and soon everyone began to file away—some with heads down, others with shoulders shaking in grief, all wondering why. Aaron guided the Lady Margaret back to Inveraray Castle where the group gathered to bear together the burden of life's greatest mystery. Each couldn't help but wonder what he would look like lying in a coffin someday, carved especially for himself. But Aaron knew exactly.

The next morning Maria still stood at the tomb, whist and pale, expressionless. When at last the sun glinted over the horizon, she drifted away.

CHAPTER

8

The newspapers were feasting on the tragedy of the Campbells in their inveterate, carnivorous manner. The thick black headlines screamed silently from the rough paper into Aaron's eyes as the decanter smashed down on the outer edge of the porcelain tub and splintered with a force spawned by self-hatred. The contents of the apartment were all but destroyed. Aaron's rage had continued for the last 30 minutes.

Bob was long gone, leaving with the setting sun. He had never seen his master come so unhinged. Frightened by the violent reaction to Colin's death, afraid of being blasted like the furniture, Bob escaped. The tirade lasted until there was almost nothing left to demolish.

Almost.

The mantel clock ticked loudly, reminding Aaron that at that very moment thousands of people were looking at the time and rushing to meet responsibilities. How could they continue with their miserable, petty lives as if nothing had happened?

As the fury ebbed, Aaron slowly crumpled down cross-legged amid his handiwork of destruction. Hands over his eyes, he rocked back and forth at a rapid pace. "No. No. No," was all he could mutter. There seemed to be nothing left worth saying. "I'm sorry" sounded absurd.

"Come back" even more preposterous. But those were the words on his heart.

Colin was lying cold in his tomb. The young man, a visionary, so beautiful, so full of hopes and dreams and a plan to change the world, would soon decay, equalizing him with every man, even the lowest criminals, who had perished before him. So much promise. So eager to bring about change. "And I destroyed all of it."

For the first time since he cradled his brother's lifeless body in the carriage, Aaron wept. Lamenting, the rocking continued, slower now, in time with the clock on the mantel, that silly, useless clock. His life had ground to a halt. There was no need for such articles in his world any longer.

The stars shone on as they always do. The people of London went to the theater, fed their children, read the latest novel, shined their shoes. Aaron, amid broken glass and splintered wood, curled into the fetal position and fell asleep. At length the clock chimed in a new day.

• • •

London was still stifled by the dark when Aaron awoke, his mind as fuzzy as his mouth. He winced, grinding his hand into the glass as he raised himself up. Disoriented, he looked around at the mess and felt a familiar craving to escape. He stumbled to the rented stall at a nearby stable, made his horse ready, and rode out into the countryside. The late-autumn air was moist and cool. Night air. He breathed deeply to clear the jumbled state to which his mind had succumbed hours earlier.

The Arabian, named Thistle by his mother, galloped in faithful, increased acceleration beneath him.

Aaron thought of Colin's resolve. Never had he known a man so committed to life. He had championed a cause, kept his holdings intact and his subordinates happy. And he loved his God. Aaron knew it was his faith which had enabled Colin to carry out his demanding responsibilities.

"I am now the Duke of Argyll," he thought. "I have but one life to live on this earth, and now I've been given the chance to make the right decisions, be the man my father always wanted me to be, avenge Colin's death inside myself."

He thought of the duties for which he had killed. He could either come down to earth and take them on with a firm resolve, or he could destroy his last chance at respectability and gamble it all away. His whole life had been nothing but a gamble until now. Could he really change? He had made so many mistakes. Yet they all seemed as chaff when compared to the events of last week.

His brother was dead. It plagued him not only with guilt and the usual longing one feels at the loss of a loved one, but with an intense physical pain. Part of him had been wrenched away. They had grown so far apart. He wouldn't have been able to foresee the torment Colin's death would bring him. For almost ten years he had driven his brother out of his thoughts. To think of him made him angry. If only he had been self-righteous and condescending. If only Colin hadn't made known so many times the love and concern he felt for his brother, even if Aaron did feel suffocated by it. How could he have believed the lies the Carlyles fed to him?

His heart had been torn out. Ripped in half at the very least. The fact that he would never see his brother again, that was the least of it. Soon the connection between he and his twin would fade forever. Never again would he feel instinctively, almost literally, the pain his brother experienced. With no one else would he be so vitally connected. To look in the mirror was afflictive, for he could not gaze upon his own image without seeing the face of Colin.

"Find the Savior." Colin's dying words resounded.

"I'm not ready," he whispered as he rode. He couldn't give himself over to God—not yet. The only solution was to try to make restitution himself. He would do it. He would follow in his brother's footsteps and so redeem himself of the murder. Truly, he would become worthy of the title he had so worthlessly inherited.

The ride continued slower now as Aaron pondered his course of action on the lonely road. His seat in the House of Lords was the place to get started. The thought made him grimace. Those old toads whom he despised would become his colleagues. But he would do it. Sacrificing his dislikes, the inconvenience of dealing with men he hated, was a small thing when compared to what he really deserved. He had to try.

Still ... Aaron knew that an honorable man would confess to what he had done. But what good would it do? Someone had to take over the estate. And if Colin and Father could materialize beside him, wouldn't they tell him not to let the estate pass out of the direct line? Surely they wouldn't want him to hang!

He turned back toward the city. It was 1 A.M.

Foxhall rose before him, and he was shown immediately into the library. Lucius Carlyle sat in his dead father's chair. The fire was the only source of light, and it made Lucius look like a satyr in its yellow flame. A tortured satyr granted, but a satyr nonetheless. He didn't look at Aaron, but bade him come closer with a careless wave of his hand. Aaron darkened him with his magnified shadow. "You know I didn't make it in time."

Lucius' head snapped up, eyes glittering. "What?"

"The man I hired had already left the inn. I didn't make it in time."

Lucius raised his hand and nodded. "So we are both left grieving."

"Was it worth it?"

His words were dull. "No. Not as I see it. Father is just as dead."

"So is Colin. Your father was old and sick and would have died anyway. Colin was young with many years before him. Can you live with it, Lucius?"

"Do I have a choice?"

"No."

"Neither do you, Aaron."

"No. Neither do I. But from now on our lives will be nothing more than a collection of past regrets and future fears."

Lucius stared into the fire. "Regret can die." He stared at the palms of his hands. "Regret *will* die."

"For some, but not for me. And the fear will never leave you, Lucius."

"Nor you."

"Ah, but there's where you're wrong. The fear is gone, my friend. For if Scotland Yard knocked upon my door and led me off in chains, I would welcome them."

The Duke of Argyll walked out silently, leaving the Earl of Beresford alone with his haunted grief and the promise of many future riches.

Aaron moved into the family's London townhouse the next day. It was one of the largest. A Mayfair house, five stories tall with over 30 rooms on Grosvenor Square. Complete with stables around the back. Horses were an old love for the new duke, but as he walked in the front door he felt only the cold hand of remorse wringing out his innards. This was no victory. It wasn't even remotely comforting. Claiming this property merely served to soak the blood on his hands far deeper into the subcutaneous flesh, saturating to the very marrow of his bones.

Bob came back. Aaron knew it was only a matter of time. Jamie MacKenzie, unable to bear the thought of serving his former master's undeserving brother, had returned to Scotland and eloped with Bonnie. Instead of assuming his brother's bedchamber, Aaron took an attic room previously used as a studio by an ancestor long ago. He had to plan his metamorphosis carefully, away from the eyes of servants, away from silent reminders of Colin.

The servants didn't quite know what to do with the melancholy man. If he wasn't up in his room, he was tucked away in the library, going through paperwork, trying to learn his newfound responsibilities, earnestly seeking to understand what was required of him. It was no small task. Many things he never knew about his brother surfaced during that time. And the more he learned, the more depressed he became. Colin's love of politics had taken its toll in other areas. The estates had been neglected. Inveraray Castle was in grave need of repair, and rents had not been collected for two years. There was so much to be done, and Aaron had no idea where to start. Instead of glorying in Colin's hidden failures, they caused Aaron to grieve all the more. For the more human Colin became, the more Aaron remembered how much he had once loved him.

Notes frequently arrived from former compatriots inviting him to parties and card games. But he refused to reply. That was all behind him now, wasn't it? In the meantime, when the sun set and the servants thinned their voices to hushed exhalations around the kitchen table, there was always brandy.

For an entire month the routine wavered not a bit. Aaron didn't dare to venture forth from the house. To gather the fortitude necessary to take his seat in the House of Lords was the way he excused himself for living like a hermit. And the longer it took, the better, as far as he was concerned. The more time his peers had to adjust to the idea of Aaron Campbell actually serving among them, the more likely they would be to afford him their acceptance. Hopefully the news of his intent was getting around. Still, it wasn't going to be easy.

How could he expect everyone to believe he had changed, when he didn't believe it himself?

A light tapping sounded at the door to his room. "Yes?"

The door opened, and a burly footman peered round, then walked in. "Mr. Robert Mayfield to see you, your grace."

"Tell him I am not at home, Seth."

"As you wish, your grace."

The door clicked shut.

As you wish.

This life wasn't at all what he had wished for, was nothing like he imagined it would be. He was alone in a world of his own making. Alone, drunk, and miserable. If he didn't venture out soon, he would wither away to a broken husk of a man. What would be worse was that it might take another 50 years of daily dying for the end to finally come, as he wished it would.

• • •

Head down, hat crunched low on his brow, Aaron made the walk to her house. That first step out the door was like diving into the loch without testing the temperature. He was about to resume the first of his responsibilities. Maria. He had promised to take care of her. And take care of her he would. Although he didn't quite know how *Maria* would take to such tidings of overt male domination.

How was she? he wondered, recalling her reaction to Colin's death. He had told her himself. She had been waiting in her dressing room, glued motionlessly to her chair in front of the dressing table. Her makeup rested in cakes over her pale complexion. There were no tear streaks, no physical evidence of torment. She just sat, as unanimated as the toiletries and perfume bottles near her icy hands.

"Maria?" he said.

No response. Not even a blink.

"Colin is dead. He was stabbed. He wanted me to tell you he was sorry."

He saw her nod ever so slightly. And she continued to stare at herself in the mirror, unaware of anything else around her. He quietly shut the door. In the hall he had heard the sound of breaking glass.

The last he saw of her, she had been standing by Colin's tomb. Where was she now? Aaron rounded the corner and proceeded up the street to her house near Covent Garden.

"For Lease" told him that Maria was gone.

Immediately Aaron thought of the opera house. Not caring who saw him, he ran as fast as he could across the street and up the park. He rapped on the door of her dressing room. No answer. He knocked again. Nothing.

Tentatively opening the door, he found the room was empty. The dressing table stood sturdily with a bare, dusty surface. The open closet was empty. Maria had even taken her scent with her and left nothing behind but a bare, forlorn room.

"She left over a month ago," a voice behind him said. Aaron wheeled around.

"Did she say where she was going?"

It was Molly. "No, m'lord. Just told the head man she was takin' a long 'oliday. Said she didn't know when she was comin' back. Told him to find another soprano for 'Tosca.'"

"Do you know where she went? Her house is up for lease."

"No, m'lord. Nobody knows. She was so quiet when she left. Cordial enough. Of course, she always was. Not like some of them singers we get round 'ere." Molly sighed. "I'm afraid the death of your brother is the reason she left. But I don't mean to be impertinent, your grace. We'll miss her sorely here, m'lord, an' that's a fact. I 'ope she decides to come back."

"So do I."

• • •

In the midst of whispers and glances filled with amused skepticism, Aaron Duncan Campbell, the thirteenth Duke of Argyll, donned his robe and wig. He was assuming his inherited seat in the House of Lords. Aaron wasn't nearly as nervous as he thought he would be. Greed, pride, or the love of power were not why he had come. He was here because his honor demanded it, and strangely enough, he took comfort in his unselfish motives.

The chamber buzzed and hummed with activity as Britain's nobility took their seats or congregated in the aisles chatting and arguing. Aaron found his seat and quietly sat, head up, but not haughty. He had told himself repeatedly that he would not snivel before these men. Yes, he had been irresponsible in the past. He had been a shameful example of British nobility. *But at least I wasn't a hypocrite,* he thought as he looked around. Some of the faces were very familiar. They knew he knew what manner of men many of them were—when their wives weren't looking, that is. And maybe they hated him for it. He knew they despised him in any case. But no more than he despised them.

No, he would sit quietly for a long time, years perhaps. Mind his own business. Cast his votes and prove himself dignified and stable.

The session was called to order with the normal formalities. The first order of the day was some minor proclamation regarding a holiday honoring the queen's birthday. *So far so good,* he thought, glad he decided to emerge.

His good feelings were soon quenched when Lord Carsdale took the floor. Lord Ashley's Act was up for discussion yet again. Aaron looked on, praying that he wouldn't be noticed or, perish the thought, singled out.

"M'lords," Carsdale began, voice already sarcastic, lips blubbering with each word, "again we are being forced to ruminate upon Lord Ashley's Act. Nonsense that it is!" There was cheering and booing. Carsdale smiled cruelly as he glanced in Aaron's direction, ready to take any step to discredit the legislation in question.

He gestured sweepingly with his hand. "And *who* have we here? Aaron Campbell? The Duke of Argyll! Shall you be joining us in the debate?" There was a moment of pause, and several hid their embarrassment with nervous laughter. Aaron sat like stone. He expected something like this would happen, just not so soon. "I suspect not, not unless it is a debate over whether one should bet it all on a full house?" The laughter spread among Carsdale's cronies. Aaron would not cower before his brother's enemy. His gaze locked onto Carsdale's, and his eyes hardened with the glint of a marble pillar. Cold. Hard. And the only thing holding him up at present.

"Nothing to say for yourself?" he mocked, warming up to the audience and failing to note Aaron's eyes. "Maybe you should have consulted the dowager duchess of Winston about this. She seems to have been a lucky person."

No, this wasn't what he imagined at all. The laughter was spreading now. Carsdale wasn't content to wound him; he wanted to castrate him as well. The man's fat jowls wobbled as he continued on, his pocked face wider and more polluted than the Thames. "How about the Lady Letitia? I'm sure she would have only been too happy to have given you counsel."

Me and how many others sitting here? Aaron thought.

By now, the whole chamber was in an uproar, except for a few loyal men who had been devoted to Colin. Aaron couldn't move. But his resolve kept his eyes fixed on Carsdale, not shrinking from the accusations. Finally Carsdale noticed and began to quell the tide of his loud speech. Aaron was winning a small victory of intimidation, saving the small bit of pride left to him. He absorbed the laughter, willing it to make him stronger, feasting on its callousness. More than one man in the chamber noticed him sitting quietly, head up, shoulders back, taking Carsdale's juvenile behavior like a man. Truly he was acting like the lord he was. The grace with which he held his head, the firm jut of his chin made them remember his brother. Some took note, wondering what future posturing would be necessary concerning the new Duke of Argyll.

"Come now, Carsdale! Hasn't this gone on enough?" Lord Ashley drawled condescendingly. "Let's stop all of this tomfoolery and get on with business. You've had your fun. And I hardly think you have any right to question *anyone's* morality!"

The laughter died down slowly. Men wiped their brows, smiling and breathing heavily. Business was finally underway.

Aaron didn't hear a word after that. What was left for him? Maria was gone. He was the laughingstock of the House of Lords. The two major responsibilities entrusted to him by Colin he was incapable of fulfilling. *It had been stupid to think I could really give myself a higher calling,* he thought bitterly. Besides, he was angry. It was one thing to be ridiculed for a cause, but he didn't believe in anything strongly enough to warrant such abuse. He wasn't a crusader or a radical reformer the likes of Colin. And he would be hanged if he would take such nonsense merely to fill a seat.

When it was over, Aaron filed out silently.

Lord Ashley weaved through the crowd, his gray head inches above the majority of the members. He stood eye to eye with Aaron as he put his hand upon his shoulder.

"Good to see you here, Aaron." His eyes held hope and kindness.

Aaron nodded from side to side, but smiled graciously. "Thank you, Lord Ashley. Thank you for shutting up Carsdale."

Ashley looked at him with eyes of compassion, and Aaron turned away. He would say no more.

The robe and the wig were put away. As far as Aaron was concerned, he need never look at them again.

• • •

"Deal me in."

Robert Mayfield looked over his shoulder in stunned surprise as Aaron pulled a chair up to the table.

CHAPTER

9

Quickly recovering, Robert pulled out the vacant chair beside him. The gentleman's club was half full. George Lindsay and Alex Fairly were there as well. The old group was complete. "I'd be delighted to deal you in, old man," Robert said, dealing the cards with efficiency and lightning speed. "I didn't expect to see you around here, Aaron. Thought you'd forsaken your Brothers."

"Yes, well, it seems the life of a duke isn't everything it portends to be."

"What? All that money and power? Come now, it's what most of us sitting here dream about every night. Except George there. He's already got the money and the power."

"Give thanks for small favors," Aaron said, putting a cigar between his teeth. "Well, gentlemen, let's see if it's harder to lose when it's your own money!"

"At last," Robert bantered, "maybe you'll start folding when you've got a lousy hand. I'm tired of always trying to call your bluff."

"Ante up, Mayfield. How I'll play now that I'm as rich as Croesus remains to be seen." He picked up his cards. Instead of resting in his hands like the hand of an old friend, they seemed uncomfortable, foreign.

A brandy arrived in front of him.

"Ahh," he sighed, raising his glass in a toast. "Here's to a stiff drink, a good hand, and a better woman!" The four men laughed as they touched their glasses together. Aaron drank, rolling the brandy around in his mouth. It burned its way down to his stomach. He took another sip and stared at the glass in his hand.

"Have they changed their brandy around here?" he asked Robert.

"Which one? They have many. Maybe they forgot and gave you the wrong kind."

The hands came in rapid succession. Aaron didn't bother to pick up each card as he usually did in anticipation. He waited until the whole deal was dealt before picking up his pile.

"Cards boring you, Aaron?" asked George Lindsay, the Earl of Crawford, noticing the change in Aaron's style. "You seem as if you could not care less about what your hand holds."

"Keep going, George. I've yet to gamble my fortune away."

"It's your funeral." George, suddenly realizing what he had said, looked up apologetically. "Sorry, Aaron. We were all shocked to hear about Colin." Alex Fairly nodded. Robert, of course, had been at the funeral.

Aaron clenched his teeth, maintaining control. The cards weren't holding their same allure, the brandy tasted funny, and now this comment regarding Colin's death had come across the table. Aaron resolved not to lose his composure. He clapped his hand on George's back.

"That's all right, my friend. Think no more about it."

"But it's not all right, Aaron. Your brother actually cared about Britain. He cannot be replaced. Does Scotland Yard have a good lead as to who murdered him?"

"No. Naturally they questioned me extensively."

"How were you on the scene so quickly?" Alex Fairly asked.

"I was invited by Maria. She wanted me to make up with my brother that night. So I went in hopes of reconciliation with him."

George shook his head. "But you were too late."

"Yes. I was too late."

The face of Lucius Carlyle materialized in his mind's eye. Each word of the conversation when the fateful card was played repeated itself at lightning speed. He was delighted the old man was dead. To have believed for one moment the earl and his son cared about his well-being showed what a fool they thought he was, what a fool he turned out to be. They were ruthless, and he had allowed himself to forget that fact out of his compassion for Julian's illness. By handing him the queen, Lucius sealed Colin's death warrant. It was *his* fault ultimately that Colin was dead, Aaron decided just then.

"Let's play cards, gentlemen. I came here to forget about my brother, not talk about him." The hand was dealt. George drew three cards, Robert two, Alex two, and Aaron one. With a surprise full house, George Lindsay sat in his chair ten pounds richer.

"Has anyone seen Lucius lately?" he asked.

Robert relit his cigar. "Yesterday he was here at the club, wheeling and dealing amongst the Brothers. I've heard he's making a fortune from the family mining interests."

Alex took a sip of whiskey and blew Robert's smoke from his face impatiently. "He hasn't played cards with us since his father died."

"Well, let's face it, lads," Aaron slumped in his chair a bit, "Lucius Carlyle was always a bit of a step up from us anyway, wasn't he? Especially before you and I came into our titles, George. We've always been in the Brotherhood because of the men sitting right here at this table. At least that's true with me. But Lucius, he's taken full advantage of the rights and privileges Brimstone affords to those who love it."

Alex, much more soft-spoken than the rest of them, said, "Not like me—the 'them that fear it' sort." He ran a slim hand through his brown hair.

Robert was instantly suspicious. He loved the Brotherhood with his whole heart. "What do you mean, Fairly?"

Alex licked his lips. "Don't you ever feel it here, Robert? Dealings . . . private, far-reaching dealings take place under our noses here every day. And though we are in the same room, let's face it: We're not even in the same class as many of the men here now. Lucius included. There's more to the Brotherhood than we know."

They all noticed Lucius as he strolled into the main room.

Robert laughed. "Alex, I always thought you a bit of a girl. Now I know it's true! Brimstone is powerful, yes, but the only reason we are not included with the elite is because all we do is sit all day and drink and gamble!"

Alex looked annoyed but conceded. "Perhaps you're right. But what about you, George? You're titled, wealthy, and I've seen you work a roomful of potentates like a Bolshoi dancer."

George Lindsay's face flushed. "I choose not to take care of business within the confines of the club. Brimstone affords me friendship, nothing more."

Aaron took note of Lindsay's discomfort and slapped a hand on Alex's shoulder. "Alex, perhaps there's more to Brimstone than meets the eye, but I doubt it. And even if there is, you won't have to worry your pretty little head about it. You've got, I estimate, another year before your money is completely squandered, and then it's off to some college to teach or to a boy's school to be a headmaster."

Alex chuckled. "You are precise. Father left me only so much. And when it's gone, you can be sure my brother will not be throwing crowns in my direction! Now your brother, Aaron, he was a man of a different mettle. Tell me, now that the money is yours, would you have been so generous?"

The question cleared up any doubt in Aaron's mind as to his brother's generosity. "No. I would not have been as generous as Colin."

Just then Robert noticed Lucius Carlyle standing nearby.

"Lucius, come join us for a quick hand of cards!"

The small, dark man extricated himself from the group of gentlemen and smoothly pulled up a chair. "Don't mind if I do, gentlemen. Believe it or not, I didn't come to the club tonight to talk business, but to gamble. A fellow needs to have a little entertainment once every so often, eh?"

"All work and no play makes Jack a dull boy," Aaron said wryly, his cigar clenched in the right side of his mouth.

"The Duke of Argyll!" Lucius chimed as he picked up the deck of cards and began to shuffle smoothly, a rapid succession of quick snaps. "I haven't seen you here in months, since the death of your brother. I was so sorry to hear of it."

"And I was equally as pained to hear of the death of your father, the earl."

"Thank you. But you know, Aaron, that evening you dropped in to chat meant more to him than you could ever know. He died with a smile on his lips, and it was due to your kindness in coming to call."

Aaron felt his hands clench in his lap. Lucius was right. Regret can die, and the new earl of Beresford was a living testimonial.

The cards were dealt.

A waiter bowed near Lucius' arm. "Excuse me, gentlemen. Would you care to have your drinks refreshed?"

Aaron shoved his glass forward. "More brandy."

"Scotch," said Robert, doing the same.

George nodded. "Same for me."

Alex shook his head. "No more for me, thank you."

The waiter took mental note. "Very good. And for you, m'lord?" he turned to Lucius.

"Bourbon. And Jerry, bring around some more cigars, will you?"

They were all looking down intently at their cards. Lucius kept a firm hand on the deck, waiting to deal out the cards requested. Aaron sat to his left.

His blue eyes told nothing. "Two."

With crisp movements, Lucius slid them off the pile.

"Three," Alex said quietly. Too bad for Alex.

"Two," Robert requested, and the cards slid in his direction.

"And one for me," Lucius said breezily as Aaron lit one of the cigars Jerry had just laid on the table. They all took silent gulps of their new drinks.

The bidding began.

Lucius was in a reckless mood. Apparently he had been lucky that day in his business dealings. Higher the stakes crept. Alex folded right away. George and Robert left at 20 pounds apiece. But Aaron, sheltering four tens, wasn't about to fold.

"One hundred pounds." He threw the chips across the table and drank a large sip of brandy. Lucius' face gave nothing away.

"I'll see your hundred and raise it two."

Aaron didn't hesitate. "I'll see your 200 and raise you five."

"Blast it," Robert whispered, "you both are mad!"

Alex nodded.

Lucius looked over his cards. Aaron held his against his waistcoat.

A few men sauntered over, seeing how silent the small group at the table had become. Five thousand pounds lay on the table in the end, when Lucius pushed across the final stack of chips.

"I call."

By this time, gentlemen of many sizes but only one texture stood around the table. High-stakes poker was cause for excitement, even at a place where business deals of a hundred times that size were made every day. But a game like this was more gutsy than most present would dare to get.

Aaron laid down his hand and took a large pull on his cigar. "Four tens."

The men behind Lucius, the elite, smiled as he laid his hand for all to see, snapping each one onto the surface of the table.

"Four queens."

On top lay the queen of spades. Lucius smiled and stripped bare the expression high society had soldered on his face for years. It was ruthlessness, opportunism, and cruelty formed into one pointed, fleeting look of triumph.

Aaron took another hit of brandy and stood to his feet. "You're a worm, Lucius Carlyle. You were born a worm, and you'll always be nothing more." He bowed to the occupants, who stood staring down at the playing card. "Gentlemen, good night."

He walked out of a building for the second time that day with head held high and shoulders back. "Poor sport... ungentlemanly conduct..." and other such comments were whispered around him. But he didn't care. They knew the significance of a queen of spades, but not *that* queen of spades. He simply didn't care what they thought anymore—any of them!

Swinging his cape around him as he walked down the outside steps, Aaron Campbell turned his back on the venerable building.

"Aaron Campbell! Wait, my boy!"

The large voice caught his attention briskly, and Aaron turned to see the Society's oldest member hurrying after him. It was Sir Silas Barringer, the head of one of Britain's oldest banking dynasties. He caught up to Aaron with no trouble, despite the fact that he was in his seventies.

He clapped Aaron on the shoulder. "Sorry about that mess in there."

Aaron's gaze was hardened. "I'm not. I've been looking for an excuse to never come back for quite some time."

The great white eyebrows arched. "So have I. I keep trying to make someone angry at me, but I can never seem to do so. Sometimes having all this money can be a thorn!" He looked on Aaron kindly. "Just give it a few days, Aaron. I'm sure you'll be welcomed back into the fold. The Brotherhood isn't something one can just throw casually from his shoulders like a garment."

All too true, Aaron thought, but said with a forced smile, "No, Sir Silas, no. There is no place for me here among these men."

"They're all a bunch of cowards, if you ask me," Silas nodded. "Hiding behind an empty ceremony, taking comfort from a scar."

"Why do you still come?"

He smiled compassionately and lightened his words immediately. "The brandy, Aaron. We have the finest anywhere."

"It's not enough for me anymore. I must be off, Sir Silas. Most probably, I will not be seeing you anytime soon."

"'Tis a shame, Aaron. You always were good for a well-said bit of humor."

Aaron turned his back again and a wall built up, quickly separating him from the Society of the Brimstone. It's construction was thorough—built thick enough, strong enough to last a millennium.

· · ·

Lucius Carlyle did not kill your brother. You did.

It had been easy enough to lay the blame on another's shoulders. But now in the darkness of his room, his pistol beside him, he saw his own visage where Lucius' had been since Colin died, and he deceived himself no more.

Inhaling deeply, he lifted the gun, felt his teeth bite the polished barrel. The sight softly brushed the roof of his mouth, and a metallic taste filled its moist, dark cavern.

CHAPTER
10

I cannot. I cannot.

Eyes thick and grainy, his head shook from side to side. Slowly the gun lowered, a shaft of moonlight glinting off the polished barrel, and Aaron Campbell went to bed not only a murderer, but in his own eyes a coward as well.

He never wanted to see London again.

• • •

Grady Chastain—a small, white-haired man, recently widowed—breathed in deeply, walked around the back of the townhouse, and knocked at the service entrance. His wiry body moved from foot to foot, and his knobby fingers, with nails just a tad too long, fiddled with the rim of his bowler. A shot of sunlight caught his clear, ice-blue eyes, and he inspected the tidy courtyard as he waited.

A young under butler, with a thick neck and calves to match, finally answered with a growl. "Yeah?"

"Grady Chastain, here to interview with the Duke of Argyll for the position of secretary." The servant chomped down into an apple as he leaned against the doorpost. "You got an appointment?"

"Certainly," the old man smiled, his bushy white eyebrows rising at the insolence of the young. "Ten o'clock." The young man truly reminded him of a bear. Not that he had ever seen one up close after living the city life for his entire 68 years. But he knew a bear when he saw one.

"All right, come in then," he said with a sideways nod. In one hulking movement, he pushed his brawny shoulder into the door frame, shoving off and turning on his heel. Through the large kitchens they walked, down a dark hallway, and into the main entry hall. Chastain almost expected him to lumber on all fours. The young man knocked at a closed door on the right. Gaining permission from the room's sole occupant, he straightened up, threw his weight on his heels, and entered—all traces of pretext left in the hallway. The bear had turned cub in an instant.

"Your grace, a Mr. Grady Chastain is here to see you."

"Thank you, Seth. Send him in right away."

"Yes, m'lord."

Seth, the old man thought. The name even sounded like it belonged to a bear.

Grady Chastain entered the study. It was lined with books. A large, ancient globe, hopelessly out of date and contrasting with the new deep-blue drapery, stood in the corner. His feet sank into the gold carpet. The fire burned gaily, and not an object was out of place. *Except the young man seated at the desk,* Chastain thought when he saw Aaron's haggard face, bloodshot eyes, and nervous hands which he sought to hide by the employment of lighting a cigar.

Aaron looked up at the old gentleman and patted the pile of papers in front of him. "I'm lost." The sparkle was gone from his eyes. And though Chastain had never before been in the Duke of Argyll's presence, he knew the cloudy eyes had once been clear and mischievous.

"I can help you, your grace." He said the words in earnest, sending a prayer upward.

"How?"

It certainly was the shortest, most singular interview question the old man had ever received. But as he spoke while Aaron continued to smoke, giving his references, telling of his skills, more than just job-related talents issued forth. And Aaron suddenly remembered the phrase, "Wise as a serpent . . . harmless as a dove." But he could not remember from where it came. *Probably John Donne or something.*

When Chastain had finished listing the reasons he should be hired, Aaron rose to his feet and put forth his hand. "Tomorrow, 7 A.M. Chastain, you are to arrive with your belongings. I shall order your room prepared today."

"Thank you, your grace. It will be an honor to be employed by the Campbell family."

"Believe me, old man," Aaron rubbed his eyes with the thumb and middle finger of one hand, "you will more than earn your salary."

Chastain bowed and took his leave.

"Well, Rosie," he muttered silently to his late wife on the way back to his small room in the west end. "Our Lord took you to be with Him, and left me with a job to do."

And with a cigar smoker, too, he grimaced. Well, the Lord never promised life would be lived with the scent of roses and perfect circumstances. But Grady Chastain knew working for the young Campbell was God's will. He was more than content with that.

• • •

Grady Chastain began working at his post the next day. It didn't take long to pack his belongings in a small, scratchy black-leather footlocker. It was all he required for three shirts and one suit. Resting between his slippers and flannel pajamas lay his Bible and Rosie's bridal bouquet—shrunken and dried, terribly fragile, infinitely precious.

When Aaron told Grady they would be leaving for Inveraray Castle as soon as possible, the new secretary pared the servants down to a margin and closed up the townhouse. Bob followed suit, gathering Aaron's personal effects, looking forward to getting back to his native Scotland.

"Well, m'lord," Grady said as he hitched into the duke's study at two in the afternoon (Aaron rarely rose before noon these days), "all is ready. The extra servants have been dispatched and places found for all of them."

"Good. Thank you, old man."

"Think nothing of it, m'lord. Just doing my job. It's worth it just to have something to think about besides Rosie's death."

Aaron walked over and picked up his faithful decanter. "I think I know how you feel, Chastain. My brother died three months ago."

"I heard about that, m'lord. He was quite a man, your brother. Hard shoes to fill, if you don't mind my saying so."

"Not at all." He took a huge swallow of whiskey. "I couldn't agree more. I'll never be the man he was. It would be foolish to try."

"I wouldn't give up hope. With the help of God and a lot of prayer, it might not be as difficult as it seems."

Aaron held up his glass. "And a little less of this."

He finished the rest of the drink. "Are you a Christian, Chastain?"

"Aye, m'lord. So were my parents. And Rosie was, too. I'll tell you this, sir, I wouldn't have been able to make it through her death without the loving Savior walking by my side each step of the way."

"She must have been a very special woman. How long ago did she pass away?"

"Not long after your brother died. Perhaps they're together up in heaven looking at us down here. Rosie would be talking his ear off, if I know her!"

"And Colin would be listening graciously. He was like that, you know."

"It's wonderful to know that it all doesn't end with death."

Aaron shook his head doubtfully. *To die is gain.* Colin's words ravaged him.

Chastain took note and continued. "Well, your grace, the fact that you doubt doesn't make it any less true. I'll be praying that someday you will come to believe it."

For some reason Aaron felt comfortable with this humble old gentleman. It was probably the drink. "Thank you, Chastain. For the first time in my life I can take comfort from that," he said with a sincerity that surprised himself. Feeling a little foolish, he cleared his throat, "Well, I guess we'd better be going then, old man."

"Certainly, m'lord. Your carriage is waiting."

"I'll be there in a few minutes."

Aaron walked through the house, still clean, still free of dust. All was whites and shadows now as the furniture huddled beneath white cotton drop cloths, and the mirrors became resigned to the world of a painting, showing only one scene from now on, no movement caught along their beveled edges, no life found inside their gilded frames.

He said good-bye forever, his boots thudding softly, their low echoes accompanying him as he walked. London. Brimstone. All he thought he was or would ever be he left behind. A feral creature made impotent, silenced by its own brutality. A useless, fanged thing which would roam the halls, leaving no impact, not even a reflection when the door was shut for the rest of a tortured lifetime....

Aaron locked it himself.

• • •

February 1843

The carriage rolled across the border into Scotland.

"Why, Aaron," he remembered his mother saying on his first holiday from Oxford, "you have lost your Highland way of speech."

Aaron had laughed then. But it was true. He had worked hard to forget the land of his birth. Across the moors now he looked at lowland Scotland before him; he looked back as well to England. A storm was advancing from the southwest, darkening the land he had chosen 14 years ago to be his home. Life there had been one tempest after another. It was all so clear now.

He turned his head back to his homeland before him. The sky, clear and deep and higher than anything he could ever imagine, filled him with a sense of vastness, as though his lungs held more air, his mind more sense, his heart more desire.

I should have come home long ago, he thought. *Perhaps if I had...*

Thoughts of Colin filled him in an even more bountiful pain. By the time the coach reached the last inn of the journey near Glasgow, the inn's bar was empty, and Aaron had to be carried up to his room.

• • •

The following day Inveraray Castle was blanketed with a light snow. The late afternoon sun lit up the venerable building as though it were Atlantis rising in golden splendor from a sea of foam.

A few weeks before, Aaron sent word that he would soon be arriving. Fully expecting to find Lady Margaret waiting for him, he hurried into the castle.

"Mother!" he yelled as he opened the door, "I'm home!"

A bright fire was burning in the fireplace of the green-hued drawing room. The castle was freshly swept, each piece of furniture polished. Clocks chimed in unison. Five o'clock. The butler, a squat man named Jacobs, welcomed him in stuffy tones. He had only been hired last year, and no one understood why Lady Margaret had taken to such a condescending, pig-snouted individual. He ruled the staff with an iron fist. Aaron hadn't liked him from the moment he laid eyes on him. And he made it a point of telling him so.

He bowed. "Your grace, welcome home."

Mrs. Rider, the housekeeper, scuttled into the room on his heels. She had been with the family since Aaron was a child. In contrast to Jacobs, Aaron had always loved the gentle yet firm woman with her jet-black hair, which she brushed back in wings over her rather large ears. They heard everything. But the wide mouth never revealed the secrets she knew.

She looked up at him, stricken. "Master Aaron. M' lord," she corrected herself, glancing surreptitiously at Jacobs, then shaking her head sadly, "your mother's not able to come and meet you."

"Mrs. Rider," Jacobs interrupted condescendingly, "let us leave his grace alone to recover from the journey. I would speak with you."

Aaron bristled. "You'll do nothing of the sort, Jacobs. Don't play the pompous fool with me. Whatever Mrs. Rider has to say about my mother, she may say, and say it now." His eyes made a quick circumference of the room, searching for something to drink. "Get me a drink, you hooligan! What is wrong, Mrs. Rider?" he asked, apprehension spreading throughout his body with elongated, feverish fingers.

"Oh, m'lord," she began, trying not to cry. "She's gone." A tear slipped from her eye. He had never seen her cry. Jacobs handed him a glass of scotch.

"What! Where did she go?"

"She wouldna' say, your grace. An' she swore us to secrecy until you returned."

"Why wasn't I told about this, anyway?" Aaron barked, unable to control himself as he threw the glass of spirits against the wall.

"Oh, m'lord!" Mrs. Rider wailed as she succumbed to tears. "There's a note waitin' for ya in your room."

Aaron bounded up the steps to his bedchamber. He hesitated when he put his hand upon the brass knob. The thought of what lay inside the letter frightened him. This was so unlike Lady Margaret. Although she had been eccentric, she had always been open and predictable.

He entered the room.

All the curtains were drawn, and the only light in the room was the fire on the hearth and the violet hues of sunset draining its dying light through the opened draperies. A small maplewood desk stood in the far corner of the room, its matching chair tucked neatly into the knee well. The letter rested upon its gleaming surface, a square of purple light thrown across the brittle parchment. *Son* was written in the familiar, educated hand. Aaron could imagine the small, bejeweled fingers as they penned the words. He saw her fold the paper, turn it over, spill wax onto the flap, and press her seal into the molten red substance.

The echo of his boots against the stone provided a hushed, haunting rhythm of isolation as he neared the desk then picked up the letter with dread and regret bearing down on the top of his head. He broke the seal and read.

My Dearest Aaron,

Right now you are most certainly displeased with your mama, yet I can only pray that you will understand why I must go.

As I write I am indeed experiencing a dark time of the soul. No parent should be forced to linger longer upon this dreadful earth than her child. Your brother's death left me more alone than I could have foreseen. But then what mother expects to mourn the son of her womb? I have become tortured with his death, rehearsing over and over again what he must have felt as he died: the pain, the confusion, the agony of knowing his life was coming to a close without time to prepare or say good-bye to those he loved. My one consolation is that you, my Aaron, were by his side when he traveled from this world. The heavenly Father was kind to me in that regard.

But I feel as though He is far from me now. I've rambled about the castle for the past month searching for a sign that He is still here. Yet I find nothing. I pray, and only silence answers. And I continue to plead for even a small bit of warmth from His Holy Spirit. And I feel more alone than before. I cannot stand it any longer.

For this reason I am going off on my own crusade. To find Him again. Perhaps if I bring my pain to the place where He suffered in agony, Golgotha itself, I shall feel His presence once again and renew the joy of my salvation. How long I will be gone I cannot tell you. As long as it takes, I suppose, for the journey to the Holy City will be long and arduous. But as I go, dearest son, I shall remember you before the Father. I have always believed He will take hold of you for His own one day.

I love you, darling, with all that I am and will remain always your loving,

Mama

Aaron cried for the third time since that dreadful night. He had forsaken her in her hour of need—had only seen his own grief, guilt, and shame. And now she was gone.

• • •

The castle stood silent, withdrawn in the dismal winter. Servants scurried to and fro, intent on their assigned duties, but lacking the joy they had previously experienced inside those once-happy walls in the service of the previous duke. Their new lord was morose and quiet. His general mood, although he was rarely seen, permeated the staff. Even Chastain's attempts at humor during suppertime did little to raise their spirits. Perhaps it was the freezing rains and iron skies that kept everyone in a dreary fog as well.

As February wore on, Aaron became accustomed to the glances of misgiving aimed his direction when they thought he wasn't looking. He couldn't blame the staff. Chastain and Mrs. Rider were the only humans he would bring into his presence regularly. The rest knew him not at all.

This irked Jacobs to no end.

Of course, it was different with the men who worked the stables. Aaron had known them all by name within a week of his arrival. Angus, the stable master, middle-aged and friendly, was eager to have the company of the lord of the manor who was, he felt, the only man he had ever known who loved the graceful beasts as much as he himself loved them. The horses were the one thing in life that never changed for Aaron. Even at the most troubled times of his youth, he daily frequented the warm equestrian world hidden inside the large stable. Peace became somewhat his.

The month of March began with a two-day snowstorm so severe it seemed as if all the snows of yesteryear congregated again for one single, blasting reunion. At 4:30, lantern in hand, Aaron walked through the castle courtyard, the whiteness gyrating within the circle of light. Despite the severity of the weather, he was compelled to go as usual to the stables. The brick building with its high windows and heavy cross beams invited, warmed, and soothed. Its ministrations of comfort were automatic and so needed. Aaron could feel his harried heart ease its frantic pace.

Up in the loft he sat and pondered before Angus arrived, listening to the sound of the noble beasts moving about in their stalls, exhaling softly through their nostrils. Ten mares were pregnant, and they were all looking forward to fruitful colting when spring came.

"Human beings could learn a lot from horses," Aaron had always said. No duplicity. No ulterior motives. If you were good to them, they were good to you. They held you on their backs and did your bidding simply because that was what they were expected to do. Aaron had no time for breaking in a temperamental stallion to suit his needs like he had done so many times when he was younger. He wanted unconditional love and reassurance. He had spent months trying to tame himself, and so far had failed miserably. He didn't need to waste his energy on a wild creature. There were enough of them in the world—he knew that firsthand. Give him a creature that was tame and gentle, responsive and patient, with legs that could run swifter than the sweet breezes which raced across the surface of the loch.

From his perch Aaron could see through the nearby window the sun rise on a clear morning, or hear the hypnotic sound of rain pattering on the roof above his head. Now all was black as the snows continued to fill up the courtyard. Prayer seemed an attainable thing. But the right words failed him. How does a man talk to the One who made him, the One whom he has failed miserably and scorned all his life? Aaron was always at a loss for words when he looked up at the dawn heralding one more new day that he would be allowed to live. He had sense enough to know that tomorrows were something he did not deserve. Forgiveness...how could a God, even the deity Colin magnified as merciful and loving, bestow it so freely, so blindly? Restitution must be then made. And there was only one way he as a man could make amends. But first he would talk to Chastain regarding what it would take to nurture the Campbell holdings back to their former glory.

"Your grace!" Angus called from below, his bald head reflecting softly the light of a lantern to his right. Great black brows arched like caterpillars above his deep-set eyes. A full nose sat perched over a mouth whose teeth were crooked and large. When Aaron looked down on him, it smiled wider than seemed possible.

"Up here, Angus."

He began to ascend the steep, narrow iron staircase from the loft.

"Have ya been here long, m'lord?"

Aaron nodded. "Naturally."

"Early to bed, early to rise, eh, your grace? Wish I could get to bed real early m'self. But there always seems to be somethin' that needs a bit o' doin' after I put in my day here."

Aaron just smiled pleasantly in return. He didn't want to tell Angus that sleep had recently become an activity for those who deserved it. He didn't want the stable master to know that only at 1 or 2 A.M. would sleep overtake him after his body, through sheer exhaustion, finally won out over his spinning mind. Switching from brandy to scotch had made no impact in aiding him to a faster oblivion, either.

"The snow has tapered off," Angus said as he unwrapped his scarf.

"Good. I'm sure the horses will be glad to get their exercise."

"And it'll make the way in easier on the lads."

"Yes . . . of course."

When the grooms arrived ten minutes later, puffing the cold out of their lungs, Aaron joined in the tasks. He enjoyed the manual labor and the freedom it gave when he resigned himself to a menial task and exercised his muscles. Listening to the men talk and commiserate together was something he needed desperately, even though he didn't join in their revelry as they sang and joked with one another. The shared tasks rendered the commonplace conversation interesting, in Aaron's opinion. *Life is so simple for the common man*, he thought mistakenly, having never worried for one day if there would be enough firewood for warmth or flour for sustenance.

After the new hay was spread and the horses were exercised, the men would take a short break in the tack room. Aaron heard about the problems their families were facing—problems that all families deal with no matter what their status.

"How's the wife, Stephen?" he asked one of the grooms that morning.

"Weel, m'lord, she's doin' just aboot right for a woman her age. 'Tis true an' altogether unfortunate that she canna seem to shake off that cough she got this winter." He rubbed his roughened hands together. "Could be worse, I suppose. She isna' confined to the bed."

"Has she seen a doctor?"

The groom donned a puzzled expression. "Doctor? Why no, your grace. We are plannin' to go drink from the holy well doon at Scotlandwell as soon as weather permits. They say Robert the Bruce was cured of his leprosy because of that well."

"Why don't you let me send Dr. Linton over to her, Stephen? Scotlandwell is a long way from Inveraray, and who knows how long winter will take to go along on its way?"

"M'lord, that would be kind of ya, it would. I'm sure Fiona would be most grateful to ya."

"Then I'll contact him as soon as the storm clears. Tell your wife to expect him."

Aaron made his way back to the castle to bathe, change clothes, and ready himself for the day. He thought of Stephen and people like him all over Scotland, still blending the pagan traditions with Christianity. *Holy well, indeed.* He shook his head sadly, and wondered how many people had gone to their graves because they refused to use their God-given common sense.

And he knew he was no better.

• • •

Chastain came to Aaron at his summons.

"Sit down, old man."

The secretary gratefully complied. "Thank you, your grace."

"We've been here a month now. You've had a chance to look over the books in detail and assess the estate, including the castle. What must be done?"

Chastain sighed and laid a stack of papers on the desk in front of him. "Well, your grace, as much as I hate to say it, your brother, though noble in his ideals, neglected his domestic affairs."

"I know. It is what I feared." That 5000 pounds he lost to Lucius seemed to be worth a bit more suddenly.

Chastain hurried to reassure him, leafing through the papers and pulling out several sheets. "But I don't think it is as bad as all that. I've already warned the tenants that their rents will be collected in full this year, with a ten-percent increase. And with your permission, of course, I thought it would be a good idea to bring in some more sheep to graze in the area a few miles west of here."

"Isn't that farming land?"

"Yes, your grace, it was. But the crofter died two years ago. He had no sons, and the fields have gone fallow."

"Good, then. We'll bring in more sheep. Is there any other way we can raise our capital?"

"I believe so, your grace. I'll be back in just a moment."

He went to the library and came back with a volume of handwritten pages. "I found these two weeks ago."

"What are they?" Aaron reached forward and picked up one of the pages, yellowed to almost brown with age.

"They're work of an ancestor of yours. Duncan Campbell."

"Ah, yes, our family's greatest scholar. I'm named after him. I'm also named after his cousin Aaron Campbell, the playwright."

Chastain nodded. "Anyway, m'lord. This is a volume of his poetry translations that I believe has not been published. Of course, you would know better than I would about such things, but I checked the section of the library that contains his published writings, and I do not see any containing these."

"Then you have assumed correctly. We have all his

published works. I wonder how this fell through the cracks? I thought all of his research was published years ago."

"Shall I begin to arrange for it then, m'lord?"

Aaron was leafing through the poetry, gathered in the Highlands by his ancestor almost 80 years ago. On the left half of the page the words were in Gaelic, on the right, in English.

"Please do. Now, what about the castle? Have you made any assessments as to what repairs are needed?"

"Yes, your grace. I still haven't completed it but, first and foremost, the roof needs to be repaired."

"Repaired or replaced?"

Chastain shrugged apologetically. "Actually, m'lord, it *does* need to be replaced."

"Do we have adequate funds?"

Chastain laughed and spread his arms wide, "Of course, m'lord. You're still a very rich man."

Aaron breathed an inward sigh of relief. "Good. That means it won't take me as much time until I can make final res . . ." His words faded.

"Final what, your grace?"

"Nothing, old man. Go on and get started on the roof arrangements."

"As you wish."

Aaron was left alone. *Final restitution* he had been about to say. He knew what he had to do. The estates must be restored. And when they were ready to hand down to his cousin, he would turn himself over to Scotland Yard. For the first time in his life he wished he had a son. The direct line of Campbell chiefs would finally be broken when Aaron hung from the gallows.

• • •

March

A slight snore rose from behind the chair as Chastain entered the library. The wind had been roaring all night. Rain fell heavily in a flood-promising rhythm. Long legs stretched before the glowing embers of an old fire. Their feet were pointed out in total relaxation. Chastain smiled with a bit of amusement as he stared at the stockinged feet in front of him. In all his years of serving aristocrats, he had never met one so averse to wearing shoes.

A strong affection for his employer had grown steadily since the talk they had in London four months previous. "If there's one sure way to care about someone," Rosie had always said, "it's to pray for them." Chastain had followed that piece of wisdom for years, even employing it with those whom he rather disliked, or who merely grated on his nerves. After a few months of prayer, he would start seeing strengths of character he never knew they possessed. Perhaps they worked hard, perhaps they forgave others easily, perhaps they had the courage to do right. Then he found he rather liked them when it came down to it.

With the duke it had been different. He had taken a liking to him the first time he walked through the door, bent on receiving the position he desired. He had needed that job. For his disquieted mind and his grieving heart, he needed to become the secretary to the Duke of Argyll. What a pair they made! Each needed the other just as badly. And now he had been here at Inveraray Castle all winter, walking over the snow, breathing in the fresh air, talking with the villagers, many of whom were brethren of like faith. He could see the influence Aaron's father had had upon their constituents. Rosie still occupied his thoughts during much of the day. He missed her so, having never pictured himself alone and getting older by the minute. But as he saw life going on all around him, her death became more and more natural. Something he could accept. He could finally look up at the sky and say, "Yes, Father, it is good."

The clock whirred on the mantel, its inner workings gearing up to produce two tinny notes about the room. The long legs bent, and the stockinged feet came down squarely on the floor as the last echo receded into nothingness.

"Your grace," Chastain said softly.

"Aye, Chastain." Aaron sat up straight in the chair and rubbed his face with his palms. "Two o'clock is it? I must have fallen asleep."

He reminded Chastain of a raccoon just them. The dark circles that had spread under Aaron's eyes the past few months didn't help. "Yes, m'lord, you certainly did. Sleeping like a baby, you were. Are you planning on retiring to bed now, sir?"

"I don't think so." Aaron turned around in his chair and looked at the old man with sudden curiosity. "What has you up and about at such an hour?"

"Couldn't sleep, m'lord. I thought I'd come and finish going over the accounts for the week, but when I came by I saw the fire here and went down to the kitchen to make a pot of tea. Would you like some, sir?"

Aaron was in the rare need of close companionship.

"Yes, Chastain, I think I would. I have no wish to retire yet. But I don't really feel like doing anything at all constructive. Would you care to sit down and join me?"

"Your lordship, I..." Chastain hesitated. This was somewhat unconventional.

"Oh, come now, Chastain," Aaron chided lightly, friend to friend, "it's two o'clock in the morning and neither of us are bent on sleep. Everyone else will still be down for at least three hours! Let's break tradition, old man. I'm in need of some conversation. If the whole thing bothers you, don't worry, I won't tell a soul about it come tomorrow morning!"

Chastain chuckled and set the tray down on the table that rested between the chairs before the fire. Porcelain clinked against silver as the objects shivered from the impact. He groaned slightly as he bent over to pour. Aaron brushed his hands aside.

"Take a seat, Chastain. I'll do it." He lifted the pot.

"But m'lord, this is quite unseemly for you to ..."

"Nonsense. Give me a chance to serve. I've never been much good at it, you know. It's time I learned. Besides, you're hardly the status of a parlor maid, and it sounds as if your back is giving you some trouble tonight."

"Yes, your grace, it is. And I thank you." Chastain nodded and felt stirrings of encouragement in his soul. There was a lion inside that raccoon just waiting to lunge forth. He knew it.

Aaron handed him his tea, threw another log onto the fire, and they settled back in the armchairs in companionable silence. The warm liquid felt good in the chilly room. But the communion of two sleepless souls was even more comforting. *Insomnia was meant to be shared*, the duke thought. Better than suffering alone and breaking the commandment, "Thou shalt not covet."

"You make tea just as I like it, Chastain, good and strong."

"Thank you, sir. Rosie, she liked it that way, too. We had to skimp on a lot of things during our life together, but tea was one thing she wouldn't cut back on. Strong and hot. That was the way she liked it."

"Sounds more like a coffee drinker." He drank the hot tea quickly down a throat long desensitized from years of hard drinking.

Chastain smiled. "Yes, sir, it does. But she would never try the stuff. 'I'm an Englishwoman, and English-women drink tea,' she would say. And that was that."

Aaron poured another cup and downed it likewise. "Sounds like she was a fine woman, your Rosie."

"Yes, sir, she was."

"Did you ever have any children, Chastain?"

"No, sir. We tried. We hoped for years that we would be blessed with a baby. But Rosie never conceived."

"I'm sorry, Chastain."

"Ah, don't be, sir. That's all water under the bridge. For some reason the Lord just wanted it to be me and Rosie. We were still very happy together."

"Do you still miss her badly?"

"Now, that's funny you should ask that, m'lord. Why today, when I took my afternoon constitutional, I came to a real clearing of the head about it all."

"What do you mean?"

"Well, sir," he began, his face peaceful and pleasant as the now-blazing fire lit up his small features, "I've had an awful time of missing her. But I told you that before. You know, since I've come here, it hasn't seemed quite so bad. The surroundings are different. Lots of duties to keep me occupied. Lovely people all around. It's been rather good for me, all of that." Chastain hesitated.

"Go on," Aaron encouraged him.

"I had strolled to the village and over to the church-yard. And I stood there looking out over the graves. Of course, that reminded me of Rosie's funeral. It always does when I go there." He took a small sip of tea to wet his mouth before continuing. "I fully expected to weep, like I always seem to. But I couldn't. Not today. It was all somewhat strange to me. Being in a state of mourning yourself, m'lord, I know you'll understand how it is with grief. At first he comes on you unwanted, unsought, dreaded for so long. But he comes nevertheless dressed in sackcloth and ashes, gloating in the fact that it's not up to you anyway. For a while you push him away with all that's left inside you. And when you get weary of all that exertion, you give in. 'All right, old fellow, I see you won't leave, so maybe we can reach an agreement, a truce. You can stay. But try not to make things too difficult for me, all right?' Well then, before you know it, he becomes your most faithful companion. Always there. Night and day. Breakfast, teatime, and supper. Sitting right there in the pit of your stomach. And pretty soon you find you like having the old man around. He's something you can count on. Something to hang your hat on in a world that has changed so dramatically, so quickly.

"I almost looked around for him as I was standing there. And suddenly I realized that over the past few weeks he'd been walking farther and farther behind me. Of course, he's never gone completely. There's always an impression left behind somewhere. A sign that he'd been there for quite some time. But as I looked over the graves, I felt happy for the first time since she passed. And I knew I could go on." He paused and looked at Aaron earnestly. "Do you mind if I speak of the Scriptures, sir?"

"Not at all, Chastain. Go ahead."

"They talk about peace which passes all understanding. I've read such passages relating to God's peace many times in my life but, until that moment, I never actually knew what it meant. I felt as if Rosie were looking down upon me there in the snow and saying, 'It's all right, Grady, my sweet, I just got here before you. If you could enjoy heaven the way I've been, sitting at the feet of the Savior we've loved for so long, you wouldn't grieve at all.' And I lifted up my eyes and thanked the Lord that He had given me the privilege to love so wonderful a woman while He lent her to the earth." His eyes were glistening as his face radiated the peace within his soul.

Aaron yearned.

"So, your grace, in answer to your question, yes, I still miss her. But the Savior has proven Himself to me as faithful and loving. He'll take better care of her up there than I ever did down here."

Chastain turned his head suddenly and looked boldly into Aaron's eyes. "M'lord, He's taking care of your brother also. The way that he died was terrible and so hard to understand. But he is with the Savior now. You must take comfort in that."

Aaron peered deeply into the eyes of the old man he had so unexpectedly come to trust. Seconds protracted to minutes until finally...

"There can be no comfort for me," he whispered softly, knowing the time had come at last. "I am responsible for my brother's death, you see."

Chastain, forgetting years of training, reached forward and grabbed the younger man's hand, holding it tightly. "You must not blame yourself, lad. That's the first thing everyone does, blame themselves. Don't be so hard on yourself."

Aaron nodded his head from side to side. "No, Chastain, you don't understand. I arranged my brother's murder."

The confession was out. And it stung like an adder.

Unable to look his newfound confidant in the eye, Aaron gazed into the fire. Still holding his hand, lending support with the strength of his knobby old fingers, Chastain sat there silently, the importance of the moment weighing heavily on him. Surprisingly, even to himself, he felt no shock, no surprise. Full knowledge of why he had been sent to this tormented young man washed through him like the floodwaters gathering outside. *Help me, God,* he prayed silently.

"Tell me," Chastain said in a gentle tone. No judgments. No condescension. Just tones of strength and understanding in the soothing command.

The words of confession flowed from Aaron's lips fully and freely with no excuses or disavowments. He related it all. Chastain simply sat and listened as the Spirit of God blessed him with calmness and the surety that He was working His will. This was the first step for the Duke of Argyll.

On the grate, the fire burned down, its red-hot cinders glowing and moving about in heated undulation. Chastain could not see Aaron's features as he spoke, but the duke's heart was open and illuminated by the burning rays of a truthful confession.

"This winter..." Aaron finished his story, "has been the most severe season my soul has yet to bear. And yet... I relish the cold, hoping that spring will never set its delicate foot again in Argyllshire. Would that I could disassemble the sun, fold away its burning sides, pack up its blinding light, and banish it from my world forever. Each day I wish to grow colder and colder, more removed from all that I hold dear, going through the motions because there is nothing left for me to do. 'Go!' I wish to yell at that flaming orb that steals into my existence daily and makes me see myself as I am. Aye, old man, how welcome is the cold, the darkness, the numbness. Not to feel, not to think. That is my wish. And yet each morning light falls upon my eyelids, burning its way with cruel heat into the very chambers of my heart, every fold of my brain, saying, 'Look upon this, Aaron Campbell. Look upon yourself and see.' And I look. For I cannot help myself. And I see. And I pray again for the cold to take me away."

CHAPTER
11

May 1843

Spring came anyway.

"The tailor is here, your grace," Jacobs, standing in the garden, shouted up to the men on the roof. His eyes squinted against the sun.

A blond head looked over the edge. "What did you say, Jacobs?" Aaron was inspecting the new roof himself. Predictably, Chastain volunteered, but despite years of training, Aaron laughed at the old man's bravado.

"The tailor, sir, he's come for your fitting!" Jacobs shuffled a bit, trying to hide his irritation.

"Good!" Aaron shouted back. "Send him up to my chambers. I shall be there shortly!"

"As you wish, m'lord."

He showed a Mr. Peter Campbell up to the duke's dressing room and made his way back to the kitchens, for the staff would be taking dinner shortly. Jacobs shook his head in bewilderment as the cook bustled in front of him, adding salt to the stew, butter to the beans, and vinegar to the cabbage. She stopped still, looking at him primarily out of one squinted eye, the other closed completely against the steam. The smells blended together to form a misty potion designed to induce hunger in the most finicky of eaters.

"What's got your mind turnin' aboot like a windy day, Mr. Jacobs?"

Jacobs looked around to make certain no one else could hear. Mrs. Gray was the only person he deigned to engage in friendly conversation. After all, he loved his sweets more than anyone, and it seemed if he was nice he could always talk her into making a big pan of cinnamon buns for dessert.

His nails tapped on the butcher block. "It's just his grace..."

"Aye? What's he up to?"

"Brought in Peter Campbell just now."

"Peter Campbell? Now just what would a smart London-type like his lordship be wantin' from the services of Peter Campbell? Dinna tell me he's goin' to have some tartan weaved for himself!"

"Aye, Cathy, I overheard him talkin' to Chastain. Said he wanted a kilt!"

Mrs. Gray chuckled, crossing her pudgy arms over a spreading bosom. "Goin' back to the Highland ways, eh? Good for his lordship, I say!"

Jacobs shrugged, feeling not nearly as magnanimous as the cook. "It's as if doin' the work of stable hands, and goin' over papers and readin' day and night, always yellin' for more wood on the fire, didna' make him peculiar enough. Add to that the fact that he never wears shoes around the castle, I suppose him goin' about in a kilt is somethin' we should've expected! He was actually up on the roof when I gave him the news!"

"Well, at least he's been no trouble. He mayn't talk to many of us, but from what I hear he's always cordial, an' stays out of the way. I do believe I've only seen him once or twice since he's come home."

"Aye, gets his ridin' done early he does," Jacobs said. "Well, if he doesna' sleep much, he certainly does justice to your cookin', Cathy."

The cook beamed. "It's all that's needed to win my heart over, Mr. Jacobs."

"Speakin' of your cookin'..." his eyes glanced over at the oven.

"They're in there, Mr. Jacobs. I'm surprised you didna' smell them when ya walked in. Ya usually have a nose for such things."

Jacobs breathed in deeply and smiled. "You're a love, Cathy..." he began. A scullery maid walked in just then, a bucket full of dirty water pounding against her thigh. The pompous butler looked at her sternly, cleared his throat, and pulled on the bottom of his vest as he proceeded to sit at the table.

• • •

The warm weather forced Aaron somewhat from his state of melancholy. The heather-scented breeze and the lively green of spring beckoned him on long hikes through the hills and calm times of reading and reflection in the garden. The fresh air caused him to sleep better and the sunshine warmed his sallow skin. He began to at least appear alive once more. By June he was visiting the villagers frequently, helping them whenever he could, be it with a needed shilling or sending over a servant to help out during a time of sickness. Having been a gentleman by birth only, now he was truly gracious by word and deed. But he was unaware of the transformation as he watched the progress of the estates like a hawk, waiting only for the appointed time when he could leave it all behind and rid himself of the guilt through a peaceful oblivion.

"Has his grace been by today?" the village women would ask one another.

"Aye, he came through earlier this mornin'. Has started strollin' about the hills since the spring has come. Wearin' a kilt, too!"

"Ah," one of the daughters sighed with love-struck eyes. "There's no finer lookin' man alive than the Duke of Argyll in his kilt and fine white shirt."

Aaron's days were kept busy with his duties and his rounds. Chastain purposely saw to it that his employer had no time to let depression ease itself into his day. His nights were spent in the quietness of the library, reading or talking to Chastain into the wee hours of the morning. With great expectation he awaited a letter from his mother, but so far he had heard nothing.

Recently, Aaron had been keeping up with the reformers, following Lord Ashley's every move. Having read the Children's Commission report and the Coal Commission report, he became enlightened to the atrocities inflicted upon the industrious class. *Maybe someday*, he thought, *I'll be counted among the ranks of warriors like Colin.* The memory of his one experience in the House of Lords would have caused a weaker man to reconsider what his duties entailed. But Aaron, now fed and nurtured by the Highlands and her people, realized that someday he would return. Perhaps this next session. After all, it would take at least three years before the estates were built back up. Perhaps he could do some good, be of some help before then.

In the stable loft, the cool morning wind blowing softly, he became acutely aware of the emptiness inside him only God was capable of filling. Chastain repeatedly reminded him that God would forgive if only Aaron would believe that He could. They had many discussions concerning faith, the old man's eyes shining when he talked about the love of God. *But Chastain didn't understand*, Aaron kept telling himself. Chastain had never sinned as he had.

Aaron looked out over the dewy fields. A silver morning sun had intrepidly begun its daily trek through the vast blue sky, when the answer surfaced from the gloom of his thoughts. The next day Aaron set out on horseback for Oxford. He would talk to Colin's mentor, Dr. Luther Eliot. And on the solitary journey he would try and figure out just how to ask that very man why God would forgive a sinner like himself.

• • •

A week later

The don sat in a faded damask chair by the cold heating stove. His tawny eyes looked curiously at the familiar face opposite him. Surely he knew the face that looked at him in sincerity, but not the man. He scratched the side of his beard, puzzled at this unexpected visit.

Aaron's eyes traversed the untidy study. Books strewn everywhere. Dust flying about the room at all times. Professor Eliot preferred it that way. He waved his hand in a sunbeam, causing the dust particles to mill about like a frenzied school of minnows.

"Sunbeams are better seen if they have more substance," he winked. It was Aaron's turn to look puzzled.

Substance—Eliot was always searching for substance. In people. In books. In music and art. The only true substance he had ever found was God. God was as real to him as the young man sitting opposite. More so, actually. If the Lord Christ came and sat down in his study, it wouldn't be as hard to guess why. With Aaron Campbell it was different. He could only assume it had something to do with his brother, Colin.

Even now his heart ground painfully with gears of remorse and sadness. How he had grieved when he heard that his former student's life had been taken from him. Naturally, with a relationship as close as theirs had been, they had kept in as good a contact as two busy men were able over the past ten years. To think that the lad was now gone, gone to heaven admittedly, well...he had tried not to think much about it. But it was hard not to remember as the same face, throbbing with youth and life, was now looking at him in earnest. The blue eyes were clearly troubled.

"So, your grace," he began.

"Please call me Aaron, professor."

"Aaron? Aaron and Colin. A bit cute of your mother, considering your nobility, don't you think?" He just couldn't resist.

Aaron smiled broadly and relaxed a bit more in his chair. "If you knew my mother, you'd understand."

"Oh yes. Lady Margaret. I remember Colin speaking about her. A bit on the eccentric side, if my memory serves me correctly."

"Yes, sir. A bit eccentric but no more so than someone trying to make a philosophical statement about dust-filled sunbeams."

Eliot nodded appreciatively. "And how is she now?"

"I don't know."

"What?"

"She left on a long trip shortly after my brother's death. I thought she would be coming home soon. But lately I wonder. It would take a powerful force to bring her back to a house so burdened with memories."

"Well, then, we'll just have to pray that God will bring comfort to her soul."

Eliot arose to grab his pipe off his desk. As he was lighting it, he continued speaking. "You and your brother had grown far apart. Am I correct in saying so?"

Aaron was more than eager to discuss Colin. Besides, he wasn't exactly sure how to phrase what he wanted to ask Eliot anyway, even though he had rehearsed a hundred different versions of the conversation on the trip down.

"Yes, sir. Although we are almost identical on the outside, we couldn't have been more disparate inside."

"Tell me about it. Your brother was truly my friend. I'd be interested to hear."

Aaron nodded and began. "Things came rather easily for both of us. Not as easily for Colin, mind you. It took him a bit longer to pick up ideas, but once he did he was like a bulldog, sunk his teeth in up to the gums and wouldn't let go. Whereas once I grasped something, I set it down just as quickly. I think, being the younger of the two, I didn't see the sense in being so conscientious. After all, Colin was the inheritor of the title, not myself. That's the way it had always been. That one difference as children became larger and larger as we grew, until it consumed all our similarities, and we were nothing alike.

"I made it through Oxford with honors...and a blasting headache every morning. Colin was more studious. He needed to be. And what was more, he enjoyed the challenge. The only challenges I enjoyed were base ones. But fortunately for me, I absorbed my studies with no effort. Not that it mattered. After we graduated, I did nothing but gamble and carouse anyway."

"You and thousands of others," Professor Eliot interjected dryly. Aaron gave a bitter laugh and continued.

"Yes, well, when we were older children, 12 or 13 perhaps, I remember so clearly the day Colin found me in the stables and told me he had given himself to God. It was then that our relationship began to crumble. He was so excited, the joy was apparent on his face. And I... I just sat there... staring at him. I asked him if it was hard to do. He said no, that it was easy. And I knew right then that if it was easy for Colin, I'd have nothing to with it. Of course I'd heard about Jesus Christ all my life. I could be found in church with irritating regularity. And though I heard the gospel preached each Sunday, I never could understand how a person could simply believe Christ died for his sins and that would be that. And Colin's enthusiastic approach to salvation didn't help matters any. It was all he talked about.

"The rift between us grew steadily wider. Prior to his conversion, we did everything together. We worked a little garden patch. We'd ride. Or we would sit in the library together for hours reading Bunyan or Addison quietly and discussing what the author was trying to say.

"When we were about 14, Father took a keen interest in Colin. I took it personally... I suppose I was jealous. No... I *know* I was. It was actually the beginning of his preparation for the future. They would ask if I would like to go on the rounds, but I always refused. They sought me out to attend church functions with them, and I refused those offers as well. I blamed Colin's future title, and his and Father's shared love for God. After a while I became so consumed in my hatred for both of those that I sought to widen the gulf between us yet further.

"When my father died, Colin became the duke. I shut down any feeling I had ever had for him. He was the duke—a title which made me feel left out and cheated."

"Did you see your brother much after college?" Eliot interjected.

"That was the sad part of it all. The only time I sought him was when I was in a particularly bad spot and needed him to bail me out."

"Gambling debts, isn't that right?"

"Yes, sir. He would tell me my feet were trodding the path to nowhere. That I needed God. I would sit there and pretend to listen. I figured it was due penance when his signed check made its way into my hand." Aaron held out his right hand, palm up. Professor Eliot noticed the scar across his palm. Aaron noted his gaze and swiftly shut his palm.

"The summer before he died, we were in the library at Inveraray Castle. After a particularly cruel trick I pulled, he had finally had enough of me. So in an attempt to thoroughly humiliate him, I told him what a fool I thought he was for paying up all the time. How all of London thought he was insane for doing so. I told him I wouldn't be in his shoes if my life depended on it. And here I am, the Duke of Argyll," he said with irony. Aaron paused. Professor Eliot nodded for him to continue.

"That was all he could take. He told me to leave the castle. The next exchange we had was the night he died. I was the first to get to him after he was stabbed. He died telling me that he had always loved me more than anyone else."

"He did, too," Eliot nodded. "I've never seen a man so concerned about his brother."

"I know."

"Why are you here, Aaron?"

"Sir, I have inherited one of the elements that separated my brother and me, the title. Now I want to know about the other element. What does it really mean to be a Christian?"

Ever the tutor, Eliot lounged back in his chair and folded his arms across his chest. "What do you think it is?"

"By confessing my sins, accepting Christ's work on the cross, in believing by faith."

The professor smiled. "Is that the hard part for you?"

"No, sir."

Eliot was taken off guard for a moment. Most of his students had a hard time with the whole faith bit. "Really?"

"Sir, it's easy to have faith in something else when you have no faith in yourself. I don't know who I am anymore. My old life has ceased to fit. I'm like a ghost roaming about the manor, tending to my duties."

"Aaron," the old man looked at him earnestly, "what is it then? What keeps you from turning to the Savior?"

Aaron's answer was soft and heartbroken. "Forgiveness is something for which I don't deserve to ask."

The professor arose out of his chair and pulled on his coat. He now knew why the Duke of Argyll had been sent to him. "Come. Let's walk a bit, shall we?"

· · ·

The quadrangle was alive with irises and roses. The sun shone flamboyantly, seizing the moment before the afternoon clouds would appear. Students shuffled hastily to their sessions or the library, eager to start their day—or not so eager, but giving in to the inevitable.

They walked along the banks of the River Cherwell. The air, still smelling of morning mists, coated their throats with its cool humidity.

"I understand your quandary, Aaron," Eliot said, abruptly breaking the silence as they continued walking. "I know what it is like to feel unworthy. To feel tainted and stained beyond all hope."

"I don't think you do, sir."

Eliot held up his hand. "Let me speak, Aaron."

Aaron looked at the professor's hand. Although time had softened its edge, the scar was still visible across the smooth-skinned surface of his right palm.

The professor took a deep breath and exhaled slowly through his nostrils. "I believe in the providence of God. I believe that nothing can happen unless He has ordained it. I believe He is sovereign.

"He sent you to me. Of that I have no doubt. I do not know what you have done that makes you feel unworthy. Most Christians would tell you—and in absolute correctness, I might add—that no one is worthy. And it is that which makes salvation so beautiful, so typical of a merciful God. They will tell you that if it was completely up to us, we would all fail. And I assure you we would. The book of Romans attests to that. It is God who shows mercy. But many of those people have never committed a sin of such magnitude as murder or rape and so on, have never experienced a hatred so black it affects all the senses. Therefore, they have no idea what a torment that kind of guilt affords. How it accentuates the feelings of unworthiness, magnifies them until they are all-consuming and visible in every thought, every action. How it eats at the very core of one's existence until nothing is alive but that self-same guilt. I do have an understanding of what the queen of spades can demand of an unlucky soul."

They stopped and sat down on the grassy bank. "I shall tell you how it was with me."

Aaron looked over at him and felt a strange sensation. This man, a Brother, had much to say. And he was more than willing to let him say it. It was why he had come. Why the Father had led him here. Aaron knew that now. He fixed his eyes on the students punting along the Cherwell, giving the professor an added measure of privacy.

"I was an Oriel man myself. *Man...*" he almost spat the word. "There was nothing *manlike* about me when I arrived at Oxford so many years ago. I was a boy, and I stayed that way throughout the first four years. My father, a shipyard owner in Bristol, shipped me off to Oxford with these words: 'In four years you'll come home, and if you haven't passed, dear Luther,' he spread his arm over the scene before us, the bustling yards, the people racing around, 'none of this will be yours. It will be given to your sister.' So off I went in the year 1799. My tutor was a quiet genius. He had never married, and no one really knew what kind of a private life he led. I assume he loved to read, and he wrote quite extensively on the topic of Republican Rome. He was quite accomplished in the field of ancient history which I had chosen to study. At first I rather enjoyed our sessions, but then Brimstone found me. And although I *could* blame the Society for all that went wrong, it was just as much the Brothers that I found myself buddying up with. Perhaps I led *them* astray... who knows? At any rate, my studies took a decided turn in the wrong direction. And I found myself at the end of four years ill-prepared for my examination.

"You know," he said, relief evident in his voice, "I haven't spoken of this for so many years. I can hardly believe how easily it is coming back to me."

"Professor," Aaron began apologetically, "you do not have to go on."

"No, no. This is what I meant about nothing happening apart from God. I never before could see the use of what happened. But if He wants me to share it with you, who am I not to comply?"

"Submission?" Aaron questioned.

"Precisely. Now, where was I? Oh yes, the examination. A month before the appointed time, Dr. Ellenburg had warned me that he wasn't going to go easy on me during the oral testing. I panicked, naturally. And all my years of irresponsibility suddenly became my professor's fault. How could it be *mine?* I thought then. As *luck* would have it—and I use that word loosely, Aaron—the Brotherhood had completed its Stonehenge ceremony just weeks before. I didn't waste any time at calling in the debt."

"You *used* your card?"

"Yes, Aaron. I was desperate. My blood Brother was the . . . never mind about who he was . . . Suffice it to say he was from one of the most influential families in England. If his father, or himself for that matter, said anything about anybody, it was regarded as infallible. He was more than happy to help when I met him with the queen in hand. The plan was simple. My friend reported to his father that Dr. Ellenburg's unmarried state was not from shyness but from sexual preference."

"He accused him of being a homosexual?" Aaron's eyes widened slightly.

"Yes. The rumors arose more quickly than a storm over the Channel. My Brother went so far as to even have some of the Brothers come forward and lie, saying Dr. Ellenburg propositioned them. I did the same, requesting then that I be examined by another don. My Brother had agreed as part of the bargain to bribe another professor to pass me with an easy examination."

At that point, needing something to do with his large, somewhat clumsy hands, Professor Eliot reached into his pocket for his pipe. He lit it and puffed until it was going strong as he continued staring off into the distance.

"So, it was all arranged. Dr. Ellenburg had lost every bit of his credibility and was on the verge of being asked to leave. He went about silently, as usual, and waited until the committee he was to appear before met. Naturally, he was hoping to clear his name and his reputation. But matters didn't turn out the way he had hoped. He was relieved of his post in disgrace. Many society families were in an uproar, demanding nothing less, believing he had compromised the purity of their precious sons.

"The next morning Dr. Ellenburg was found hanging from the rafter in his study. A note protesting his innocence lay on his desk. And I killed him, Aaron. If I had pulled a trigger and shot him directly in the skull, I would not have been any more a murderer than I was already." Silence engulfed them both. Aaron exhaled, not having realized he had been holding his breath. Eliot was lost somewhere in the corners of his mind. He placed a hand on Aaron's sleeve after several minutes.

"The point is this: God forgave me, Aaron. I had done the unthinkable, and He still forgave me. Although, as you can well imagine, I've never forgiven myself."

Eliot lifted up his right palm and showed it to Aaron. "We have been taught honor all our lives, lad. We think we know what it means to keep a promise. But let me tell you this: Our feeble honor is nothing compared to the honor of God. When His Holy Scriptures tell us that 'If we confess our sins, He is faithful and just to forgive us our sins and to cleanse us from all unrighteousness,' we can believe it, and we can take comfort in it. Did He not forgive David of Uriah's murder? Did He not forgive the thief on the cross? Forgiveness is so central to who God is, probably because we all need it so badly."

"Even having God's forgiveness," Aaron ventured, "how did you manage to live with yourself?"

"Years after I believed in the Savior, I found his sister and told her the whole story."

"What did she say?"

"She was shocked, naturally. But she was ill and said she had not the strength nor the will to pursue the matter. It changed my life forever. The reason you see me here, as a professor, is that I went back and finished my studies and excelled. I could not accept my inheritance. It was blood money. I took up Dr. Ellenburg's mantle, studying Republican Rome and continuing his work. But through it all, the Savior is beside me. And I would rather have Him than all the money and shipyards England holds."

"Does it bother you, the fact that you gave up your inheritance?"

"No. It was a choice I made. And each day that I speak of Rome, I make restitution, although it gets easier each year. God is kind, Aaron. I've had to live with the consequences of what I did. But He was good enough to make it all bearable. Your brother was a tender gift. And the other lads, well, they make everything worthwhile for me now."

The two men sat in silence for a long time until Aaron stood up, straightening his clothes. He helped Professor Eliot to his feet and shook his hand. "Thank you, sir. I'd best be off."

The old man smiled. Knowing Aaron's need to leave the grassy bank and be alone he said, "You go on. I'll stay here awhile."

Aaron nodded gratefully and turned, finding the pathway again.

"Son!" Eliot shouted. "I can always be found here."

Aaron lifted his hand in a wave and kept walking.

• • •

The streets of Oxford are perfect for walking all day, alone in one's thoughts. Nobody bothered Aaron to ask directions or talk about the weather. They respected someone in contemplation. Aaron spent a lot of his time walking around Christ Church College—"The House," as most called it. The great vaulted ceiling of the chapel with its intricately carved stonework spreading across the ceiling in fans could hold one's attention while he lost himself in thought. Cardinal Wolsey had built this college, so long ago. *And look where it got him*, Aaron thought. *Look what happened to Wolsey's contemporary, Sir Thomas More*. The affairs of religion had always confused Aaron. It all seemed to come down to honor. Wolsey only cared about his own honor; Sir Thomas More, the honor of the Church of Rome. And Henry VIII, the man who sentenced both to die, told himself he was merely guarding the honor of the English throne.

Honor. In its name it led men to do horrible things. All, really, for the sake of pride. For the thrill of power. Hadn't that been Lucius Carlyle's motive when he called in the promise?

And what did any of them know about honor? Some schoolboy melodrama with ancient monuments, robes and candles, playing cards and blood. There was only one source of honor. And any true manifestation of such could only be found through Him. And His forgiveness was there for the taking as well.

The sun was setting as Aaron started back to Inveraray Castle. *Yes*, he decided. *I will give myself to God. But not here. Not on this road. It must be with Colin.*

• • •

A grating wail sounded as Aaron pulled open the gate that was connected to the iron fencing surrounding the Campbell family tombs. The night was chilly, with a clear sky and a full moon. He had taken his cloak from the saddlebag, protectively pulling it about him. Colin's stone tomb, four feet high, was carved with a rope design around the edge. On top it was inscribed:

Colin Archibald Campbell
The Twelfth Duke of Argyll
Born September 5, 1810
Died November 6, 1842
I know that my Redeemer liveth,
and that he shall stand at the latter day
upon the earth. Though the worms destroy this
body yet in my flesh shall I see God.

Aaron sat down on the tomb. How he wished Colin were with him now in spirit as well as body. Inside this tomb his twin rested. And it was his own doing.

The night was still, and a soft breeze blew through Aaron's hair. He ran his fingers over the carving, tracing each letter. As he traced he talked softly, pouring his heart out to his brother as he should have done years before.

"Colin, I'm sorry. I know you've forgiven me. But how much it hurts to sit here on your grave. To tell you of what I've been going through lately, and not be able to see a smile lighting up your face.

"You really loved me. More than anyone ever did. And now, through your death, I'm ready to make the commitment that you had prayed I would make since we were 12."

He took a deep, ragged breath, his fisted hands shaking as he tried to get out the words, lost in a squalor of self-disgust. "But I was so proud and ... and so jealous. I was blinded by my own petty emotions."

He rubbed his face in an effort to calm himself, and he smiled slightly. "For the first time in years I look back on our childhood memories and smile. The tricks we played on everyone. Except Mother, of course." A small laugh. "The other night I was thinking about when we were seven and we were stricken by scarlet fever. I passed through it easily enough, and I felt so guilty that it had taken you down more ferociously. I remember sitting on Mama's lap into the wee hours of the morning as you tossed and turned and cried out in your delirium. One night, in particular, I thought you were going to die. And Mama held me tightly, and we cried and cried. I remember her praying, calling on God to heal you and bring you back to us. You had been unconscious for hours.

Suddenly you opened your eyes and gave us a lopsided grin, and I had never been so happy in my life. The thought of losing you was frightening beyond belief.

"Oh, Colin!" he wept as he lay face down against the slab, great sobs racking his body, "I missed so many years with you. You died, and I didn't know you. We were one, Colin. One flesh. One person. And I ripped us apart over the years. And if that wasn't enough, I destroyed forever the bond we had shared."

The weeping continued as Aaron took hold of his grief and embraced it. It wouldn't be the same for him as it was for Chastain. As long as the grief was stirring in his heart, he was paying for what he did. He could never let it go.

After a while, tears refused to come, and Aaron knew he must do what he came here for. He knelt by the tomb, and the love of God enfolded him like a heavy blanket. Aaron, with his face between his knees, humbly, quietly, and with great suffering spoke to God for the first time since he was a child.

Darkness overtook the land as the breeze died down in homage to the Lord. Aaron surrendered.

CHAPTER

12

Forgiveness is a powerful force. And Aaron found even more startling and infinitely humbling the ease with which God forgives. Aaron Campbell was a new creation, and inside of him God's forgiveness and love flowered, a newness of life so refreshing, so utterly beautiful, all he wanted to do was sleep. The battle was over. And to the Victor went the spoils... Aaron's heart. Aaron was vanquished. But the Victor had fought for love. And that made all the difference. Once enemy territory had become home.

Walking into the castle, Aaron was relieved to see the glow of a fire spilling into the hallway from the library.

"Chastain!" he called as he entered the room.

"Welcome home, your grace."

"Chastain, I'm home in more ways than one."

"What do you mean?"

"Your prayers have not been in vain, old man."

"I did not believe for one moment that they were, m'lord."

"You are a wise man, Chastain. I wish I could be as certain, as full of faith as you."

"Simply trust, Aaron."

Aaron smiled. "Yes, I suppose that everything comes down to trust."

"Yes, your grace. God has a purpose for your life. He will reveal His plans for you and will show Himself real. Make no mistake about that, your lordship." Pausing slightly, his emotions overtook him. "Welcome to the family, m'lord." He held out the knotted old hand.

Aaron reached to shake his hand, but pulled the old man into an embrace instead. "Thank you, Chastain. Thank you," he said, heartfelt, realizing the debt of gratitude he owed the man. "Thank God for you."

• • •

Aaron's appetite for Scripture became voracious and ongoing. Spring and summer were filled with study. Thinking he remembered so much from childhood, it became apparent he was starting his new life in Christ with a shallow foundation. The late-night sessions with Chastain stepped up considerably, and Aaron was impressed, as well as delighted, with his secretary's broad knowledge of Scripture. And he learned how to pray.

In the mornings, Aaron sat in the loft with his Bible, once Colin's. His brother had reached from beyond the grave to encourage his twin with words of praise to God and discovery of personal spiritual truths written by his own hand in the margin of the worn book. That time of meditation had become precious to him. Reading. Pondering. Wonderment and peace filling him with each verse he read, each prayer he uttered. His Savior became more real with each turn of the page. *God's joys truly are new every morning*, he would think as the sun christened the new day's sky. The bitter cold of his past was behind him.

"I am amazed," he said to Chastain one day as they were going over accounts, "at the simplicity of mind and heart the Savior brings. London brings a shudder deep within when I recall the life I lived. A nocturnal world, Chastain. I remember the whisper of the cards as they swished into place in front of me . . . and I hear chains. I recall the way my favorite brandy would slowly trickle down the back of my throat each night . . . and I feel flames. And the women, ever ready for me, with open arms and empty gazes . . . I remember their kisses and their mock affections . . . and I feel smoke, thick and suffocating, wending its way into my nose and mouth, through my lungs, and winding around my heart."

"Sin is a powerful force, m'lord."

"It must be, for someone to endure such emptiness for that long. Not just endure it, Chastain, but look forward to it."

"You are a new creature, m'lord. And whether or not the Redeemer saves us from cards, drink, and women, or pride, prejudice, and greed, we are all just as new, putting off those things which are behind."

Putting off.

Aaron realized that some things can be put off forever. But some things must be paid for here on earth. And with even more determination in his heart, he vowed to do right. He must step up his preparations and build up the estates more quickly. And when the time did come for him to walk to the gallows, he would go with the words of his brother on his lips.

To die is gain.

• • •

Sir Silas Barringer, the owner of one of Britain's most respected banking institutions, was shown into the drawing room of Aaron's Edinburgh townhouse. He was distinguished, philanthropic, and fabulously wealthy. And when Aaron had contacted him regarding his investments, old Silas had been only too happy to make a visit to Edinburgh. The man truly had only one love in life ... money. And he wasn't ashamed to admit it to anyone.

"I've much business to do in the 'Athens of the North,'" he had written in a firm hand with thick, black, inky strokes, "and I should be happy to put you on my schedule, your grace."

Aaron waited for him in the library. And when Sir Silas Barringer entered, he couldn't help but be impressed. His black suit was cut to perfection, and a single diamond of fabulous proportions held his cravat in place to the front of his shirt. The blinding white of his hair contrasted with his arresting eyes, which were piercing, very dark, and heavy-lidded. But the singular feature which made Silas Barringer stand out in a crowd was the size of his hands. Like two great man-o'-wars they were. He shook Aaron's hand with a firm grip that Aaron easily returned. A moment later they were sitting in chairs, the soft light of the afternoon coming through the sheers as they enjoyed a glass of sherry. Neither mentioned the night Aaron had lost so dismally to Lucius Carlyle.

"I haven't got much time to waste," Aaron was saying. "I want to double my current investments in land holdings. Is it true you are selling off some of your holdings in America?"

"It's true. I'm going to invest in the South."

Aaron raised his brows. "Where is the land you wish to sell?"

"Long Island, New York. Boston. And some water-front on the Patapsco River in Baltimore."

"Is the shipping industry growing there?"

"Oh yes, it's quite a port."

"Why sell it then if it stands to make you money in the future?"

"Cotton, pure and simple. I think I will make more in the South. You would be wise to consider that avenue as well."

"Well..." Aaron considered, but not for long. "You are probably right. And in the near future I might consider it as well. But for now I would like to take another route."

"Well? What do you think then? Are you interested in purchasing the properties I mentioned?"

Aaron stood to his feet, "Yes, Mr. Barringer. Yes. I believe I am."

Just then the butler announced dinner, and Aaron ushered Silas Barringer into his dining room for a meal of roasted pheasant.

"How is London these days?" Aaron asked as he began eating.

"The same, the same. Tell me, are you planning on taking your seat in the House of Lords this fall?" He sat forward.

"I think so."

"And... will you follow in the footsteps of your brother, the late duke?"

Aaron nodded his head. "I am not sure what God is requiring of me, sir. Right now I need to secure my holdings. Perhaps I shall do *some* good this session; however, my brother let the estates slip a bit, and I have much to make up for. I won't have the opportunity of enjoying politics on the grand scale he did."

Barringer cleared his throat. "Quite a man, your brother. Quite a man." But he was more than happy when Aaron turned the topic to one of finance.

• • •

It was October when Aaron finally received word from his mother. The note was short, yet holding the affections of a mother for her only living son. Having taken up temporary residence in a convent outside Jerusalem, she still did not know when she would return.

• • •

Chastain walked with Aaron over the hills. Aaron kept his normally brisk pace down to a saunter as Chastain read the figures on the pad of paper in his hand.

"Barley...20 percent increase. Oats...35 percent increase. Hay...25 percent increase. Wheat...19 percent increase. Add to that a 15 percent increase in livestock and the planting of over 2000 new trees, and I'd say your first year as the Duke of Argyll has been a profitable one, your lordship."

Aaron smiled down at Chastain and clapped him gently but firmly between his protruding shoulder blades. "Old man, you are one deuce of a secretary. Thank you."

"Don't thank me, m'lord. Give glory to the Savior. For some reason He's chosen to bless you mightily."

"That he has, old man."

But only Aaron knew why.

• • •

Late November

The sky was colorless—a 10 A.M., woolen kind of sky where a blanket of clouds, neither dark nor white, snuggles up to the sun, making the breeze seem a bit more chilly than it should. Thistle's hooves sounded very dull, and Aaron dismounted and tethered the lithe beast to a small beech tree at the edge of the meadow. November 6. *One year ago today*, he thought as he walked forward, his kilt swinging with the rhythm of his stride. *One year ago today he died, my only brother.*

The churchyard, surrounded by iron fencing, lay about a hundred yards before him as he mounted the last hill. Raised tombs seemed to hover above the ground. Tombstones leaned with exhaustion, having proclaimed the graves' occupants for centuries and seemingly growing weary of the task. Many were unreadable, but still they stood, leaning against one another in defiance to the fact that they had become meaningless pieces of stone. He gazed over the graveyard, his eyes lighting upon a small figure huddled beside Colin's tomb.

"I'm not the only one to remember," he whispered. To know that Colin was not so easily forgotten brought satisfaction. He quickly began to negotiate the distance between them.

Apparently it was a young girl. Her full, dark cloak was draped over her kneeling frame. In her intentness, she failed to notice him as he drew closer. There were no outward signs of grief. She simply sat back on her heels and stared at the tomb in front of her, not moving an inch, barely breathing. Her slick black hair was pulled back tightly into a long braid—a severe style that echoed her almost puritanical clothing. She didn't look like a commoner. Her bearing was too proud.

She turned toward him, and he saw the white streak of hair along the side of her head. The woman stood up and began to hurry away.

"Maria!" Aaron yelled.

CHAPTER

13

"Aaron?"

He hurried over to her, taking off his cap. "Aye, Maria, it is I."

"In your kilt you look so ... so Scottish! What are you doing in the Highlands, your lordship?"

"I suppose I could ask the same question."

She nodded. "Yes, I suppose you could, m'lord. But we'll ask later. Will you remember your brother with me this day? I thought I wanted to do this in solitude, but now that you've come, it seems fitting somehow."

"Aye, I shall remember him with you, Maria. For the past year I've had to remember him alone. You were his friend when I was not. You knew him as a man. All I have are boyhood memories."

"Well then," she smiled sadly, her gray eyes ancient, "between the two of us, we have a complete picture."

Aaron stood next to her and took her arm in his. The quiet of the morning settled about them like the dome of a cathedral. Birds chirped in a faraway manner. No breeze accompanied their mourning.

Her presence couldn't have been more profound.

Many moments passed in speechless remembrance. Words were unnecessary as they let their minds wander through the twists and turns of the past. The man in the tomb had been loved by so many, in contrast to the two lonely people who mourned him. Finally, Maria lifted her eyes to Aaron.

"I'm ready to go, your grace."

"Would you come back to the castle and warm yourself before you leave?"

She nodded yes and walked to the carriage waiting on the other side of the church. A moment later she was back at Aaron's side. "I told the driver to pick me up at Inveraray Castle in half an hour. I should like to walk there with you, by way of the loch, if you please."

Putting her arm through his, she breathed in deeply.

Silence accompanied them on their walk as well, but finally, when the castle was in sight, she spoke. "I've been waiting for this day all year, wondering what it would be like when it finally arrived."

"As have I."

Maria's eyes took on an earnestness Aaron had never seen in their gray circles. "M'lord, he died because of you, you know."

The statement hit him as a soldier's arrow seeks only the heart. "What do you mean?" Aaron bristled as his mind chilled with a misty fear.

She spoke with some difficulty "Your grace, your brother cared more about you than you could ever realize. Do you see that spot of ground there by the water?" She pointed. "Under that tree?"

"Aye."

"The day before the masquerade ball, Colin and I sat together there. He poured out his soul, telling of the pain your separation from him brought. Even more, the pain of your darkened heart. And we prayed together," her voice caught, her cheeks reddened from a shyness, an embarrassment at laying bare her soul, "we prayed . . .

for your soul, m'lord. Colin petitioned God to bring you to Himself no matter what it took. And so I've taken up where he left off." She continued looking down at the ground she crossed over. "Oh, your grace, you've been in my prayers each day."

Aaron placed his hand on her arm, a tenderness for this tiny woman beside him enveloping his heart with a powerful, sweet bondage. "Maria, your prayers have been answered. I surrendered." His words were quiet, yet sad, speaking of depths left to plunge, of hauntings she would not ever understand.

Maria's eyes shone with unshed tears. "How did the Master subdue you, your grace?"

Inveraray Castle stood before them. "I'll tell you tomorrow, if I may. Where are you staying?"

"At Castle Lachlan."

"With Anne's family?"

She nodded. "After Colin died, I had some performances in Rome as well as Paris. When I was there, I received an invitation from Anne's mother to summer with them. Summer turned to fall, and now fall will soon turn to winter, and still I am here. I've been teaching music at the orphanage."

"Don't you miss the opera?"

She shrugged in that feminine way she had. "At times. But the sabbatical has been very good for me. Besides, the children give me joy to spare, and I've learned so much about living from Anne's great-aunt."

Aaron's eyes lit up. "Is old Aunt Violet still around?" he asked of the spinster maiden who had been running the institution ever since anyone could remember. She was the youngest daughter of a Maclachlan chief who fought for Bonnie Prince Charlie.

"My, yes. She's almost 90 years old. But you'd never know it. I've always heard it said that marriage ages a woman!"

Aaron laughed. "Maybe. But it also mellows a woman. Makes her like fine brandy, rounds off the rough edges enough to heat up the palate but not set your entire head on fire!"

"It sounds as if you know by experience, m'lord."

"Unfortunately, I do know the difference of having a relationship with a married woman and an unmarried woman. And if you had asked me last year which I preferred, I would have told you married without having to think for a moment. But now..."

"You've found the Savior. Your grace, He's lovingly led you through a wilderness of your own making. I can hardly believe you, one of London's greatest sinners, are now a child of the Creator."

"I do not deserve His love, and yet, Maria, it is mine."

Just then Maria's coach pulled around.

"So much for warming myself. I had no idea the time was escaping us so rapidly."

"You are still welcome to come inside. Why don't you stay for lunch?"

"Thank you, m'lord, but no. The day is quite young yet, and I have much to do."

"May I call upon you tomorrow?"

Maria stepped back a couple of feet and looked at him. Studying him closely. Weighing in her mind what the outcome of his call might mean eventually. He was still the image of his brother, but there was more now. His eyes were still different—they had seen so much more than Colin's ever had. But they looked upon her with warmth, and she could see that a new light shone from their blue depths. What harm could it do?

She finally decided. "Yes, you may come, your grace. I think I should like that very much."

He helped her into the carriage, and it rolled down the road as the morning breeze finally rushed down from the hillside. Aaron shivered involuntarily as he made his way to the stables.

• • •

Around Loch Fyne, Aaron traveled to Kilbride, Maclachlan territory. The two clans had been closely tied for centuries. Their ties consisted of shared blood and neighboring earth. And though the Campbells were a wealthier, larger, and much more influential clan, they never forgot their bond with the Maclachlans.

Aaron sat on a new stallion he had purchased only two months before. Given the name of Damascus, the great chestnut horse, with black mane and tail, thundered underneath him as he made his way to Maria. On a single mount, Castle Lachlan was only an hour away. He hadn't been there since Colin's wedding years before. Remembering the last time he rode away from the great baronial manor house, he couldn't help but smile. *May my eyes never rest upon these religious fools again!* he had thought then.

"And now I am one of them! And more foolish than most, perhaps."

He galloped past the ruins of the Maclachlans' medieval castle, destroyed by a British frigate almost a hundred years before. There was little left of the building now, yet time hushed itself in the old fortress' presence. Aaron felt weighted with insignificance when he rode by, knowing that in a hundred years it would look much the same and he would walk the earth no longer. How much easier it would be if each human were made of stone. Heart and all. *There is so little time given a man,* he thought. And though he had wasted much of his life, he knew there was much he could do before the earth claimed his body as her subject.

Several minutes later he approached the grand manor, its delicate arches and beautiful stonework an airy contrast to the old, earthbound edifice. The drive rounded gracefully to the front door. Aaron reined in Damascus and jumped down. Immediately the front door opened.

"Your grace," a stocky footman bowed his head as he took Aaron's coat and hat.

"Aye, I am here to call on Mrs. Rosetti."

He bowed again. "Very good, m'lord. She is expectin' you. The drawin' room is this way if you'd prefer to wait there in comfort."

"Thank you." Aaron followed him to the drawing room off the right side of the entry hall, his feet traveling without sound over the mosaic floor. In a glance he checked himself in the hall mirror. It was the first time in his life he was unsure of his appearance.

"I'll fetch Mrs. Rosetti."

"You'll do no such thing, Fergus Maclachlan!" a voice from the corner of the room ordered. "Not until I've finished with him."

Aaron wheeled around as Fergus bowed and left the room, quietly shutting the door behind him.

In a straight-backed chair sat the oldest woman Aaron had ever seen. She was dressed in a full gown the color of crushed raspberries, and her hands sported jeweled rings on all but two fingers. A hint of rouge livened the papery cheeks. Her eyes, colored the bleached blue of having seen almost a century of sunlit days, flashed visibly and most saucily.

Aaron bowed and walked across the room. "Aunt Violet. How lovely to see you again."

She waved a hand at him, the jewels glittering in the sunbeam that fell across her lap and casting dots of light on the bodice of her dress. "Please dispense with the formalities, Aaron Campbell. Do sit down! Duke of Argyll or no, I cannot abide to speak to someone who towers over me so. You're even taller than my dear father was, God rest his soul."

"Thank you for allowing me to come to your home."

"Well, coming is one thing. Staying is another. I remember the last time you darkened our doors. It's not a very pretty memory, mind you."

He had arrived for Colin's wedding more than a little inebriated. "Yes, well, that was years ago, Aunt Violet. As you can see," he spread his arms wide, "I bear no trace of drunkenness."

"I don't believe you."

"It's true, I assure you."

"Breathe into your handkerchief and pass it over to me."

Even as his brows raised in surprise, he chuckled, pulling out his handkerchief and humoring her. He wouldn't have dreamed of doing otherwise.

The wrinkles on her forehead became more pronounced as she sniffed the white linen square then pressed it back into his hand. "All right, you must be telling the truth," she announced grudgingly. "So you haven't been drinking, but you want to see Mrs. Rosetti, and you've been known to consume more than just liquor. She is gracious, a wonderful lady, Aaron Campbell, and if you have designs on her that are anything other than upright, I'll make sure our family never sells you another draft horse as long as I live."

Aaron arched his brows.

". . . and I intend to live another 20 years! As if I didn't know what you were thinking, you upstart."

"No more of the famous Maclachlan Belgians? I do not know if my plowmen would ever forgive me, especially after this year's successful harvest. Believe me, Aunt Violet, my motives are whiter than snow. I wouldn't think of putting Mrs. Rosetti in a compromising position."

Suspiciously she squinted one eye at him, the folds of her lids closing around it. "How do I know you're telling the truth?"

Aaron's eyes locked into hers, blue eyes to blue, and the words issued forth true, clear, and without apology. "I've come to know the Truth. And He has set me free."

In walked Maria.

Aunt Violet's brows arched this time. "So a rogue the likes of Aaron Campbell has become a Christian. God save the church!" she said with a twinkle in her eyes. "Seriously now, Aaron, your salvation must have been hard-won."

He nodded.

Her tone softened immeasurably as she reached for his hand. "Good. So was mine. And I am all the more thankful for it. Testify of it to me, child."

Maria sat down on the sofa next to him. "Yes. Tell me, too, Aaron. How is it that, after a life of fancy and folly, you have found yourself redeemed?"

Quietly and reverently, Aaron told them of God's quest for him and his surrender. He focused not so much on his sin, but on the mercy God extends to those who believe. By the end of the ten minutes it took for him to testify of God's saving love, Maria Rosetti and Violet Maclachlan were breathless in Christian joy. Their hearts expanded, nourished afresh by the deep waters of God's overwhelming love.

"I, too, came to know the love of God after years of rebellion," the old woman explained. "I left Scotland for five years to study the arts in Paris. I couldn't wait to get away from my family, and once I was out from under Mama and Papa's rules, I became reckless. Men, jewels," she displayed her ringed hands, "champagne, parties. I came home from France as old as I am now. Sometimes I envy those who become Christians at an early age, who never fully experience sin and its miseries on a grand scale. Yet at the same time, they do not have as full an understanding of just what it is that God saves us out of."

Maria agreed. "I just came to the Savior two years ago."

Aaron basked in the close communion of the saints, sharing what the Lord had done for them. But he knew his sin outweighed them all. And it would always be thus, no matter who he should share his testimony with. If only one could go back ... then the hauntings of the past would be no more.

The clock on the mantel chimed. Aunt Violet looked up sharply, checking the watch pinned to her dress. "Oh, my heavens, 11 o'clock already! I need to be getting over to the orphanage. I'm teaching the older children the fine art of watercolor."

"Aunt Violet's still a wonderful artist," said Maria.

Violet shook her head. "My work is nothing like the work I produced in my youth, but it's still in the mind even though my fingers refuse to hold the brush without shaking. And there is one girl who shows much promise." She slowly rose to her feet with the aid of a cane, refusing Aaron's help. "Aaron Campbell, you are invited to dine with us this Friday."

"I shall come happily," he said as he politely stood. "Thank you, Aunt Violet."

Bit by bit, the grand lady made her way out of the room to the front hall where Fergus was waiting with her cloak. Maria and Aaron watched from the window as she was helped into her carriage. The going was slow and painful, evident to any who watched, but Aunt Violet never grimaced or complained. She held her head high and waved the driver on.

Aaron looked into the upturned face of Maria. Jovial confusion swept over his face at her sudden laughter.

"What do you find so amusing, Maria?"

"You, m'lord. If you stood any taller, I should have to shout to be heard."

Aaron joined in her laughter. Their eyes locked, and even though the humor remained, he forgot the road behind him and found himself walking only along the gray path of her eyes.

"How tall do you stand?" he asked.

"Four feet, 11 and three quarters inches tall, and not one bit less." She straightened her shoulders back a bit. "How tall are you, your grace?"

Reaching forward, he took her hand in his. "Six feet two inches, give or take half an inch. So let me see, that means there is one foot, two and a quarter inches between your lips and mine. I believe I can negotiate such a distance."

Maria turned away from him, her midnight-blue dress trimmed with black velvet swinging gently with her movements. "Perhaps you can...."

"But..." he prompted, rubbing a thumb along her cheekbone.

"I shall not make it easy for you, m'lord," she said, despite the fact that she did nothing to remove his hand from her face. "Just remember, surreptitious kisses caught by garden walls are one thing. Marriage, loving for life is another altogether. It will take more than expert lips and eloquent protestations of affection to win my heart."

"How do you know I want more than what you and Colin had together?"

She laughed. "I'm no fool. I've been in most of the great houses of Europe, and I've dined with kings. I've served ale in pubs and prayed for my next meal, your grace. Human nature across the social strata is something in which I rightfully claim an expertise. And deep in your eyes there now sparks a flame only a man can exhibit for a woman. I've seen it many times."

"Perhaps you are right," he admitted as he led her into the hall and they began to don their wraps for a walk up to the old castle ruins, "but you must realize I would never force myself upon you. If all you care to experience is the same platonic love you felt for my brother, so be it. I would never pressure you to the contrary."

She fastened the cloth-covered buttons on her ink-blue ermine-trimmed cape.

"Your grace, you may have the best intentions in the world with that sweet little speech you just gave. But I know differently. Platonic love? For the rest of your life? *You?* Oh no, my lord duke. I could see it in your eyes the day after we met. A passion runs through you—an earthy passion that devours all that's sweet, feasts on all that's lovely. You would be no more content with platonic love with me than I would with you. You're not a fool, m'lord. When our lips first met across that one foot, two-and-a-quarter-inch span, we knew life was never going to be the same for us, that we would go on in bliss or misery, but never like before."

They stepped out into the winter breeze. "Before you kissed me, I was beginning to think that maybe I *could* love your brother. After our episode in the garden, I knew that would be impossible. You will not be satisfied with anything other than what I am equipped to give. And yet I wonder if you still are a man that relishes in the wanting of a woman, but despises after the taking is done."

"I am changed, Maria. I would not do that to you or any other woman now. It would be wrong."

Her laugh was suddenly harsh, and Aaron knew the artist-husband wasn't the only one who had hurt tiny Maria.

"Tell that to countless men and women whose hearts have been broken by such individuals, sanctified or not. I will not be yours—my lord duke, hear me well—I will not be yours until you realize that to your heart I am air, light, food, and drink, complete and utter necessity. For I shall never be cast aside. And when someday you crave my love so strongly that you grasp for your sanity, I shall willingly become yours. But not until then."

He was caught in her trap, and he knew it. Just then he forgot that such a proposition was truly cause for alarm as he tucked her compact hand in the crook of his arm. "That may be sooner than you think, Maria."

"We shall see then, won't we, m'lord?" was all she said.

The subject was clearly closed.

They walked past the massive stables built by Violet's brother, Lachlan, the chief who started raising the prize Belgian draft horses. Men called to one another, horses whinnied and exhaled forcefully through their snouts. The coach house came next, its vehicles polished and ready for the whims of the chief and his family—Iain and Anna, Anne's parents.

"Castle Lachlan in the summer is lovely," Maria said as they quit the yard and began to walk beside Loch Fyne and up to the ruins. "The flowers are breathtaking. And now they lay dormant. For that reason, winter saddens me so."

"Have you ever read of an imperial palace in Russia, complete with indoor gardens?" Aaron asked.

"No! How lovely that would be! To walk on a stone path, through lush grass, a pebble-bedded stream meandering close by," she imagined.

"Fed by a musical waterfall," he finished, "with ferns and bushes."

"And flowers. Don't forget them. There would have to be lots of wisteria, their purple drops and twisting vines growing up to the roof. Is this room made of glass?"

"I believe so."

"Well, then," she tapped his arm, "I think you should make such an addition to Inveraray Castle."

"And give Dorian MacCall one more area to tyrannize like a despotic preacher? I should say not!" But the whole idea pleased him, she could tell.

Maria pouted. "And I thought you, m'lord, were a romantic."

"Don't tempt me, Maria. I've swept more women off their feet than I can remember."

Her voice deepened. "Yes, I know. And surely I wouldn't be immune to your charms, now would I?"

"I'm not sure. For the first time in my life."

They continued. The snow of a few days before, now mostly melted, huddled under the trees or around rocks and hedgerows, trying to escape the sun. Some lucky patches of white were still visible on the hillside, looking like sheep whose time appointed had almost arrived. The ruin stood before them, belligerently poised on a wide peninsula that jutted into Lachlan Bay. An island, overgrown and used for nothing but scenery, lay in the frigid waters.

Vines, now winter bare, covered the crumbling walls, their brown veins snaking up the sides and over into the mysterious inner sanctum of the old castle. Only the foolhardy ventured into the center of the ruins anymore. A local boy had been killed 30 years before when the highest-standing wall of the keep, then four stories tall, had crashed upon him.

"So your family has been connected to the Maclachlans for ages?" Maria asked as they slowly circumferenced the fortress.

"Aye. Although it seems that the marriages for the past 70 years have ended up fruitless as far as heirs are concerned. Anne and Colin had no children. And Aunt Violet's sister, Alix, married an uncle of mine, our family's greatest scholar, but he was murdered before their child was born. It was a girl, so two years later off Alix went to the Colonies with her new husband."

"What happened to the daughter?"

"She's still living in Virginia. Owns a large tobacco plantation along the James River. Perhaps one day I shall travel to see her. She is a cousin, after all."

"You'd better make it soon. She's probably getting old."

"Aye. That's true. Maybe we'll go to the States for our honeymoon."

"Lord Campbell, you are enough to drive even a patient woman like myself to unmitigated derangement. Please let us change the subject."

"As you wish, fair lady. When do you think you will be heading back to London?"

"I'm not sure. Someday, surely, I shall return. But that life lost all its glory for me when Colin died. You see, I didn't bother to make other friends when he was there. There's really no connection in that great city for me. Besides, I love teaching, and I'm finding that life in the country suits me far better than I could have previously imagined. If I want to sing again, I've a standing offer to tour America. However, I don't think I should take it anytime soon."

"Well, I for one, Maria, am glad to hear it. And I couldn't agree with you more. Scotland is beautiful no matter the time of year. I cannot believe that I stayed away for so long."

In pleasantness and genial conversation they walked back home. There were no uncomfortable lulls, no ill-timed sentences. They danced in verbal harmony over subjects ranging from themselves, to singing, to their favorite daily paper in London. But always they seemed to return to the Savior. The rest of the afternoon was whiled away in the drawing room, playing whist and laughing at their awful luck. And after Aaron departed for his castle, Maria sat in the parlor as one amazed and not a little frightened.

In one day she had fallen exhaustively, entirely in love with Aaron Campbell.

CHAPTER
14

If Chastain had been a weaker individual, dispossessed of self-control, he would have laughed. But he had an overabundance of the stuff, so he pushed the urge down with a firm swallow and a conscious tightening of his stomach muscles.

Aaron paced before the fire, the agitated young man he had previously been surfacing once again. "How could I have been such a blasted fool!"

"Your grace, you didn't do anything wrong. Maria Rosetti is, I'm sure, a lovely lady."

"She is that. And maybe that is the problem. I was temporarily blinded by her beauty and charm. Not only that, I think I'm in love with her."

"What is the harm in that? I think it's *wonderful* news! Does she love you?"

"Yes."

"You're positive?"

"I know women, old man. Nothing can change that."

Chastain nodded. "Well, come sit down, m'lord. I'll pour you a cup of tea."

"I'd rather have a scotch right now."

"Yes, I'm sure you would." He picked up the teapot anyway. "Perhaps I'm getting old, and I've forgotten the ways of the young, your grace, but..." he hesitated.

"But what?"

His smile was broad—he just couldn't help himself. The duke...in *love*...what a wonderful, wonderful turn of events. "Well, sir. When a man is in love, and the woman he loves feels the same way about him, that usually constitutes cause for rejoicing...not agony!"

"Usually. But not for me."

"*Why*, your grace?"

Aaron sat down in his customary chair. "Chastain, there is a reason I have been working you like a draft horse this past year."

"To build the estates back up."

"Yes. But there's a reason I want them increased so quickly." Aaron's hands began to fidget, so he picked up the cup and saucer. "I'm preparing for my death, old man."

"Aren't we all, m'lord?"

"Well, yes. But I mean my imminent death. Chastain, as soon as the Campbell holdings are back to what they should be and I can pass them down to my cousin with a clear conscience, I am going to confess to the murder of my brother."

Chastain's mouth opened in shock. "M'lord..." was all he could begin to say, he was taken by such surprise.

"It's true, I assure you. And now, with Maria..." He stood to his feet and began pacing. "Don't you see? I cannot love her or let her love me. I am a *dead man*, Chastain. What shall I do? I made advances; I accepted her terms."

Chastain's heart was filled with love for his spiritual son. His olden eyes wished to fill with tears of sympathy, but he controlled himself.

"Oh, your grace," he said gently, "do you honestly feel it is what God is requiring of you?"

Aaron nodded.

"Are you sure?"

"Reasonably so ... I thought so ... maybe not ... oh, blast it, I don't know!"

"Your grace, I don't think God expects you to turn yourself in and hang for the murder. You were under duress. And besides, think of all the examples in the Bible where men committed atrocities and God forgave them without having them serve one day of formal punishment for their sin."

"Who?"

"Why, David when he murdered Uriah. And what about Paul? He was responsible for the deaths of many Christians. Are you above men such as these?" He had to make him see the foolishness of such a commitment. His heart commanded him to keep Aaron alive as long as he could.

"No. Surely I am not. But Chastain ..."

"I'm not expecting you to change your mind. Just think about it tonight. The Savior is a gracious, loving God, your grace. I do not believe for even a second that your hanging from the gallows will give Him cause for joy."

• • •

December 11, three weeks later

Maria couldn't wait to see him. For the past three weeks Aaron Campbell had come by almost every day. And each day the sight of him grabbed her breath from her throat afresh. She knew she was a pretty woman, although not a beauty like Aaron's mother had once been, she admitted easily. But she never dreamed she would end up with a man who looked like the Duke of Argyll.

"That's the fourth time you've avoided my lips today."

The sun was coming through the large window by the table at which they sat. His hair was lit up to a blazing blond, and his eyes, that strange blue-green color, glowed like aquamarines. Keeping his lips from hers had been nothing more than torturous. And she stared at their firmness as she spoke. It drove him crazy.

"I haven't noticed any signs of lovestruck insanity on your part yet, m'lord. Although I must say, you are persistent."

"Is the memory of your last kiss too sweet to defile?"

Maria looked out the window of the breakfast room and poured them both another cup of tea. "Perhaps. He certainly was an expert, or so I was told."

"Who? Who was it?"

"I do not kiss and tell, my lord duke."

"As far as I can see, you don't kiss at all. Knowing that, you're probably just saying it to make me jealous."

"Is it working?"

"Aye, Mrs. Rosetti, it certainly is."

"Would you feel better if I said I was teasing you?"

"Perhaps I would."

"Well, I'm not teasing. My last kiss was a wondrous thing. Given to me by a Russian nobleman."

"Who was he?" he repeated his question.

"I shall never tell. But tell me this, your grace, am I driving you crazy yet? Are you going insane with love for me?"

His eyes blazed fiercely into hers. "I think you know the answer to that."

"Let's change the subject," she said, caressing his cheek with her small hand. "I don't yet see any evidences of complete lunacy. But when I do, trust me, darling, my lips will be yours to do with what you will. And then..."

"What?"

"I shall be your wife. When summer comes and the flowers are blooming once again."

"How shall I convince you that I am falling headlong into madness over you, Maria?"

"Oh..." she kissed him quickly on the cheek, "I have perfect confidence that someone as full of life as you will have no trouble figuring that out on your own."

"May we have tea together in Strathlachlan the day after tomorrow?"

"I shall look forward to it, m'lord. Perhaps, just perhaps, I shall let you kiss me then."

Aaron laughed. "Believe me, Mrs. Rosetti, if kissing you were my only objective, there would be nothing you could do to stop me."

"So you're still confident in your charm, eh?"

"No. If I had relied on that, we would have been married a week ago. I want it to be your timing, my love. Then you will know it is what you truly want. I've known that you are my destiny since we walked to the castle ruins."

She walked him to the entry hall. "Till Thursday, then?"

"Aye, till Thursday." When he bent down to kiss her forehead, it was all Maria could do not to throw her head back and pull his mouth to hers.

• • •

London, 3:00 A.M.

By the docks on the Thames, two figures stood near the murky river. The smell of the polluted water wafted up in each breath they took, despite the bitter cold of the night. No moon shone upon their faces, and their voices were just husky whispers in the darkness. Down by the street in the distance, the faint, lonely clop of a solitary horse and wagon could be heard as the thickened water flowed underneath the pier on which they conversed. One man, thin yet fit, was dressed in the elegant evening clothes he had donned hours earlier and worn to three parties and one dinner with a lady friend. The other man, middle-aged yet successful, was clearly of a lower class—his clothing expensive, yet not comparable to the elegant garb of his companion. His blue eyes, their color faded in the shadow of his top hat, looked confused.

"Your grace," he pleaded, "how can I do what you ask? My wife? My family? What will become of them?"

"Great care will be given them until I send them to you. If you do not go tonight, Mr. Dickenson, I am afraid you will die. As will I."

"But sir..."

The gentleman's eyes flashed angrily. "Just do as I say! I promise you, you will not regret it. If I do not kill you, then someone else will. You can depend upon that, sir."

"But my business..." Tears filled the corners of the man's eyes. All his life he had worked from morning's darkness to evening's end, and now he was wanted by people he didn't even know.

"...will be dismantled after your 'death.' I assure you, I will send you more than the sum of what your business is worth. Now hand me your coat."

"What for, m'lord?"

"Why, Mr. Dickenson, have you not read the story of Joseph and his coat of many colors? And now hasten, the boat is coming. You shall be taken to Liverpool where you will board a ship bound for New York. From there you will take a train to Boston."

"Boston? Why Boston?"

"I hear they throw marvelous tea parties."

The man's brows knit in puzzlement.

"Never mind," said the gentleman as the sound of oars dipping quietly into the water drew closer. "There's the boat now." He glanced quickly around to verify their privacy. "It is taking you upriver about 11 miles, where a carriage will be waiting to take you to Liverpool."

"When can I expect my family?"

"They will meet you in Boston in a month and a half. Here..." he thrust a full purse into the man's hands, "Ten thousand pounds. Another ten will be sent with your wife and children. Enclosed are contacts in New York as well as Boston. The latter is especially important, as he will set you up in your new home. What business you choose to start or buy is up to your discretion."

Mr. Dickenson put it into his black satchel. "M'lord, I don't know why you're doing this. My life is being turned inside out because of it, and yet I feel compelled to thank you. I know that you are indeed saving my life and bidding me go with your own funds."

"Not all of us noblemen are scoundrels, my friend. But please, do me one favor. Change your name and gain U.S. citizenry. I will forward the instructions of how to do so with your wife. Now go! Time is most precious. They will be wondering what is taking me so long."

The shipping magnate squinted in the darkness. "Who are 'they,' m'lord?"

"You do not want to know," the gentleman said softly. "Believe me, Mr. Dickenson, you surely do not want to know."

• • •

Christmas Eve

Jacobs stomped the snow from his feet as he made his way into Inveraray's kitchen. Snow was thick on the ground, but the duke had given firm instructions that two giant wreaths were to be hung on the iron gates down the long drive. He commanded Jacobs to do the job himself. *Just to make my day miserable,* Jacobs was sure that was the motive behind it.

The staff were gathering for their dinner and were more chatty than usual.

"Enjoy a hearty level of conversation this day, staff," he said officiously as he hung up his coat and hat. "I'll let you get away with it simply because it's Christmas Eve."

Cathy and two kitchen maids appeared with large platters of food, which were passed around quickly.

"Did they finish the new pavilion?" she asked the butler.

"Aye." He tucked a forkful of tender venison into his mouth. "Finished three days ago. Thank goodness."

"These past four months they've been a complete disruption if ya ask me, sir." She hovered over the table, refilling glasses and making sure that each man and woman present enjoyed the simple fare. Leaning over near his ear she whispered, "I do believe his grace has finally lost his mind."

Jacobs shot her a disapproving look, but nodded in agreement.

"I've never seen a man so in love," offered one of the upstairs maids, her eyes dreamy.

"That'll be enough talk from you, young lady," Mrs. Rider admonished. "It isna' up to us to offer any opinion as far as his lordship is concerned."

The lass dropped her eyes in contrition. Across the table a young underbutler gazed adoringly at her, but she failed to notice.

Soon the meal was over, and Cathy hurried everyone along. "I've a grand meal to prepare for tonight. Give me peace and quiet while I cook."

Jacobs would not be undone. "That's right, we need to finish puttin' up the decorations, and the silver must be repolished. Hurry now, there's much to be done!"

Grumbling good-naturedly, the staff rose to their feet.

• • •

Aaron was waiting impatiently in the entry hall when Maria arrived by sleigh. She had never looked lovelier, he thought, as he helped her off with her cloak. Clad in a gown of silver-blue satin, Maria straightened the gathered lace which fell from an embroidered, mid-arm cuff. Tiny tucks made up the ivory underbodice. The full overskirt was embroidered in the same fashion as the overbodice and the sleeves with ivory flowers and smoky-green leaves and stems. The ivory underskirt was made of a soft, heavy brushed silk. Flowers and ribbons adorned her curled hair.

"You are lovely, Maria." Aaron's voice was deep, hushed with emotion.

She smiled with ruby lips and took in his attire. The midnight-blue cutaway coat with slim-fitting black trousers showed off his athletic physique. The wine-colored, lightly embroidered waistcoat contrasted with the linen shirt, the cravat of which was tied to perfection around his throat. "You look quite lovely yourself, your grace." Her insides were shaking at the sight of him. She wanted to scream since she felt so pent-up, so aware of the man standing in front of her. He reached out, letting one of her curls glide between his fingers. "Come into the drawing room, Mrs. Rosetti. Before we eat I promised my secretary that he could meet you. This is the first time you've been here since the masquerade, isn't it? I'll go fetch Chastain in his office." Clearly it was the last thing he wished to do right then with her face upturned to his.

"You beast!" The mood lightened instantly.

He turned back around, confused. "What did I do now?"

"Making that poor old man work on Christmas Eve. . . . I'm appalled!"

His smile erupted. "I can see it now, Maria. Someday soon, when the flowers are blooming naturally, you will become the lady of the manor. And very soon after that, the servants will be lazing about, taking ten minutes to answer the bell, and you won't understand why."

"Be gone with you, m'lord!" she said with a wave of her hand. "I'll wait here."

Maria pulled her chair closer to the fire. As the sleigh ride had chilled her thoroughly, she kicked off her slippers, wiggling her toes as close to the flames as possible. The heat soaked in slowly like massaging fingers, from her toes, to the arches, then through to the tops of her feet. Dancing on the hearth, the flames mesmerized her as her mind wandered over the events that had brought her to this place. How could she have known that Aaron Campbell would become so loving a suitor, so fine a gentleman? She laughed when she thought of that kiss in the garden. It seemed ages ago, and yet she never forgot him, although at one time that had been her fondest wish.

"I see you and my master are more compatible than I suspected."

Chastain stood next to her chair.

Maria shoved her feet quickly back where they belonged. "Pardon me?"

"I am Chastain," he bowed over her hand. "And I have come upon the duke more times than I care to count with his stockinged feet pushed near the fire like your own were just a moment ago."

"It was such a chilly ride ..."

"There's no need to explain, Mrs. Rosetti," he chuckled. "It is a dear pleasure to make your acquaintance."

"And I, yours. Won't you have a seat?" She gestured gracefully. "His grace should be back soon."

"Thank you. Are you enjoying your days in Scotland?"

"Yes. Most definitely I am. And how about you, Mr. Chastain? How does a transported Londoner like yourself find this area?"

"Wonderfully therapeutic. This summer when the heather was in bloom," he remembered with closed eyes and a sniff, "I realized what heaven indeed would be like."

Their eyes smiled into one another's, and the conversation flowed easily from that point onward. They both knew of each other's heartache, but convention bade them keep silent. So they kept to the familiar: London. Music. And the Duke of Argyll.

"He's changed completely since I was first hired on. Matured. Deepened. Has truly become a man."

"I agree. For some it's harder than others. Takes well into adulthood. For others, a lack of a proper childhood brings it on much sooner."

"I take it your growing up wasn't in the most loving of circumstances?" he prompted.

"Early on it was. But my parents died when I was a youth. After that I had to fend for myself mostly. I was too old for an orphanage and too young for any proper position. The contessa I worked for heard me singing one morning as I was polishing the grate in her home in Venice. God had His hand on me even then, I suppose." Chastain nodded yes, that it is always so. "And she sponsored my singing career. I owe her much."

"Is she still living?"

"Goodness, yes. When I go back to Italy, I always stay at her villa. She is 70 years old and walks three miles every day. A wonderful woman."

Just then the mantel clock whirred then chimed.

"What could have happened to his grace?" she mused. "He's been gone for at least 15 minutes. I thought he would be right back."

Chastain stood slowly to his feet. "Have you warmed yourself thoroughly yet, Mrs. Rosetti?"

"Yes."

"Good. I'll have your cloak brought around then."

"What?"

"It's a surprise. If I tell you, the duke will fire me, to be sure. And I so want to be around next summer when the heather is in bloom!"

Her cloak was brought in, and she was ushered conspiratorially to the front door by the old secretary. Waiting out front was a beautiful sleigh recently purchased by Aaron. Painted a deep green with gold-leaf trim, its runners sat on the snow and a team of six mammoth Belgians, Maclachlan Belgians, stood patiently waiting. This was light work for horses of such strength. Holly garlands looped around the sides, and wreaths were placed around the lights. The footman, whose top hat sported a sprig of holly, helped her inside, his caped coat fluttering about him.

"Let's get ya wrapped up nice an' warm, ma'am," he said with a hearty smile and cold-reddened cheeks. A large white mink wrap was placed around her shoulders, and an ermine blanket covered her feet, which he had placed on a warmed stone on the sleigh floor. Aaron had thought of everything, down to an oversize muff handed to her by the old secretary himself.

"This is enchanting," she said to Chastain. "But where am I going?"

"Never you mind, madam. You'll find out soon enough. Be kind to him, for he loves you greatly."

He turned on his heel as the driver snapped the reins, and they were off.

Maria couldn't help but feel a tad confused at the mysteriousness of this adventure. But instead of trying to figure it out, she decided to enjoy it. Though frigid, the night was calm. The heavens were more generous as the clear sky blessed the night with more stars than she ever remembered seeing before. And as the sleigh turned off the drive and proceeded across the meadow, she noticed several deer standing sentinel near the woods. The full moon shone on their brown, soft coats, and they moved not at all.

Over a hill the sleigh continued as the cold put redder roses into her cheeks and a brighter sparkle in her eyes. In the distance a light shone. Oh, not the singular light of a candle or a window, but a glowing entity, diffusing its warmth somehow into the clear atmosphere around it.

"What is that?" she questioned the driver.

"We'll be comin' up on it soon, ma'am" was the completeness of his answer.

Whatever it was, it made her feel warm simply by resting her eyes on its golden hue. The night enveloped it like a garment, yet faded into insignificance in its presence.

Small bells jingled softly as the horses brought her closer, and she could see what was casting such an unusual light. She had never seen anything like it. Her heart stepped up its beat as she realized it was indeed a building—a building made entirely of glass, except for the iron skeleton which supported the large panes. Its dimensions were about the size of the large banquet room at Inveraray Castle. The sides were 20 feet high, and on top a Slavic-style dome painted blue with golden stars pointed to the image it sought to mirror.

The sleigh stopped, and still Maria was in awe. As the footman helped her alight, she couldn't take her eyes off the delightful building. Like a Moorish arch the door was shaped, its clear panes worked much like stained glass forming the images of Adam and Eve. No serpent was present.

Opening the golden handle, the driver ushered her into a small world of beauty and wonder. Maria couldn't move as she stood there amid the heavy sweetness of the moist air. Finally, the kind man gave her a little nudge. "Go in, ma'am, it's all for you. And ya dinna want to let in the cold."

She found her feet upon a stone path. The stones were brook stones, made smooth by countless years of running water. To the right and to the left a carpet of lush grass extended to the walls of the building, and a stream in a pebbled bed ran from a rock formation in the center.

The water fell musically from the top of the ten-foot tower, dipped gracefully under a small bridge and into a large stone basin. And flowers bloomed. Lilies, orchids, and amaryllis. Wisteria, unable to grow so quickly, was painted underneath the dome, the big, purple blooms almost real enough to touch. The scent was sweet and full. She drew the warm air through her nose and deep into her lungs. Candles burned in holders placed by every other pane of glass, and Chinese lanterns hung from the two orange trees heavy with fruit. Lining the path on either side, flames danced in footed iron holders.

"He is insane," she whispered. "Aaron Campbell is thoroughly and utterly insane."

Aaron appeared from behind the waterfall. "I was hoping you would say that."

CHAPTER
15

He walked toward her, each step purposeful, yet agonizingly slow. "You said my name, Maria. Say it again."

Puzzlement skated over her features.

"Say my name, Maria. Not 'm'lord,' not 'your grace,' not 'my lord duke.' Say it, Maria. Say 'Aaron.'" The aqua eyes bore into hers, generating a heated, magnetic field between them. His words were soft, washing over her, stroking the secret, needy places of her heart. And he finally stood directly in front of her.

Aaron's hands encircled Maria's waist, and he pulled her closer to him, but not yet against him. Her body sang with physical tension, and she obeyed him, whispering. "Aaron."

He lowered his lids; it was his name. Not just a title. "Say it again."

"Aaron. Aaron." Her hand went up to cradle the back of his neck. "My Aaron."

"Yes." The eyes were still closed. "Your Aaron." The admission from the lips of such a man was more potent and every bit as igniting as a passionate caress, and Maria thrilled.

His left hand moved up her rib cage, around to her upper back, and he pulled her against him.

Finally.

The length of their bodies touched, her head rested against his muscular chest, and he swept his fingers into her raven curls, relishing in their silky caressings against the backs of his hands.

Both sighed. Maria's eyes closed as well. Behind them they could hear only the gentle music of the falling water. Inside they were aware only of their thundering hearts forcing blood, heated and thick, through their bodies to pound within their ears. Then Maria spoke. She could contain herself no longer, and words she had not uttered for many years came out with a whisper.

"I love you. I love you, Aaron Campbell."

Aaron now thrilled, the declaration more intoxicating than brandy, more potent than the love of a thousand women. He had known only her just then, all others completely forgotten, forever banished.

"And I love you, Maria Rosetti. I love you so much so that each day surprises me."

"Then kiss me. Please. End this torment, my darling Aaron."

He obeyed, bending down to reach her upturned mouth. Softly his lips caressed hers with a cool fire. He had kissed many woman, knew the art well. But he let go, forgetting form and practice, and with his heart he kissed the only woman he had ever loved. Her hands wound into his hair once more, and her body shook when he finally pulled his mouth from hers. Aaron knelt down, then sat on the lush grass carpet, cradling her in his arms. His expressive eyes looked lovingly into hers, communicating a commitment far deeper than words could ever tell. Maria thought she had loved him before walking in through the exquisite door that night. Yet in the space of several minutes her emotions increased a hundredfold, and she realized that she had always been meant to love this man. The crumbling walls, erected by a painful past, completely shattered into dust.

Both had made many mistakes, but life and love were starting anew, and this time, the Savior who saved and restored, was guiding them.

His eyes glistened. "Maria?"

"Yes, my darling love."

"Will you marry me?"

She hesitated, looking up at him through a little squint. "On one condition, Aaron Campbell."

"And what is that?"

"That you'll always kiss me like that."

"Gladly, my little phoenix. I can kiss you in no other fashion than what my heart demands. And my heart dictates to love you utterly—today, tomorrow, and for the rest of our lives."

He bent his head again, and both were lost to a heady existence consisting only of gentle waters, sweet flowers, and the enveloping warmth of one another.

. . .

March 1844

"Mistress Mary, quite contrary, how does your garden grow?" The children's voices mingled their clear, strident tones with Maria's mellowed full ones as, with swinging momentum, the jump ropes sliced through the air in wide arcs. The springtide air was fresh and slightly cool. The late-morning sun was shining through the cottony clouds overhead. It reflected off the children's shiny hair.

With the blooming flowers, the squeaky-clean smiling girls, and the tiny raven-haired beauty laughing as she jumped, it was truly a lovely scene that Aaron beheld from the other side of the gate.

The orphanage, built originally as a house almost a hundred years previous, was a sturdy structure. What had started out as a midsize home for a prominent Maclachlan and his new bride, grew and grew over the years. The stone building was quite large and housed the establishment quite comfortably.

The girls obviously adored Maria, and she delighted in them as well. Though she never mentioned that she, too, had no parents, somehow the orphans felt differently toward her than they did toward the kindly spinsters who ran the home. They knew that she was one of them, though they didn't know why. Maybe it was because she played games with them, running races, skipping rope, or playing hopscotch. Maybe it was because she would overlook a pea in flight at the dinner table. Whatever the reason, the girls, big and little, were thrilled to have her among them. The maiden missionaries who ran the institution were happy as well with Maria. They had seen years of hardship and misery. To them, an orphanage of happy children was a blessing beyond description, a taste of the heaven to come. In these children, in Maria, they found a renewed youth, a forgotten vigor. Before Maria's arrival, the Strathlachlan Home for Foundling Girls had been run quietly, pleasantly, and always with efficiency. Now, however, it was an oddity not to hear laughter or someone singing a hymn or chanting a nursery rhyme as she walked the echoing halls. Everyone who lived within the walls knew that their orphanage was the happiest one in all of Scotland.

"Good day, your grace," a young girl, eight-year-old Penelope Graham, shouted from a tree branch above Aaron's head.

"Hello, Miss Penelope," Aaron answered with a straight face, bowing formally. "May I gain admittance into your beautiful gardens?"

Penelope giggled, a hand covering her mouth. "Oh, m'lord," she managed to get out, "you're a funny one, ya are!" Suddenly she had a horrified look on her face. "Your grace, please forgive my impertinence!" she begged. "I didna' mean to be disrespectful!"

Aaron's look became mockingly stern as he held up his arms. "Young lady, come down this instant." Then he smiled as she jumped into his arms. "What you need is a good toss!" And he threw her high up in the air, catching her in his strong arms a second later. Gently he set her down, patted her head, and dismissed her with an "Off with you now." Penelope ran down the path with a skip, yelling at the top of her lungs. "Mrs. Rosetti! Mrs. Rosetti! He's here! His lordship is here!"

Maria jumped out of the swinging rope, not missing a beat, and hurried over to him, eager to see him as always. He bent down and kissed her hand and studied her again in her pale-blue muslin gown, a white shawl embroidered with pink roses thrown carelessly about her shoulders.

"I can see that, as usual, my beloved," she said with sparkling eyes as he lowered her hand from his lips, "you continue to charm the girls and keep adding to your retinue of lovestruck females. Of which, I might add, I am chief."

Aaron looked at her with satisfaction in his eyes. He never could get over her quiet beauty each time he saw her. Yet more than that, her strength was fascinating to him. And she had eyes only for him! "Aye, fair lady," he said theatrically, "and a lucky man I am to be loved by such a damsel of priceless worth as yourself!"

She laughed, a hearty, throaty laugh, as she took his arm and guided him back toward the play area.

"We're giving a concert next Friday night, Aaron," she said as they sat together on the bench. "Would you come?"

"Of course. You know I would love to. What is the occasion for this one?" He knew Maria didn't need much of an excuse to put on a concert. The little girls loved getting involved, and once word had gotten around the countryside about the enjoyable evenings, gentry and common folk alike attended. This would be the third concert given since Christmas. Maria's natural showmanship, love for music, and vast experience made it impossible for her not to throw herself wholeheartedly into the music program of the home.

"The orphanage desperately needs new beds. We're just trying to raise a little money."

"Why didn't you ask me, Maria? I would have been happy to have bought..."

"Come now, darling Aaron. I think you've done quite enough with modernizing the kitchens and the new heating stoves. Besides, the girls are so excited to be helping out in their own small way."

Just then the bell rang and the girls, all wearing navy sailor-style dresses with no ornamentation, began to file into the building to finish up the morning's lessons. Aaron looked around him in all directions. "Are we alone?"

Maria nodded with a jaunty sparkle in her eye. She pushed Aaron to the far corner of the house, and they slipped around it out of view of any who might be watching from the window. He pulled her against him. "Do you ever get enough, little phoenix?"

"Of you? Never."

He kissed her and left her breathless. He felt breathless, too, but he didn't show it. "Tell me, my tiny darling, have my kisses erased that of the Russian nobleman?"

Maria put a hand up to her mouth and began to chuckle. "Actually, you kiss almost exactly like he does. Very proficient, I must say. But no, not better."

Aaron groaned in exasperation. "If I find out who he is...tell me, Maria. Who was he? Chastain and I have exhausted the resources of our minds trying to figure out what Russian nobleman was even *in* London during that time!"

One winged eyebrow raised. "It really bothers you, hmm?"

"Don't play with me, Maria. You know it does."

"It's terribly funny, you know."

"I can see that."

"Oh, darling, think about it. My last kiss. A *Russian* nobleman. Doesn't that give you any idea?"

"No. But if I ever find him..."

Maria interrupted him. "He was a cossack."

"A coss..." the words trailed off. "Why, you really are a cat, aren't you?"

She nodded up and down, finally letting herself succumb to raucous laughter. "*You* were my last kiss. Oh, darling, if you could have seen your face just now when I told you your kiss was no better!"

"Just wait, Maria. No one has bested me yet when it comes to matters like these. You'd best be on your guard."

"Oh, punish me now and get it over with, Aaron Campbell."

He did, his mouth bearing down firmly on hers. And when they came up for air, Maria began laughing all over again.

• • •

The soft patter upon the tin roof of the orphanage awoke Maria before it was light. Two weeks previously, the headmistress, a Miss Lovett, had asked her if she could possibly stay at the orphanage for several weeks. Two of the ladies who were sisters were going to Aberdeen on holiday to visit their brother. Naturally, Maria was very willing and only too happy to help.

There was much to do that day in preparation for the evening concert. She sprang from her bed and got ready quickly, looking forward to a cup of tea. The cook, Miss Sinclair, would already be in the kitchen, and the thought of a scone hot out of the oven, not to mention the quiet conversations they always had before dawn, made her hurry down the hallway. She had become an extremely early riser since she had started staying at the home. It gave her a chance to think and a time of solitude in a place other than her room. But what she looked forward to the most in the hour before dawn was practicing.

The large music room was her territory. With her own funds she had it painted a pale, yet warm yellow, a welcoming color that had made the room a gathering place for most of the girls. Blue rugs and draperies brought the hue of a summer sky indoors, and several comfortable chairs upholstered in a floral pattern sat near the mahogany piano.

Miss Sinclair was extremely busy, having started baking the refreshments for after the concert, and there wasn't time for the usual chat. So, with cup in hand and a small plate laden with steaming-hot scones, Maria entered her cheerful haven. With a long sip and quick bite, she sat at the piano and started running scales, her voice lovingly accompanying each note. Practicing each morning, her voice was as clear and strong as ever. After the exercises were done, she sang her favorite song from her favorite work, Handel's "Messiah." "I Know That My Redeemer Liveth" had become her theme of late. Knowing that her Savior lived was a comfort to her. Father was dead, mother too. And Colin had died and so had her Lord. But He had risen from the grave, whereas the others had not. He would stand at the last day upon the earth, and she would be with Him. It touched the inner sanctum of her soul when she pictured herself standing next to the Savior. His presence in her life was already so real. The joy at gazing into His loving face would be utterly overwhelming, entirely beautiful. The thought of that future meeting brought tears to her eyes each time she sang the song.

This morning was no exception.

• • •

The little girls assembled like nervous field mice in the salon next to the music room, where all of the seats were filled. Many more people were content to stand. The singers' compact little hands fluttered as they sought to calm one another down, to no avail. Everyone knew the continuation of civilization itself hinged on whether or not they were able to reach that high F, didn't they?

Maria, dressed in a simple navy satin gown with black piping and embroidery, gathered the girls around her with an encouraging, warm, and knowing smile. An acquaintance of hers who owned a cotton mill was only too obliged to honor Maria's request for 50 yards of bleached muslin to make the girls matching outfits. They certainly were lovely in the calf-length dresses with large round collars upon which some of the older girls had embroidered daisies. With their hair freshly washed and braided, their faces flushed with excitement, and their eyes fairly glowing, they couldn't help but remind those assembled of an angel choir.

Maria imparted words of encouragement and reminded them that God would reward their long hours of practice. After all, because they were there to give glory to Him, He was pleased already. Then they all bent their heads as Maria prayed a quick but sincere prayer, asking the Lord to calm their fears and enable them to show His love to all who were gathered in the room.

The headmistress, Miss Lovett, opened the program with prayer, then it was time for the concert to begin. The choir was made up of 15 girls, ranging from ages 8 to 14. They filed in silently and took their places at the front of the room next to the piano. Maria followed them, smiling pleasantly when she took her seat at the piano.

Aaron's heart jumped to his throat. To see her here, doing something she loved so much and doing it so well, caused a feeling of admiration to spring up within him. She, unlike his former self, had always been someone who fell headlong into doing what she loved. She reminded him of Colin in that respect. The introduction began, and the strains of "Hark the Voice of Jesus Calling," issued forth, paying tribute to all the missionary ladies under the roof. The clear voices of the children, the subtle harmonies, and Maria's lilting accompaniment enchanted everyone in the room. More hymns followed: "A Mighty Fortress Is Our God," "And Can It Be That I Should Gain," and "When I Survey the Wondrous Cross." Each arrangement more beautiful than the last. Maria sang with them, guiding the choir gently, but not overpowering their voices with her own. She was truly a professional. And her fiancé couldn't have been more proud of his talented, capable, lovely wife-to-be.

After the hymns, Penelope Graham stepped from the line to stand beside Maria at the piano. Maria had been most pleased with the young girl's talent. As the introduction began, Aaron felt a lump in his throat. He recognized those strains. "And He Shall Feed His Flock" by Handel. Glancing sideways at the ladies sitting to his left, he saw that tears had already sprung to their eyes before a note was sung.

As Penelope sang of the Good Shepherd caring for His young, gathering them with His arms, carrying them in His bosom, her eyes sparkled with a light of inner peace and eternal security. The audience wept. Even Maria had to blink back her tears as the beautifully clear, childish tones floated across the room like white feathers, coming to rest in the hearts of each one present.

After several more selections, the program came to a much-regretted close. Maria did not sing a solo this time either, as many had hoped she would. She wanted the folks to come for the girls. Her moments in the sun had come and gone. And although the girls always begged her, she firmly refused.

• • •

Two weeks later spring had fully bloomed. In an ivory gown with a little blue jacket, Maria sat next to Aaron in the family pew of the village church. She looked fresh and young. So many of life's old cares had been wiped firmly away by the loving, strong hand of Aaron. But for now, she sat with a transfixed stare as she nervously flexed and unflexed her fingers.

"Calm down, my darling," he said comfortingly as he took her hands in his own. "There's nothing to be nervous about. The folk here are simple people who are thrilled when Alice MacDougall's daughter gets up and trills a little Sunday school song."

"I know, Aaron, but I just can't help it. It's been almost a year since I've given a solo. What if I just can't do it anymore?"

Aaron chuckled and gave her fingers a comforting squeeze. "Oh, Maria, you'll do fine. Forget about all that. I am completely confident that you'll sing wonderfully."

Just then the pastor, Reverend William MacGregor, arose for the invocation. When Maria walked up to sing, she felt faint. It was the first bout of nerves she had experienced since her training in Italy. But when she looked at Aaron's face registering all the love and support she could ever want and the accompaniment began, she forgot all else. The notes came out clear and pure, as true as they had ever been at the opera. And this time she was singing about her blessed Savior.

• • •

Spring was passing quickly. They were well into April, having spent the month in idyllic picnics and rides in Aaron's phaeton through the hills when it wasn't raining.

If it was raining, they would simply talk for hours sitting together on the window seat of Castle Lachlan's drawing room. The simple times were the most precious.

Maria continued singing in church. Summer would be coming soon, and with it, the flowers. Their wedding would take place then as well. Her excitement mounted when she thought of being unified with Aaron once and for all. But all the while Maria yearned to sing again. Really sing. To open her throat and unleash her voice to its fullest. Opera had been a part of her for so long that it wasn't easy to put it away. Aaron had discussed the matter, saying he would support her decision to go back, wanting only her happiness. She knew he was proud of her talent and would never stand in the way of her personal fulfillment. But she couldn't help wondering if really he was just saying such because he thought she would never return to Covent Garden. Besides, who ever heard of a duchess performing before a paying audience?

Aaron arrived at the orphanage early that April day armed with a bouquet of wildflowers and a glint in his eye. Maria was descending the stairs as he entered the hall. She was arrayed in a flowing aqua-blue gown made of layers and layers of fine cotton embroidered around the hem of the skirt and the jacket with violets. A small straw boater decorated with violets and aqua netting perched on the top of her head. Her hair was pulled back in a loose-flowing braided chignon.

Maria cried with delight at the sight of him in his beautifully cut charcoal-gray suit. "Aaron! You're early!"

"I hope it's not too much of an inconvenience," he said. "I have a lot planned for us today."

She smiled. An inconvenience! Seeing him standing there looking so dashing, positively exuding charm, he could hardly be thought of as an inconvenience.

"Of course not, darling," she said walking up to him.

He took her hands in his and smiled down at her. She noticed the sparkle in his eye as he kissed her hand. "You look beautiful. And your dress is stunning." He kissed her lips. "The lambing numbers are in, some of the lumber is cut and bringing in a huge profit, so it just looks like I might be able to afford you as a wife if this keeps up."

Maria laughed. "Luckily for you, my only extravagance is fashion. I've traveled enough and met more important people than I care to remember, so just keep me tucked up here in the Highlands with lots of party dresses, and I shall be your devoted slave."

"That sounds like an offer only a fool would refuse. But we must hurry."

He does seem awfully impatient, Maria thought.

"You're hiding something from me, aren't you?" she asked knowingly.

"Me?" He feigned being wounded. "How could you accuse your loving fiancé of keeping anything from you?"

Maria just laughed and said, "I'll get my parasol."

Five minutes later they were on their way. Maria loved Aaron's obsession with speed, and she held her hat firmly on her head as the open carriage sprinted down the road. "Are we heading to Inveraray Castle this morning?"

"Yes, my love" was all he would offer.

"So, are you going to tell me your secret?"

When he smiled broadly and glanced down at her sideways, she said, "I suppose not." She breathed in the fresh morning air and sighed. "Ah, what a beautiful day.

It's so wonderful to be out here." She closed her eyes and enjoyed the breeze and the wild rocking of the vehicle. After a while they passed through the gates of Inveraray Castle.

Aaron helped her out with a mysterious smile. "Your destiny awaits, my lady," he said, and Maria laughed.

"I'm intrigued to say the least, Aaron, but I've absolutely no clue as to what is going on!" Her eyes twinkled merrily. "You're still a rogue, you know," she accused good-naturedly. Aaron conceded with a bow and took her arm to lead her up the steps and into the drawing room.

She could hear the pleasing tones of the harpsichord as Aaron reached for the doorknob. When he pushed open the door, a blast of sound raced to her ears, the beautiful, golden sound of a baritone voice. She cried with delight as she saw Gianni Gipella, an extremely gifted baritone with whom she had performed throughout Europe in her younger years. He was without a doubt her favorite colleague. Dressed flamboyantly, his black hair a tad too long, Gianni looked the same as she remembered, and good memories of her opera days flooded back with a rush.

"Gianni!" she cried, running across the room with arms outstretched.

"Maria!" he said warmly as he hugged her tightly. "How good it is to see you again! You look more beautiful than ever."

"Oh, darling, you do run on!" she said in her usual tone. "What are you doing in Scotland?"

Gianni just pointed beside her to Aaron, who in turn looked at Maria sheepishly and shrugged. She looked at him with questioning eyes. "You brought Gianni here?"

"Well," Aaron began, "it seemed to me that you've missed the opera."

"Of course I have, but that doesn't mean..." she hesitated, "but now seeing him here... well, how did you know to get in touch with Gianni?"

"It was really quite simple, my love. A few letters and he was tracked down."

"You can imagine my surprise when I received the duke's letter telling me you consented to marry him," Gianni interjected.

"Believe me," Aaron said, "no one was more surprised than I."

"He also told me that you were yearning to sing again."

"You said that?" She turned to Aaron in surprise.

"Of course, my love. One would have to be blind not to know that you've been wanting to get back on stage for months now."

"So," Gianni said further, "ever since you have left the opera, I have had to endure twittering-throated, giggling, or conceited sopranos. Girls... all of them. Not a woman to be found! So when I learned where you had gone and received an invitation to see you, I knew the gods had smiled upon Gianni Gipella once again."

"But is there still a place for me?" she asked. "I've been gone so long. I cannot imagine coming back after all this time!"

"Maria, Maria. Do not let those words of doubt fall upon my aching ears! For my sanity, please come back ... or I swear I shall leave for Florence tomorrow!"

Maria's eyes darted from person to person, and she suddenly laughed. "Well, this is all so sudden. Oh, Gianni, I'm so glad you came. To be honest, I cannot make a decision right this minute, but I'll let you know very soon. And I will think about it seriously."

Gianni bowed with a warm smile. "That is all I can ask for, Maria."

"Will you be staying for a while?"

"Thank you, but no. I must be getting back to London."

"What are you working on?" Maria asked with great interest.

"Don Giovanni."

"Oh, don't say any more, I couldn't bear it!"

"I remember. That's your favorite!"

"Who's cast as the lead soprano?" asked Aaron, obviously leading up to something.

"Diana Santilli. But she's doing it temporarily until they find a replacement. She's expecting a baby in six months. Maybe you should think about it, hmmm?"

Maria's eyes shone. "Don Giovanni!" And they needed her! She knew without a doubt she would be welcome back at Covent Garden. But what about Aaron? Did he really want her singing again? She knew that a heart-to-heart conversation was in order, and the sooner the better. The only problem was she didn't yet know what her heart wanted to say.

• • •

April 1844

"Your grace," a liveried servant announced, "the Earl of Crawford is here to see you."

Aaron's head snapped up from where he was working. "Are you positive that's who it is?"

"Aye, m'lord." He handed the duke the earl's calling card. "Shall I show him into the drawing room?"

"By all means." Aaron rose quickly from his desk and donned his coat. "What is George Lindsay doing here after all this time?"

He remembered the last time he had seen George. That fateful night at the club when he had lost to Lucius' queen of spades.

Suddenly he felt vulnerable and alone. Chastain was in Glasgow. Maria was in London shopping for her trousseau and catching up on the news at the opera.

She wasn't going back.

"From June onward, I want only to be your wife," she had said the day before she left. And here he stood now, face-to-face with the past. Breathing in deeply, he strode out of his study, across the hall, and into the drawing room.

"Lindsay, old man!" he greeted his longtime compatriot.

"Aaron!" George offered his hand. They clasped together mightily and pumped hard.

"What in heaven's name are you doing all the way up here in Argyllshire after all this time?"

"I'm on my way home to Crawford," he said, averting his eyes for a moment, "and I came to see for myself if the rumors are true. Are you really marrying the soprano in June?"

Aaron smiled broadly. "You have heard correctly. Maria Rosetti has agreed to be my wife."

"Pretty little bit of a thing, she is. When did this happen? You must tell me all about it. Think of it, Aaron Campbell settling down. I'm losing money on this one, old boy, I'm afraid to say."

Aaron showed him to the sofa. "Have a seat, Lindsay," he offered graciously. "By the way, are you staying far away?"

"I'm at the Pied Bull, in the village."

"Oh, you mustn't stay there. You must pass the night here."

The earl accepted gladly.

"So . . ." George leaned forward and thumped Aaron on the shoulder with his slender hand, "tell me about her."

Aaron reached for the bell. "First some refreshment to wash the dust of your travels away."

A footman appeared and soon was off to meet Aaron's requests.

"Where were we?" he asked as he turned back to George.

"Maria."

"Ah, yes. Lindsay, she's . . ." Aaron fought for words to describe what she meant to him.

"Goodness me, you *are* a man in love. I never thought this day would dawn."

"It has, and I thank God for it." Aaron's words were earnest. George reddened in embarrassment and changed the subject.

"The club hasn't been the same without you, old boy. Not the same at all. I do believe Robert rues the day you severed all ties."

"How is Robert?" How Aaron missed him, and prayed for his once closest friend.

"The same. Drinks too much. Smokes too much. And gambles too much. But he misses you, I'm sure. He refuses to talk about you when Alex and I begin to reminisce."

"I think about him often. And what else keeps you occupied, Lindsay? Besides the forementioned activities."

"Believe it or not, I've begun to spend more times on my estates in Kincardine. I realized they would not run themselves. And London... well, my friend, I must be getting old because I find I can only enjoy it in small doses. Scotland suits me now. The Brotherhood is still alive and growing, by the by."

Aaron shuddered. And the delicate buffer of his new life and Maria intensified to blood-red with startling speed. "Oh? And Lucius... is he still up to old tricks?"

"Naturally. And adding to his fortune every day."

Aaron had to escape. "Let us ride over the countryside. I want you to see my lands."

"Wonderful," George sighed with relief. "When the conversation turns to Lucius Carlyle, I always feel in need of fresh air."

CHAPTER
16

London, a week later

"Mrs. Rosetti has already been seated, m'lord" the maître d' informed the striking duke in the beautifully tailored evening clothes. His mind recalled the days when he had said those words with frequency to the late Lord Colin Campbell. The uncanny resemblance shocked him when the new Duke of Argyll walked through the door.

"Thank you, Milton." In perfect harmony with his surroundings, Aaron handed his hat and cape to the attendant waiting beside him. Surprisingly, it was good to be back in London! He thought it was going to prove difficult, until he realized he couldn't bear to be so far away from Maria. But no, he returned to the familiar streets with ease. Maria had helped, to be sure. She was his earthly nerve center, his consummate existence. With her by his side, it was so easy to forget his old habits. Conversely, there was much to remind him of Colin. He wondered if the guilt would ever go away, and prayed that it wouldn't. For only a monster could walk away from such an act and go on to live his life like any other man.

Chastain had convinced him that God was not asking him to turn himself over to Scotland Yard, and the love of Maria was proof. Maybe someday he would confide in her, tell her of his torment, but he doubted it. It was *his* demon to fight, and to cast even a small portion of the burden on someone else would only deem him a coward. Or so he felt. He supposed it was a blessing that he had always been good at hiding his feelings, at playing a part.

Sitting at a round table in the corner by a window overlooking the gardens, she was picture-perfect in a periwinkle evening gown that brought out her white skin and black ringlets. Their relationship had taken a new turn over the past three months. The love they shared had become more compelling, freshly urgent as the wedding drew nigh. It was like a smoldering fire yearning to burn freely and in an all-consuming way. And when apart, they counted the minutes until gray eyes would once again meet blue.

"Maria!"

Her eyes opened wide with delight. "Darling! Come sit down. I've already ordered for us."

Aaron sat down with a laugh, taking her hand. "That's what I appreciate about you, Maria. You're a woman who knows her mind. And everyone else's as well!"

She chided him as she eyed his evening clothes. "Oh, now hush. You always order the same thing anyway! Who would have thought you would turn out to be such a creature of habit, my Lord Campbell?"

"Me? I've always been a creature of habit, my darling. It's just that the habits have changed."

The waiter came with the first course: a smoked-fish soup with potatoes and carrots in a creamy base. For dinner Maria had Cornish hen with preserved peaches, and Aaron enjoyed minted Welsh lamb. Dessert was a tansy pudding which neither had trouble finishing. Maria laughed as she wiped her mouth and waited for the coffee to come.

"Many a woman would love to have a man like you around to enjoy her cooking, Aaron Campbell. You consume more food than even Gianni, and believe me, that is saying something."

Aaron shrugged with a smile. "Mrs. Grey at Inveraray seems to think I am the most wonderful master in all of Scotland. And I do not mind in the least. Each meal exceeds its predecessor, which is fine with me."

"I suppose it is. You never seem to stop working these days. When was the last time you sat down and relaxed? Just stared into the fire and cleared your mind of all things tedious?"

"That sounds like a wonderful luxury," he admitted, knowing full well he would never clear his mind for the rest of his life. "But our wedding is coming up next month, and I still have much planning to do."

"Have you decided where we are going on our honeymoon?"

Aaron nodded and raised his brows.

Maria gasped. "America?"

He nodded.

"You're really taking me to America?"

"Yes."

"New York?"

He nodded and reached for her hand.

"Boston?"

He caressed the fine bones along the back.

"Philadelphia?"

His hand traveled up her arm.

"...Baltim..." Her eyes locked into his, and she couldn't speak. Her body shook as he looked at her deeply.

"There are many places I wish to take you," he said softly, his hand traveling over her shoulder. "Many places I wish to go." His eyes intensified under his desire for her.

Just then a hand landed on his shoulder, and Aaron turned suddenly at the sound of the voice accompanying it.

"Aaron Campbell! What brings you here, old man? We were wondering if we'd ever see you in London again!"

A chill ran up Aaron's spine to his brain, and his shame flared back to life stronger than ever. Forcing a smile onto his lips, he responded. "Lucius Carlyle! What a surprise, indeed!" He turned to Maria, amazed at how natural he sounded. "The Earl of Beresford and I were at Oxford together. Lucius, have you met my fiancée, Mrs. Maria Rosetti?"

Maria extended her hand, and he took it, raising it to his lips. "Delighted to meet you, Mrs. Rosetti. It is indeed a pleasure. I've enjoyed your performances for years!" His charm and graciousness were beyond description.

"Oh please, your grace! Don't make me feel so old!"

He still hadn't let go of her hand. "Nonsense. You're as beautiful as the day you first started performing at Covent Garden."

Maria pulled it back and smiled brilliantly up at him. Aaron took notice. "I see, my darling," she turned to Aaron, "that the earl must have been a source of constant competition as far as the ladies were concerned!"

Lucius laughed easily. "No one can charm a woman's heart like the Duke of Argyll, believe me, Mrs. Rosetti."

"Please, your grace, call me Maria."

Aaron looked sharply at her. "What brings you around here this evening, Lucius?"

"As usual, I am mixing business with pleasure."

"Has business been good?"

"Yes, actually. Our mining interests have been reaping heavy dividends. Father's dreams are becoming a reality. Even more so. I wish he had lived to see all his wealth return to the family and then some."

Maria bristled. "Mining interests? Coal mines?"

"Yes, Maria."

"But I'm sure you've heard of Lord Ashley?"

"Yes, of course. Who hasn't heard of that misguided gentleman?"

Aaron interrupted. "Better mind your words, Lucius. Maria was a very close friend of Colin's, and much in sympathy to his causes."

"Ah, I see." His eyes became ice, although the smile never left his lips. "Then I am correct in assuming you have no wish to hear of my successes."

"No, your lordship. Not even a word." Maria would say no more.

Lucius cleared his throat brusquely, but as always retained his composure and smiled benignly. "Well then, I shall take my leave of you. But, Mrs. Rosetti, I leave you with this thought. If the coal mines are so horrible, why are you here at Mivert's dining amid gaslit lamps and sconces? Did you think the coal gas crawled into the pipes on its own?" He smiled broadly. "Come down to the club sometime, Aaron. I certainly enjoyed our last game together! That seemed to be the start of the Carlyle family's upswing."

He bowed with a smile, turned on his heel, and walked to his table.

"Thank you for not stating your mind, Maria. I know that took a considerable amount of self-control."

"Really, Aaron. Who does he think he is?" Her eyes were flashing. "And to openly talk about Lord Ashley like that! He'd better be careful."

Staring down at his napkin, Aaron spoke. "I don't think the Carlyles or men like them are the ones who have to worry. We both know they'll stop at nothing to further their financial kingdoms."

"Nothing? Even murder?"

"Well," said Aaron, feeling eerily detached from the conversation, "even the *Times* hypothesized that Colin's murder had to do with his reforms."

"Your brother was probably murdered as an example."

"How so?"

Maria leaned forward, her voice hushed. "A few weeks before he died, he was accosted by a man in an alleyway. At knife-point he was told that if he didn't stop his crusading he'd be extremely sorry. I told him he should do something about it . . . notify Scotland Yard . . . something. But your brother was a man who felt more comfortable fighting his own battles. Besides, the police probably couldn't prove anything anyway. Colin said as much."

"I'm sure he knew what he was talking about." Aaron began to grow extremely uncomfortable.

But Maria continued on. "And Colin was just the first, I am sure. I'll have to say some extra prayers for Lord Ashley tonight. If Scotland Yard ever finds out who killed Colin, I would like to usher him personally to the gallows," she declared passionately.

Just then, much to Aaron's relief, the waiter came by to ask if they needed anything. Both declined his further services, and Maria gathered her purse and wrapped its ribbon handle around her wrist. "By the way, what did Lucius mean about the card game? What happened?"

Aaron grew visibly uncomfortable now, and for the first time his eyes were closed to her. "I lost quite a bit of money to him shortly after Colin's death. I haven't picked up a deck of cards to gamble since. Let us change the subject. Carlyle is ruining our evening."

Maria's eyes flashed. "But, darling, that is just the point! Carlyle is ruining more than that! He's taken what was once good and decent in our land and has twisted it to the benefit of his pocketbook. But you can stop him, darling, don't you see? You can assume Colin's mantle!"

Aaron felt as though he was being stabbed by her repeatedly. Each word was a twist of the already deeply submerged knife.

"After all, darling," she continued, oblivious to the havoc she was wreaking, "anyone who can build his fortune atop the misery of others is a monster. It's blood money he garners into his storehouses each day. Do as I say, Aaron, please. You could be so powerful, so good. Pick up where Colin left off!"

"No." Aaron's eyes flashed in warning. "I'm not cut from the same cloth."

"But why not? You'd be a wonderful legislator."

"I do not wish to discuss this."

"But darling, I know you, and you'd not be ..."

He was completely unnerved by this time. "Enough, Maria. You don't know everything about me. And you never will. So let's just leave it at that, all right?"

Maria looked away, and Aaron signaled for the tab. During the entire ride home, she refused to meet his eyes.

• • •

Upon arriving back at his townhouse, Aaron went directly to the attic room. It was no longer his sole sanctuary, but it was where he felt most comfortable. Seeing Lucius had exposed all the festering disease successfully hidden from Maria and almost everyone else. As long as he hid the truth from Maria, he would never be worthy; he would always hold a secret. A spot in his soul to which she would never be privy.

She deserved more than that.

Not only that, she was vehement regarding Colin's killer. Aaron knew everything would come to light someday.

He had to tell her.

They would meet up with Lucius Carlyle again, and Aaron couldn't be sure that at such a meeting Lucius would not bring out what had happened just to destroy Aaron's happiness. *But would Lucius go to such lengths?* he asked himself. The answer was obvious. Lucius was the craftiest man in England. He never would put himself in a potentially vulnerable situation. Yet the truth could surface anyway, rising in bloated decay from some subterranean cave hitherto unknown.

As Aaron got down on his knees, he knew the Father's answer before a word was uttered. Honor demanded it. Loving her required it. His faith made it a mandate. He would tell her. He must. But even if she did forgive him, how could things ever be the same between them again? Any mote of innocence left regarding her opinion of him would be shattered. Trust would lie in pieces on the ground as well. And picking up so many tiny, jagged fragments would prove to be impossible.

Whispering softly to himself, Aaron drew out his handkerchief and wiped his brow. "I have lost her. I know it. I have lost her."

Aaron stripped down completely and climbed into bed. Sleep would not be found—at least *that* was something of which he was certain. And lying there in the darkness, he relived the past and begged God's forgiveness for the thousandth time.

• • •

The morning sun, molten and glowing, was just peeking over the horizon. The sky cast a red glow on the brick face of Maria's hotel. A haunting stillness crowned the deserted street, and the trees in the park across the road shuffled their leaves in gentle, springtime somnolence. Squirrels perched atop fence posts and in trees. Sparrows sang softly, and pigeons cooed from above. Cats oozed over fences to land on the walkways in front of the houses, and the sun began to shake the chill out of the air as if it were a rug.

Maria was looking out of the window which faced the street and not seeing a thing. Two hours past she had awakened and finished a light breakfast of tea and toast. She was tired. Physically spent and emotionally drained. Sleep had been evasive. The last time she had squinted to see the clock by her bed it had been 3:30, and an hour and a half later she was wide awake once more. But still weary.

Nervously she tapped her nails on the occasional table standing next to her. Aaron had never acted like that before. Driving home last night, he was surly and extremely preoccupied. It was puzzling. To be honest, he had always seemed the slightest bit removed from her, but he had imploded in on himself in the carriage. Had even forgotten to kiss her good night. Heavens, not that she would have kissed him back anyway after the manner in which he had spoken to her in the dining room!

The sun was well over the horizon when she saw him walking briskly toward the hotel. She immediately went down to the hotel lobby. Resolve cemented his features into a hard, purposeful mask. Dread dropped harshly and suddenly into her stomach as he marched stolidly in her direction.

"You're an early bird this morning," she said, trying to sound happy, but achieving only shrillness. The sound of her own voice startled her. But his appearance was even more startling. His eyes were red-rimmed, and they refused to meet hers. She couldn't be upset at him anymore. Seeing him so tormented was like a sudden rain that caused her heart to grow even larger with love for him.

"Maria, we need to talk. Where can we be alone?"

She ushered him into a cozy parlor to the side of the lobby.

They sat on the sofa, and he took her hands in his. He stared at the carved rosewood armrest and breathed in deeply before turning to face her. His gaze was bold, and she could see he only wanted to say whatever it was he came to say, to get it over with quickly so they could go on.

"Maria, what I have to say to you will probably change forever the way you feel about me. But in light of my feelings for you, and the fact that you deserve to know everything about me, I must tell you."

"Aaron, you're frightening me." She stroked the back

of his hand and put a twinkle in her eye. "What could possibly be so bad? Whatever it is, I'm sure I'll understand."

Aaron pulled his hand away, and Maria felt a stab in her heart.

"No, Maria, it's not as simple as that. I wish it were." He arose and walked over to the window. Waiting patiently for him to begin, the feeling of dread spread from her stomach to consume her whole body. Her hands and knees began to shake in small, rapid vibrations. And she bit down to keep her teeth from chattering.

The room suddenly grew cold.

"It has something to do with Lucius Carlyle, doesn't it, Aaron?"

Slipping his hands into his pockets, he turned around. "Yes. How did you know?"

"From the moment you greeted him, the change in you was apparent."

"You're absolutely right."

"Then you'd better tell me about it now."

Aaron resumed his place beside her. Oh Lord, he wanted to prepare her for what he had to say, to ease her gently into his dark side, to escort her lovingly through the squalid labyrinth he was about to open up. But he could not. The strength just wouldn't be found. If he held back in the least, he might never do what he came to do.

"Maria, it is I who am responsible for Colin's murder."

Her eyes registered her shock, but she was powerless to respond. He continued, words tumbling rapidly over each other. Only mentioning a promise once made, he deliberately left out any reference to Brimstone. But he recalled the night with Julian Carlyle, agreeing to do the deed to keep the Carlyles from implication. With each word, Maria's horror grew, even though Aaron sought to keep from his account the sordid details. "Oh, Maria, remember... I am not the man now that I was then. I was a monster, driven to drink and gamble my existence away. You remember the Aaron of the masquerade?"

"Yes," she said dully, "I remember."

"I have truly changed. I don't expect you to understand, but you must see how I felt at that time of my life. We were only ten minutes apart! My selfishness knew no limits. My bitterness was harbored safely and lovingly away. What a gross injustice it seemed to me that, although we were identical twins, Colin inherited everything while I was to receive nothing."

He looked up at the ceiling, searching for more reasons. "I was a drunk, Maria. It all started when I was barely out of childhood."

"But, Aaron, Colin was good to you!" She was hiding now behind a facade of anger. "It was not Colin who cut you out, it was your father. And when you began to drink and gamble, Colin couldn't trust you with the money."

"Of course I know that now."

"Then why did you kill him for the Carlyles?"

"Maria, I can never give you the details or you would be in danger for your life."

Her eyes widened, and her breath caught as he continued.

"All I can tell you is that Julian Carlyle had invested the majority of their money into coal. Coal was all they had."

As he continued, she was going into a state of withdrawal, receding into a desolate desert of rage. Colin's face loomed in front of her. All the memories, the conversations, the tenderness in his eyes. He had been such a gentle soul, would never have brought harm to anyone. She came back to the present when Aaron uttered the words, "I felt I had to do it, Maria." He held his hands out in supplication. "The night that he died, I went back..."

But she wasn't listening. She looked at his hands and stood up, her eyes flashed dangerously, and she sprang like a cobra. "Get out of here!" Tears of rage fell as she slapped his right hand away. "Get away from me," she grated through her teeth. "I never want to see you again!"

He tried to take her gently by the shoulders, imploring her. "Maria..."

She pushed him. "I said I don't ever want to see you again."

"But, Maria. I'll confess to what I've done. I'll make restitution."

"Do whatever you want to do, your lordship. But do it for yourself, not for me. You've sat here for the past ten minutes and have given me nothing but excuses as to why you had your twin brother murdered."

"But, Maria, let me explain. That same night I went back to..."

She ground her palms against her ears. "Be quiet, your grace! Just go now and leave me be."

Maria ran from the room.

· · ·

That evening

Aaron sat in the stables behind his townhouse. Many nobles had given up private transportation for the hired coaches and cabs which roamed the streets. Not so the Duke of Argyll. Though he had only returned to London a week ago, his coach and six was already recognized and commented upon on the streets.

Some servants were washing the day's dust off the black coach. They had finished with the open carriage ten minutes earlier. Aaron jumped off his perch.

"Have the phaeton made ready with the two Arabians and brought round front in 15 minutes," he ordered.

"Aye, yer lordship," said one man.

"Yes, m'lord," said another.

Aaron hurried into the house to find Chastain, who was preparing to leave by train in the morning for Inveraray to settle some pressing business matters for Aaron.

Forty minutes later he and the old secretary were eating up miles of countryside in the lightly sprung four-wheeled vehicle. Aaron's hat was gone, and he drove in his shirtsleeves. Not that he cared about circumspection at that point. Chastain sat beside him, dignified and frightened beyond all imagining. He didn't show it, however (much to his credit), but kept a hand on top of his bowler as his white hair fluttered about his cheeks. His small blue eyes squinted against the wind, and he breathed only when it became absolutely necessary. The sun was gone for the day, leaving behind angry streaks of red and purple. Feeling the horses gallop so freely, so wildly, Chastain wished he was at the other side of the horizon with the daylight. Goodness, but he would rather be anywhere else at the moment.

Finally, Aaron slowed the pace of the horses. Their sides puffed in and out. Aaron walked them for a bit before pulling over to let them drink from a small stream which bordered the left side of the road.

He jumped down and came around to Chastain.

"Well, old man, could you stand to stretch your legs a bit?"

"I don't know if I can stand at all, your lordship."

Aaron held his hand out. "I'll help you down."

"I would be most grateful, m'lord."

Tenderly, Aaron placed Chastain's hand on his shoulder and cradled the bony old elbow in his other hand. Chastain leaned all his weight upon his employer and stepped off the edge. Aaron's other arm went round his waist, and he easily caught the elderly man's weight for a soft landing down on the long grass. A minute later they sat on the bank next to the horses.

Aaron pulled out a pipe and lit it. A Christmas present from Maria who said she was sorry, but she simply could not abide the smoke from a cigar. He puffed to get it going, then leaned back.

"Tell me, Chastain, is man destined only for disappointment in this life?"

"Oh no, m'lord. If he is typical, he will end up disillusioned, discontent, and disheartened as well!"

Aaron laughed sadly.

"But it is different with our kind. It's only temporary," Chastain said. "Naturally, we cannot help but feel these things. Even the most godly men become disillusioned many times in their life, I am sure. At least I hope that is the case, or I shall wonder if I am at all hand in hand with the Father!"

"You deal with such things, old man? You are always so calm and filled with such peace."

"Oh, m'lord. I deal with such things every day. May I speak frankly, your grace?"

"Of course."

"Imagine, if you will, you are 68 years old, and all

you've done your entire life is fill in numbers in account books and take care of business for those who expect bowing and scraping and never look upon you as more than a subservient wretch. Your grace, I've worked for three other noblemen beside yourself, and other than you, I was more intelligent than any of them."

"Come now, old man, you do yourself a disservice. You're more intelligent than me as well!"

Chastain shook his head. "Anyway, it isn't easy being looked down upon by such buffoons. Sometimes I think the Americans have the right idea when they say that all men are created equal."

"That's what the Scriptures say. Neither Jew nor Greek, bond nor free."

"Aye. But you know, it isn't being looked down upon that gives me cause for disappointment. It's that I feel sometimes I never really *did* anything with my life. I served those who employed me, asked no questions, took home my pay, and returned each week for more of the same."

"Surely, being an honest man and doing an honest day's work is no cause for shame?" Aaron asked.

"No. I suppose you're right. Especially with the way society is going."

"I agree. Each year I find I have less and less in common with the younger people."

"So, all in all, m'lord, I've lived my life as best as I've known how, and I did what I had to do. Yet, I wonder if that's all that is expected of us."

"To do what we have to do?"

Chastain nodded.

"I think so. And that is what I must do as well."

"Sir?"

"Maria knows the truth now, old man. She said she never wants to see me again."

Chastain didn't know what to say. Aaron let out a hollow laugh. "So, you see, I sit here disheartened and most definitely disappointed. But not completely discouraged."

"Why is that, your grace?"

"Because now that Maria is gone, my calling is sure. God wants me to turn myself in to Scotland Yard."

"Sir, are you sure?"

"I've never been more certain about anything in my life."

Chastain and Aaron sat for several minutes as the night air circulated about their bodies and the crickets chirruped. Aaron's pipe went out as more stars came twinkling into the velvet expanse above their heads. The old secretary turned to his master.

"Your grace, my father always told me a man must do what he thinks is right. And so I will not try to dissuade you. Although it is not my place, I only ask one thing of you."

"What is that, old man?"

Even in the dimness, Aaron could see the spark of vengeance in Chastain's eyes. "Do not go down alone. Take Lucius Carlyle with you."

"I've already thought of that, old man. And take him down I shall."

• • •

Two days later

Aaron was standing on the platform. The late afternoon train that Maria was taking would get her to Bristol for an overnight stay. Her ship was leaving from there in the morning.

She was going to America.

There were not many others boarding the train. Coming toward him, she was unmistakable—the small figure with the proud bearing of a queen. She walked with head held high through the steam of the train. Martha had told Aaron of her employer's plans after Maria refused to speak with him the day before.

Quickly walking toward her, he took her by surprise. She couldn't hide her feelings, and for one brief moment it was as if nothing had ever happened. But her eyes became guarded once more.

"What are you doing here, your grace?"

Her inability to say his name pained him, and his eyes implored her. "I couldn't let you leave without seeing you again." He looked down, and his voice came out hesitantly. "Maria, please, don't go like this. Tell me you forgive me."

Her small smile was infinitely sad. "I've forgiven you. But I don't think I can live with what you've done for the rest of my life."

"But, Maria, I love you so."

"I love you too, Aaron, but we all must live with the decisions we make."

Before she realized what she was doing, she took the glove off her right hand and removed the beautiful ring. "I can't marry you."

The devastation on his face cut her to the core, and her lips quivered as she grimaced to hold back the tears. Little did she realize the ring was his death warrant. She thrust the ring forward, eyes looking only at the floor. "I'm sorry. I have reasons you can't begin to understand."

Aaron shook his head slowly from side to side. "No. I won't take it back. It's yours."

"But, Aaron," she protested.

"No, my love, I'll never need a ring like that again," he said sadly as he raised his hand to caress her cheek. "How much I love you."

The whistle blew.

"I must go."

Her feet carried her to the car as fast as she could walk, and she boarded without looking back. Aaron, on the now-deserted platform, stood among the steam feeling its heat on his wet cheeks. Shaking himself, he hardened his features and walked away from the platform.

• • •

It was still early, not yet 7:00, when Aaron reached Foxhall.

For several minutes he stood by the front door, composing himself, ridding his fingers, his knees, and his innards of agitation. He would not let Lucius know what he was feeling. He must seem as strong as a lion and in complete mastery of the situation at hand.

Flat-palmed, he laid his hand upon the smooth, white, freshly painted surface of the door. Leaning his forehead against the wood, he deeply inhaled the perfumed air, then in one quick motion he raised his head and rapped on the door. He was shown into the dining room.

After a pleasant greeting on his part, Lucius offered Aaron a seat at the long cherry table. "Have you dined yet?"

"No, there wasn't time."

"Shall I have another place set?" Lucius invited. Aaron declined with a nod and an uplifted hand.

"If you don't mind then, I'll eat while we talk."

"Do you mind if I smoke?" Aaron asked, his nerves strung more tightly than steel cables.

"Not at all," Lucius answered, his head bowed over his plate. "A glass of wine, perhaps?"

"No, thank you."

Aaron watched him butter his dinner roll, his eyes resting on Lucius' lion's-head ring, saying nothing as he smoked his cigar. The smoke felt good in his mouth. It was the only familiar something to be found in the room. He studied the man in front of him.

It was a shame, really. Lucius Carlyle had all the makings of a great man, but he chose a different, darker path. If his physical qualities were not exactly those of an Adonis, his mind more than made up for it. Aaron remembered late nights at Oxford, when Lucius had imbibed a bit too freely. The discussions were truly amazing, centering most often on philosophy. Truly, Aaron knew that Lucius was the only member of their group who could outthink him. And that was what made him apprehensive just now. Naturally, when he was sober, Lucius suppressed his instinctual intelligence, hiding behind the masks of power and money. Blast it, but he wasn't looking forward to this confrontation. And yet... in other ways, he was. Yes, he most definitely was looking forward to seeing Lucius' expression when the card was played.

"What happened to us, Lucius?" Aaron asked finally.

"What do you mean?"

"Do you remember the late-night discussions we used to have? Descarte, Rousseau, Voltaire. You had such high ideals then, deep inside. I knew I'd never do anything with them. But you, Lucius, with your mind and the heart you possessed at that time, you could have done anything you wanted."

Lifting a morsel of grouse up to his mouth, he looked at Aaron, not quite meeting his eyes. "No, Aaron," he swallowed and took a sip of wine. "It isn't that simple. Only you appreciated what power lies behind here." He tapped his forehead. "Not any of the others. Not Mother. And certainly not Father. You saw yourself that the family name, the fortune, the position of the Carlyles was his life. And it became mine. I've paid for it with my soul, and I intend to keep hold of it no matter what it takes. Don't take me for a fool by bringing up the empty idealism of university days." He pushed his plate away, the food half-eaten. "Enough of this. You've come here for something. Now what is it?

"This."

Aaron tossed the card he had hidden away so many years before across the table. It was smooth and flat, held in place for years in a mathematics text. Lucius' blood, once crying out from the surface in an angry, sanguine red, was now brown and flaking off.

"So, the bloody queen has come to call upon me, eh?" Lucius asked, setting down his napkin and locking eyes with Aaron. "What can I do to help, old friend? Do you need money, or someone silenced...."

Aaron nodded. "I wish it were that simple. In two days' time I'm confessing to my brother's murder. Put your house in order, Lucius. I have been doing just that for the past year and a half."

"What is the queen for?"

"Your cooperation. Speak only the truth when Scotland Yard comes. But queen or no queen, Lucius, the truth is going to be revealed."

"You can't possibly mean..."

"I want you right there beside me at the gallows."

"This is preposterous!" Lucius drew back his shoulders and threw his napkin onto his plate. He let out a harsh laugh.

Aaron smiled, his first real smile in two days. "Is it? Is it, Lucius? And is that a prerequisite for fulfilling your vow?"

"Aaron, perhaps I sounded insulting, forgive me. I did not mean it so. Just think about it some more, dear friend. We have gained so much these past months. So much. How could you be serious about throwing it all away?"

"Oh, I am fatally serious, Lucius. I believe there is something that you don't yet know about me. I have become a Christian, Lucius. And I believe this is what God is requiring of me. My affairs are in order. My estates are secure. The timing couldn't be better. But let us not talk of me. You know what the vow entails. You must honor your commitment or surely Brimstone will retaliate."

The tables suddenly turned as Lucius sneered triumphantly. "You don't know the half of what Brimstone entails, Aaron. There is an honor far deeper than you can imagine sitting there with your silly request still fresh on your lips," he said softly, not masking the threat in his voice. "If you were wise, Aaron Campbell, you would rise from your chair right now, mount your horse, and head for Scotland. Because if you do not, you shall surely look upon this evening as the night your tomb was sealed."

"Then so be it." Aaron answered softly, calmly, an almost-insane expression on his face. "Maria has deserted me. I have nothing left to lose."

Lucius' eyes shifted momentarily, a physical manifestation of the sour motion in his blood. Then he grabbed the card, tore it in two, and threw it across the table toward Aaron. And he started chuckling. "You'll never be able to prove I had anything to do with it."

"I kept my side of the bargain, Lucius."

"Did you?" Lucius asked, still laughing.

Somehow Aaron remained calm. "I murdered my brother for you."

Lucius smiled wickedly. "Take heart, old boy. This only proves that I really am what everyone believes: a ruthless son of the devil. And I assure you, Brimstone will not take my life over this, but yours."

"Then, Lucius, I promise you this: To die will be an awfully big adventure. This matter is far from closed."

Lucius laughed. "Beware, Aaron."

Aaron rose to go. "You will burn in torment, Lucius Carlyle."

"I fully intend to, dear man."

· · ·

As Lucius was sending messengers to ride in all haste to George, Alex, and Robert, Aaron made his way back to the townhouse. A sense of resolve permeated him and calmed his aching spirit. He went over his will, looked over his account books, and walked about the house until almost 11:00. Aaron would never see Scotland again, and that saddened him beyond expectation. Before he left for Inveraray, Chastain had brought each necessary document at Aaron's request. In supportive but melancholy silence, the old man had bent over Aaron at his desk answering question after question.

And Aaron never stopped thinking about Lucius. The man still had two days to reconsider, but he wouldn't. Aaron knew that. He appealed to the honor of a man who had none.

• • •

George Lindsay, Robert Mayfield, and Alex Fairly sat around the table in a dismal mood. The club was empty except for themselves. George, looking surlier with each tick of the clock, threw down his cards. "No more for me. This place is looking drearier than usual. What say we find entertainment elsewhere?" Everyone agreed. No one was in the mood for cards anyway.

Robert Mayfield just grunted and opened his pocket watch. "We'll have to get going soon. I suppose this meeting will have to do for entertainment."

Utterly annoyed at being at Lucius' beck and call, George was clearly not looking forward to it. "What do you think Carlyle wants? And to be so secretive about it besides?"

Alex grimaced, feeling much the same as George. "Don't ask me, Lindsay. All my note said was to meet him at Fallen Gables. I don't know if I'll still be able to find my way there."

George agreed with a nod. "It seems rather silly, all this subterfuge. We haven't met at that place since summer holiday our third year."

"Well," said Robert who had always loved an adventure, "it sounds intriguing to me. Something must be afoot in the Brotherhood." The others all nodded in accordance. "Let's go."

The threesome started out under a waxing moon. Robert remembered the way, and they were soon stumbling through a thick hedge of yew. The prickly, dark trees hid the small cottage from the view of any passersby who should just happen to be wandering that way at ten o'clock in the evening.

A brick path leading up to the low wooden door, now a dusty, scratchy red, was grown over with weeds and untended roses. Like a skeptical, squat little man, the low house leaned to the right, its wooden exterior looking strained, exhausted. Slate, flat and deepest gray, made up the roof, and the windows were sporting their glass panes except for the one around the side which a branch had impaled during an angry storm the month before. A dim glow shone through the dirty panes of the three front windows. They had come here many times during university days.

Lucius was waiting.

"Thank you for coming, gentlemen." He stood to his feet.

The others sat down, two on a sofa, one on a chair. The room was actually furnished adequately, but the dust and dirt from years of neglect gave the room a suffocating quality even though the night was cool. A feeling of claustrophobia settled on them. And inevitability—a dark, irrevocable inevitability—kept guard in the dim light like a blackened gargoyle on the outside of a tomb. No one was leaving until it said so. No one could deny that the setting and the mystery caused a sudden thrill to trip along through their veins.

Robert loosened his cravat. "What's all of this about?" he questioned, direct as always.

Alex chimed in, not quite as comfortable in these surroundings as the rest. "Yes, Carlyle, this is all a bit mysterious."

"There's some trouble in the Brotherhood, men. And it has to do with our good friend the Duke of Argyll."

George sat up straight. "Aaron?"

"He came to see me this evening, actually, and I'm loath to state that it wasn't at all pleasant."

"What happened, Lucius? Get to the point." George was a bit irritated at having his evening disrupted, but he tried not to show it.

"The matter is pure and simple, lads. Aaron hired someone to kill his brother."

"What?" Alex gasped.

"His guilt has gotten hold of him, and he's going to turn himself in."

"That's preposterous!" Robert responded. "You'll have to explain more thoroughly than that, Lucius. Aaron couldn't have had his twin brother killed. I simply can't believe it of him."

"Oh yes, it's true, believe me. Didn't we hear nightly, as the brandy took hold, of the injustices of being the younger twin?"

George shook his head. "Perhaps. But murder?"

"Why not? He took pleasure in losing his brother's money, feeling some sense of revenge." Lucius sighed. "Believe me, gentlemen, I wish it wasn't true. Aaron is my good friend. He was right there when it happened."

George burst in. "If Aaron set up the murder, Lucius, why was he there at the opera? How would the assassin know who was who?"

Lucius was quick. "He wasn't there until after Colin was stabbed. Being on hand was the perfect alibi. Who would believe that a twin could be so hard-hearted? He knew it was going to happen all right. Colin died in his arms."

Robert crossed his arms across his chest. "Sounds plausible, but I'm still not convinced."

Lucius smiled graciously. "Loyal to the end, eh, Mayfield? Commendable. Blasted commendable. But you haven't heard it all."

"How do you know so much about it, Carlyle, if it was all Aaron's doing?" Alex ventured nervously.

The wind picked up outside, and the branch began to scrape against the broken glass.

"Well, men, I wish I could tell you I was completely innocent in this matter, but I fear I am not. The reason Aaron had Colin murdered was because I cashed in my queen of spades."

"What?" George was flabbergasted.

"It's true. Our estates were drastically dwindling. Father needed reassurance before he died that things would get better. All we had left were the mining interests. Colin was extremely dangerous to my family's well-being. He had to be destroyed."

Alex was pale. "Why Aaron?"

"For reasons I have already stated. No one would expect a twin to heartlessly murder his own brother. He was the natural choice, and add to that the fact that my card bore his blood, it all made perfect sense. But my foolproof plan backfired. Aaron has become a Christian, and that makes him more dangerous than I could begin to say."

Robert took a silver flask out of his coat pocket and took a swig. George reached for it and did likewise.

Lucius' voice dimmed. "One with such beliefs cannot hold dear the Society or keep its secrets hidden. As the good book says, 'A man cannot serve two masters.' Brimstone will surely be exposed. And you and I and all the Brotherhood will have to answer for it."

"What do you propose we do about it?" asked Robert. "I mean 'long live the Brotherhood' and all that, but what can we possibly do?"

An evil grin made its way to Lucius' face. "Men, Aaron Campbell must die."

George ground his cigar with his heel with a quick twist. He was having none of it. And furthermore, he was insulted that Lucius tried to hide his own involvement at first. "You've raised a cloud of dust, Lucius, and now you complain that you cannot see. This has nothing to do with us or the Brotherhood. I'll not clear the air for you. If Aaron is the good friend you say he is, you'll be able to reason with him."

Alex nodded in agreement, but not Robert. His chance to prove himself as more than some gambling, drinking buffoon had finally come.

Robert turned to Lucius. "I'll do it."

Alex was shocked. "Why, Robert? Aaron is our friend. Can you so easily betray him?"

"Aaron is the betrayer. He's betrayed the Brotherhood . . . each one of us."

George scowled. "We are betrayed not by Aaron. We are betrayed by the falseness of our own souls. Brimstone has made it thus, having given us much to hide and secrets for which to kill."

"That matters not." Robert dismissed George's disillusioned words.

Lucius agreed. "The fact is that many will suffer if Aaron does as he's promised. Brimstone could be exposed. Do you have any idea what kind of upheaval such an investigation would cause?" He held out his hand. "Thank you, Robert."

Robert shook his hand. "Aaron hasn't been around for well over a year, gentlemen. He's forsaken the Brotherhood. Clearly it is as Lucius says: He's a dangerous man."

Lucius leaned back, a slow smile of satisfaction spreading across his face as one by one each man left the dim confines of the house.

"I'll ride back with Lucius," Robert proclaimed as Lucius walked to his horse.

George looked at Robert harshly. "And just when will Judas do the bidding of Lucifer?"

"Tomorrow night. But I am not the Judas here, George. Aaron is. Brimstone must be protected at all costs."

George turned away, the breeze lifting his pale hair. *Good*, he thought, *that gives me some time.* "Come on, Alex," he put his arm round his friend's slim shoulders, "it's just you and me now."

Alex breathed a sigh of relief.

• • •

Riding through the midnight, Aaron neared the Apple and Serpent. He was going to tell Jacob Beck of his planned confession. The assassin could do whatever he wanted with the information. He didn't know where to go from here. *Have to think, to prepare the next step.* There was no way of implicating Lucius without bringing the entire Brotherhood to light. If there was a bigger, darker side to the Brotherhood as Alex suspected and Lucius implied, perhaps he could find out what it was. Perhaps he could use that to bargain with. Make it easier on himself. Why couldn't he do both? Find out just what Brimstone really did, and implicate Lucius as well? Unfortunately, it would take some time.

Maria's ship sailing the Atlantic formed pictorially in his mind. *I have more time on my hands than I could possibly want.*

In front of him stood the inn he had come to despise. In his mind it had taken on a personality of its own. A sinister place that housed with pleasure the dealings of evil men, rich and poor. The Apple and Serpent.

Aaron entered and gazed around him, keenly aware of how differently he viewed these surroundings since he had last darkened the door. A few rough types were sitting at one of the tables. The innkeeper, a large man with muscles bulging beneath his grubby shirt, asked what Aaron wanted in gruff tones and came back a minute later with a sweet cider. Aaron nodded his thanks brusquely and handed the man a shilling. The conversation of the other party had quieted to a whisper, and Aaron sat, waiting. More ruffians tumbled in at intervals until the place was over half full. *Come to quench their thirst after a hard night's work,* he thought bitterly.

Fifteen minutes later Aaron was not surprised when the noble-looking gentleman came down the stairs. He nodded and gestured to the seat across the table. The innkeeper came over with a glass and a bottle of whiskey, which Jacob Beck gratefully poured and drank down with a single gulp. Aaron's throat opened, wishing he could share in the drink. He watched Beck's hands as he poured another glass. Those fine, strong hands. The hands that wielded a small knife a year and a half ago.

Suddenly, Aaron felt trapped in a heavy, sickening world of his own making. Why was he here? What had he been thinking to come back, to see face-to-face the man who had murdered his brother? But Beck's voice returned him to his surroundings, and he stared up at the assassin, a bemused expression on his face.

"I was wondering when you would show up, your grace," Beck said nonchalantly.

Aaron was genuinely confused. Perhaps one murder led to another in most cases. "What do you mean?"

Beck threw a bag of coins across the table. "Here," he said, his voice as flat as his gaze. "It's all there. Every penny. I knew you'd be back for it sooner or later."

"What are you talking about?"

"The blood money. Judas' wage."

Aaron met his gaze. "I don't understand. Why would I want that? You earned your hire."

Beck shook his head. "No."

"I'm sorry, I still don't know what you mean."

"Someone else beat me to it."

CHAPTER
17

The surrounding inn seemed to fade into a void, and Aaron felt himself suspended out of time. Only Beck and the scarred surface of the table existed in his stunned consciousness.

"Are you sure?"

"Upon my word, m'lord. I did not kill your brother."

The world changed in an instant.

"What happened, Beck?"

Beck leaned back and lit a pipe. "Everything has its price."

Aaron retrieved his purse and slid several one pound notes across the table. Out of his inside coat pocket he pulled out a Cuban cigar and lit it.

"Tell me."

"I went to the opera as planned. I slipped in behind the curtain ready to strike. The last scene had begun, but I hesitated for just a moment. It's this instinct I have, your grace. When things are not what they should be, I always know it. And something in the air was not right. So I stayed behind the curtain, saying to myself, 'Just a minute more, and then it's time to strike.' That was when I heard your brother cry out. Naturally, I stayed put. I was there the whole time you were with him."

"Did you see the man, Beck?"

"I did. And I couldn't tell you anything more about him other than he was dressed much like everyone else there that night."

"Did you see anything that would identify him?"

"He wore a large ring on his little finger. It was fashioned after the head of a lion."

"Thank you, Beck."

Aaron walked out into the night a free man.

. . .

Riding back to the city, Aaron was filled with a restless wanting. It was Carlyle. The previous day's conversation replayed in his mind yet again. "Did you?" Lucius had asked when Aaron reminded him that he had kept his side of the bargain. It was all so clear now. The lion's-head ring. Lucius' hidden nervousness. All he needed to know, he knew.

Lucius Carlyle had murdered his brother.

How Aaron was going to prove it was another matter. Whether he should bring Scotland Yard into the matter right away was a question he couldn't answer yet. But he was almost home. A good night's sleep might help clear his mind. He had learned a long time ago that the wee hours of the morning were no time to make a decision or chart a course. *I won't do anything until I talk to Chastain.*

And there was always Brimstone to add into the equation. Obviously, Lucius knew something he didn't. Certainly, he was now in grave danger. Grosvenor Square loomed in front of him. As he turned the corner, the lights on either side of his front door sent small beacons of welcome his way. They were the last thing he saw. For waiting alone on that corner, in the dead of night and holding a steel bar, was Robert Mayfield.

• • •

A metallic click echoed dully, and Aaron's eyes opened wide. Bereft of light, the room was humid. Rain had fallen. And the midnight world was still.

Peering into the darkness, his eyes adjusted to the blue luminescence of the night. Doors of perception slowly opened wide.

"Robert?"

Aaron became totally aware of his whereabouts. He was at Fallen Gables. A blinding pain seized his skull. In answer, all he heard was heavy breathing.

"Robert?" he questioned again, leaning up on his elbow. "What are you doing?" His old friend was shaking and shivering, rocking back and forth on his knees, his pistol held loosely in one hand, the barrel moving around in clumsy circles. The other hand clenched the neck of a half-empty bottle of scotch. Carrying out the task hadn't proved as easy as he had thought it would.

The pain inside Aaron's head made it difficult to focus, but he knew exactly what was going on. "Robert, why you?"

Robert jolted into action, a fire of confusion, grief, and disappointment setting his anger aflame, giving motion to his limbs. Grasping him by the coat, he pulled Aaron to his feet. He shouted as he threw Aaron against the wall. "Because you have forsaken the Brotherhood!"

Wincing as he made contact, Aaron cried, "No, Robert. You're mistaken!" This madman brandishing a pistol was a stranger to him.

That same pistol was now shaking a foot away from his temple. "Be quiet!" Robert shouted. "You deserve to die. You'd be content to see us all hang."

"But it's not true. Lucius is lying. You must listen. . . ."

"Quiet!" Robert roared. "You've betrayed us all! The Brotherhood! Everything!"

Robert raised the pistol again. One shot. It was all he had. It was all it would take. The liquor flowing through his veins would make it a simple matter. And yet he hesitated momentarily, finding a firmer position for his finger on the trigger.

Aaron wasted no time. With a yell, he sprang from his position on the ground, his head slamming into Robert's stomach. The hefty man was thrown off balance, and he flew several yards back before slamming into the opposite wall of the cottage. But alcohol or no, Robert was a strong man. Immediately he tried to rise, but Aaron was too quick. He grabbed for the wrist that held the gun, twisted, and was behind Robert in a split second, the arm held behind its owner's back. Aaron pulled up, trying to free the gun. Robert resisted.

"For the sake of all that's decent, Robert, let go of the gun!" he shouted.

Robert struggled, and Aaron pulled up again. Somehow Robert twisted around, the gun still in his fist. Aaron lunged at his arm, forcing it over his head.

A shot rang out.

And Robert knew the chance was gone.

A fight ensued. Robert was stronger, but Aaron was more skilled and infinitely faster. Punches were thrown, kicks placed, and finally Aaron had his old friend pinned to the ground. Robert's eyes were angry.

"You may have stopped me for now, Campbell, but I will see you dead."

"No, Robert. You won't," his words turned cruel, "not at your cowardly hand, in any case. Now, you will listen to me and listen well, Robert Mayfield, for I shall only explain this to you once."

Aaron commenced to tell the tale. As he went over all the details, the scarlet bonds of friendship tightened, joining them closely together once more. And by the time Aaron was done relating what had happened that very night at the Apple and Serpent, Robert was sitting beside him on the floor of the cottage sharing a cigar.

Aaron finished the tale. "So there you have it, my friend. The whole story. Every sordid, mucky detail."

Robert hung his head. "Forgive me, Aaron. I'm sorry. The ironical part of it all is that you were faithful to the Brotherhood, not Lucius. Blast it, you would have killed your own twin to keep the vow."

Aaron nodded. "Aye. Lucius is the one who holds the Brotherhood fast merely for financial gain and personal manipulation. When his bloody queen was called, he ripped it in half and threw it at me."

"He conveniently left that out of his tale. So much for honor." Robert shook his head sadly.

"You and I both know it's more than that," Aaron said perceptively. "Be truthful with me now. Why did you take it upon yourself to kill me?"

"I had to."

In spite of himself, Aaron smiled. How familiar those words were!

Robert sighed wearily, still ashamed. "Lucius dragged us all here a few hours ago. He recited his tall tale and told us you had to die. Naturally, George started to leave, saying this was between the two of you. And Alex was frightened. But you know me and the Brotherhood. I once said I would do anything for the Brotherhood. I volunteered. Aaron, you may not understand this with your position and your wealth, but I saw it as my big chance. An opportunity to make a mark, to save the Brotherhood, and so have every last one of them indebted to me. Finally, a turnabout."

Aaron was not in the least surprised. "That sounds like you, Robert."

"Yes. And I'm ashamed to say I took no time in planning your demise."

Aaron patted him on the arm. "That's all right, my friend. You always were one to dispense of unpleasant duties quickly. Believe me, I understand. Only too well. My current status is still new, don't forget. I remember what it was like to bow and scrape. I really owe a lot to Lucius in a perverse sort of way, when you think of it. I could easily have been my brother's murderer but for him. What I don't understand is why he did it himself."

Robert, nodding his head from side to side, concurred. "So what do we do now?"

"I haven't the faintest idea. I was planning on working that out in the morning. Tell me this, did Lucius tell you to carry out the plan tonight?"

"No, he gave no instructions. But I did tell George I was going to wait until tomorrow night. Lucius knows better than anyone, the less said the better."

"Aye. We are up against a formidable adversary, Robert. We must play the game craftily and respectfully. Go to Foxhall tomorrow morning and tell him you will kill me after dark. It will give me an extra day. Lucius is a conscientious sort and more cunning than the two of us put together. Meet me back here tomorrow evening at 9:30. I'm going back to talk to Jacob Beck. If we are playing with the likes of Lucius Carlyle, we need to stack the deck in our favor."

"Beck would have killed your brother without a shred of guilt!"

"Even rattlesnakes have their uses, Robert. We must find a way to throw Carlyle off. He must suspect nothing."

"Tell me more."

"I'll tell you tomorrow when my plan is thought further through. In the meantime, I'll make the necessary preparations."

• • •

29 April 1844

My Darling Maria,

You left today, and with you went all hope from my heart. I set out to do exactly as I said I would, turn myself in. But something amazing happened, my love. Something I almost dare not believe, it is so wonderful.

I am innocent of my brother's death. I can hardly believe it myself. And although I cannot impart the details in this letter, suffice it for me to tell you that the man I hired did not kill Colin. But he witnessed the murder. It was Lucius Carlyle. I still don't know why he bloodied his own hands. But I will find out. And I will work to implicate him. Justice will be served, Maria. And it has been what I've wanted since the day my brother died. Only the recipient of that justice has changed.

There's so much I wish to tell you. So many things I wanted to say that day at your hotel. Did you know that on the night he was murdered I tried to stop it? I rode to the inn at which I hired the assassin, but he had already left. And so I raced for Covent Garden. That, my love, was why I was on the scene so quickly. But I was too late.

Come back to me, my darling, please. But wait until July when this should be a finished matter. I pray it will take no longer. Breathe not a word of this to anyone, and destroy this letter after you have read it. I love you and remain wholeheartedly,

Your loving fiancé,

A. Campbell

CHAPTER

18

The next evening

The warmth of the inn assaulted Aaron's face as he opened the door.

This place is becoming a matter of habit, he thought good-humoredly as he sat down. Barney, with a disgusted smile on his face, roughly placed a mug of sweet cider in front of him with a plunk. A bit slopped over the side, and Aaron lifted the mug to his lips, leaving a wet ring on the scarred surface of the trestle table.

To the ringing of eight tinny chimes from the mantel clock, Jacob Beck trod down the stairs. He sat down in front of Aaron automatically, no surprise registering across his patrician features.

His voice was as stone. "So you're back, m'lord." Frequenters of his lordship's ilk were ill-appreciated at the Apple and Serpent.

Aaron grinned. "Aye, Beck, it just seems I can't keep away from so fine an establishment."

Despite himself, Beck laughed one quick "Ha!" and jerked his thumb over to Barney. "Better not let him hear you say that. He's under a bit of a delusion concerning this place. Now tell me what it is you came for, and the quicker you do it the better it will be."

Aaron explained what had happened the night before. Beck listened without reaction.

"Beck, will you help me?" Aaron was asking. "I wish to stage my death."

Beck leaned back in his chair, rubbing his chin. Aaron hastily added, "Of course, I'll pay you whatever it is you want within reason." To which Beck simply nodded and lifted his hand. Clearly he was deep in thought.

After several minutes he gave his head a quick nod and brought a hand down on the table with a light rap. "All right!" he said, staring at Aaron's signet ring. "I've got it. Yes, it's quite clear. I'll help you. But my price will be handsome."

Aaron sighed with relief. "Tell me."

• • •

By 8:30 they were galloping at a breathless pace. Fallen Gables was at least an hour away, on the other side of London. With the plan well rehearsed, it wouldn't be wise to keep Robert waiting long. The sooner the wheels were set in motion, the better it would be for everyone . . . except Lucius Carlyle, of course.

The beauty of the scheme was found in its simplicity. Knowing what he knew, experiencing what he had experienced, enabled Beck to craft a flawless scheme. Aaron knew he could never have come up with the idea on his own. And it seemed to him that God had even planned that fateful meeting with Beck in the distant past, setting the stage to prove Lucius' guilt now. Because, of course, God knew all along that Lucius would do the deed. Looking back over the events that had transpired these past two years or so, Aaron could see quite clearly the hand of the Lord. He almost felt like one of Joseph's brothers, doing something evil, yet God meaning it for good. Had he been an extremely willful man, he might have resented that he felt rather like a puppet. Rather, he took great comfort in knowing that he was secure in the Father's hand. Better to let God pull the strings and change the backdrops. He had had enough of doing it himself. Even in the midst of danger, Aaron felt at peace in the knowledge that his God was in complete, sovereign control.

Jacob Beck, on the other hand, rode along somewhat confused. That he was involved in this way with the Duke of Argyll was puzzling to him, to say the least. Why was he helping the man out like this? Working to incriminate someone guilty of a crime he himself had committed many times. Granted, they had been nothing personal to him. But, nevertheless, he was still guilty. Beck was well aware of exactly who he was and where he was. And the quandary of his mind was solved as soon as he realized that he was doing it for the money, plain and simple. It was always for the money. He would kill the queen herself . . . for the money.

Robert was there as had been arranged. His eyes lit up at the sight of the two men coming into the house. Good. Jacob Beck had agreed to help.

"Robert, I'd like you to meet Jacob Beck."

"Just Beck." The assassin bowed slightly with gentlemanly grace, yet his voice held no warmth. "Mr. Mayfield."

"Thank you for helping us," Robert said, immediately impressed with the man's apparent icy capability. Maybe there was hope yet. At least not everyone involved had a personal stake in the matter.

The three sat down together. Robert pulled out a candle and lit it. He was quite surprised at Beck's appearance.

"Why, Beck," he drawled, "I am impressed. You cut as fine a figure as anyone in the Mayfield family!"

"More so, if you were honest, Robert," joked Aaron turning to Beck. "He's got three brothers, and every one of them is as unkempt and irresponsible as he is."

Robert laughed heartily, taking no offense at the truth. Beck just nodded. It was time to get to work.

He started out businesslike, the dark eyes sharp, suddenly looking like any hardened military leader explaining the next maneuver to his troops. "As I see it, there's only one way to throw the Earl of Beresford off and to save Mr. Mayfield from Lucius Carlyle's retaliation. You, Mr. Mayfield, could simply refuse to kill his grace, but he'd find another way. His type always does."

"So what do we do?" Robert asked.

"His grace thought of a brilliant plan. We'll stage his death. After that, the earl will think he's pulled it off completely—and you, Mr. Mayfield, you're off the hook as far as he's concerned. Do you think there's any chance he'll turn you in just for spite?"

Both Aaron and Robert nodded negatively. "He'll be too worried about his own head. He's up to his eyes, and the farther away the authorities are, the better," Aaron surmised.

"Smart man. Then let's set out now. It's only a 15-minute ride from here, but we want the news of it to spread to London in time for the *Times'* morning edition."

"What is only a short ride from here?" asked Robert.

"An old abandoned mill house I know of. You'll understand when you see it. By the way, Mr. Mayfield, do you have a flask on you?" Beck asked. Robert nodded. "Good. Don't drink any of it along the way. We'll need all we can get."

Robert looked confused, but he wasn't about to ask another question. Beck looked clearly like a man who didn't appreciate questions.

The horses galloped swiftly. Because they kept to fields and small lanes, the journey took a bit longer. It was imperative they not be seen together by too many people.

Thatch-roofed, vine-covered, and in a state of complete disrepair, the tiny stone mill house on the bank of a dried-up creek looked forlorn and sulky as they rode up and dismounted from their horses. Overgrown bushes and unpruned apple trees hid the building from the casual passerby. Beck pulled away some vines hanging in front of the door, pushing it open easily.

"Someone has been here recently," Aaron remarked. Beck just nodded and walked inside.

The fetid stench of decaying flesh reached their nostrils. And there in the corner was a corpse. Not more than three days dead, its smell was cloying, sickeningly sweet. Neither Aaron nor Robert made a remark, both knowing exactly how that corpse had come to be sitting there on the cot. *Best not to say a word,* Aaron thought as he put his coat collar up to his nose.

"Yep," said Beck, eyeing the dead man then Aaron, up and down. "The size is just about right." The men agreed quietly.

Beck continued to take charge. Not being completely insensitive, he knew that Aaron and Robert were trying to cope as best they could, not knowing what to say or how they should act. If they knew what had really happened here 3 days ago, they wouldn't have had much cause to worry. Disposing of someone else's handiwork was better than creating your own, he always said. But he would keep them in the dark as to the true nature of this man's death.

"All right, your grace, give me your signet ring and a cigar," Beck commanded. Aaron complied, sliding the ring off his finger and handing it to him. Beck pulled a cigar out of Aaron's inner coat pocket and broke it in half. "Mr. Mayfield, hand me the flask. We want this to look as authentic as possible, especially to the earl."

Beck took a deep breath, held it, and walked over to the corpse. The cigar he placed in its mouth. The ring he put on its finger. After pouring the contents of the flask over the cadaver's chest and onto the cigar, he placed it in the dead man's hand. Then he quickly ran out the door for some fresh air. Soon he entered the mill house again.

"Here, your grace," he said to Aaron, "take my flask out of my pocket. I don't want to touch anything after handling the body."

Aaron poured a little of the whiskey over Jacob Beck's fingers. Beck then took the flask and poured the alcoholic contents around the room. The plastered walls, wood floor, and the stray branches that covered the floor would catch fire with no problem at all.

They went outside and Beck took control again, gathering a large pile of leaves to pile around the corpse. He threw a match on the bundle and quickly left the building. Staying a minute to make sure the fire would run its course, he spoke to the men.

"The way I see it, m'lord, Mr. Mayfield here should just lay low. I'll arrange a tip to Scotland Yard and Fleet Street right away. It is imperative that the earl knows of this by morning from another source. Tell Lucius about it later if you think it would help, Mr. Mayfield. It might ease his mind, which is precisely what we want."

Beck faced Aaron now. "Your grace, you must ride to Scotland on the double. Disguise yourself, and do not stay at any inns directly along the way. Keep off the main roads, if possible. Confide with your next of kin what you're doing. If he's to pretend to become the next duke, you must draw him into your confidence. Then go underground. Don't show up at your funeral. Don't show up anyplace you are known. If you need me again, just send a message through Mr. Mayfield here, and I'll meet you."

"Beck," said Aaron earnestly, "how can I pay you for this? What do you want?"

"Arrange for 500 pounds to be delivered here in three days' time." He handed Aaron a card with an address written on it.

By now it was evident the fire would keep burning. Flaming tongues were already licking at the windowsills. Beck swung up on his horse and galloped away without a backward glance. Aaron swung an arm around Robert's shoulder. "Well, old boy, fine mess we've gotten ourselves into!"

"What's next, Aaron?"

"At the funeral, talk with Chastain, my secretary. He's completely trustworthy, and he shall direct you to where I'll be hiding. We'll plan from there exactly how we're going to trap Carlyle. But for now the first step has been taken, and I do believe we shall be successful."

"All right. Until then, my friend. By the way, when is your burial?"

"In a week's time, I should guess."

Aaron pulled his best friend into a bear hug, pounded his back, and let him go with a push. "Thank you, you scoundrel."

"Anytime, Aaron," Robert said dryly. "One thing I've always said about you, things are never dull when you're around!"

CHAPTER
19

Jacobs was irritated. The dream had been wonderful. He had never seen a woman like that in real life, and just when she was about to kiss him, he awoke to the bleary face of one of his under butlers. The underbutler's face looked ghoulish in the darkness of the room, but concerned.

He didn't bother to hide his chagrin as he hoisted himself up on his hands. "What is it, Gregory?"

"There's someone at the servant's entrance, sir. He positively refuses to leave until he speaks to Mr. Chastain. I dinna know what to do wi' him!" The young man shivered in his nightclothes.

"Well, light my candle, for heaven's sake. An' get on a robe. I dinna know what ya must be thinkin'. Are ya sure he willna leave?"

"Aye, sir. Told him to come back tomorrow, bu' he put his frame in the doorway an' I couldna' get him to move. Finally I told him to sit doon at the table an' wait."

Jacobs sighed, taking the candle the young man offered him. "All right. Go back to bed, then. I'll be takin' it from here. ya did what ya could do."

It didn't take the butler long to don his clothing, and soon he stood at the head of the table. Sitting at the other end was the most disheveled, filthy old Highlander he had ever seen. His long black hair hung down in his eyes, and by the light of Jacob's singular candle his features weren't discernible. Dirt lay in daily layers on his face, and one hand sat on his lap in a useless lump while the other played with the knobby top of a wooden cane. His kilt was so dirty the colors were hard to discern, and his plaid was nothing more than a collection of tatters miraculously attached to one another by a thread here and a thread there. Danger clung to him like a shroud.

"What do you want?"

The voice was deep and growly. "I willna' leave this castle until I see a Mr. Grady Chastain."

"Come beggin' about here, eh? Well we've no use for your sort at Inveraray Castle. You'd best be leavin'. Mr. Chastain needna be disturbed at," he looked at the clock near the window, "three-thirty in the mornin'. Off with ya now."

The man stood to his full height and threw off the cane. He held up the curled hand. "This hand may not be much to look at, sir. But the other has the power to blast ya clear doon to the loch. Am I makin' m'self clear enough?"

Jacobs laughed. "You dinna scare me with that talk. One yell an' I'll have the entire staff in the kitchen."

The stranger's eyes glowed in the dimness; they were almost hypnotizing. "Ya do as I ask. Ya do it now. Grady Chastain, I want to see him."

The haughty little man opened his mouth to yell, but the stranger was much too quick. Within the space of a minute, Jacobs was gagged, bound to a chair, and left sitting in the pantry with the door closed.

Grabbing the candle off the table, the wild Highlander ran to Chastain's quarters, opened the door softly, and stepped into the chamber.

"Chastain!" he whispered as loud as he could, shaking the old man's sleeping form. "Wake up!"

One eye opened. And upon viewing the other occupant of the room, Chastain sat up with a sudden cry.

"Shhhh!" the stranger whispered, pulling off the massive wig to reveal the short blond hair beneath it. "Have no fear, old man. It's I."

Chastain took the candle from Aaron and held it closer to his face. "Your grace?"

"Yes. Quickly now, we haven't much time. Get dressed and follow me."

An hour later Chastain opened the pantry door. He immediately began to undo the rope that bound Jacobs to the chair, purposely saving the mouth gag for last.

"Jacobs, are you all right?"

The ropes had done little to bind up his temper. "I tried to stop him, the blasted beggar! Who was he? Are ya all right yourself?"

"Yes, very well, thank you. That was Angus MacBeth. I met him one day while roaming the countryside. He's a hermit. Lives west of here. I told him if there was anything he ever needed, he shouldn't hesitate to contact me. Certainly, I didn't expect him to take me up on it in the middle of the night. I'm so sorry I caused all this trouble for you."

Jacobs began straightening his clothing. "What did he want?"

"He asked me if the castle could feed him for a while."

"What!" This was clearly an effrontery.

"Yes. You heard me correctly."

"He must be an idiot to come around askin' for such. What did ya say?"

"I told him in no uncertain terms that we would be happy to provide food for him."

Jacobs became red-faced. His volume escalated with each word. "Who gave ya leave to be makin' decisions like this, Chastain? When his grace returns, he's sure to have somethin' to say about it. And what of Cathy? One more mouth to feed! She's not goin' to like it one bit! An' neither do I!" He stomped his foot for emphasis.

Chastain tilted back his head and grew cold. "It just so happens that his grace knows all about my dealings with Angus MacBeth. The duke is a charitable man; he'll respect my decision. As for Cathy, she's not a stingy woman with her time or her food. And," Chastain's anger was clearly evident, "it's not your place to like or dislike it. You are the butler, the but-ler, and you should remember your place, sir! Tell Mrs. Rider to come to my office in the morning, and I shall explain all the details."

• • •

The solid-gray walls whispered the final enchantment of the Middle Ages as Aaron came upon a ruined castle a mile away. It had survived centuries—a tribute to an ancestor's folly long ago. The chief who built it 500 years before had been killed by a raiding clan before he ever moved in. Everyone thought it was cursed, and so it sat now as it did centuries before: empty, unused, and (some people claimed) haunted by the men who built it.

The stone keep, hostile in its uselessness, rose three stories high with a wide, carved arched doorway at the bottom. Its four corners were towered and caught the wind like stalks of tall, dry straw. Half of it was overgrown with vines which softened its appearance. It was a lost traveler's dream.

Daybreak began to lighten the landscape, and the sun had not yet risen. The castle seemed to hang suspended out of time in the pearly light.

Aaron walked through the door. He knew this keep well.

The great hall echoed around him, and the smell of moist stone, ageless dust, and time made its way to his nostrils. A hearth showed signs of decay, yet strangely was not blackened by fires of some past occupant. Sturdy beams divided the room halfway up, shrouded by thick cobwebs. And high windows slit in crosses cast their sacred markings on the dusty stone floor.

To the left of the large room a staircase ascended to the upper floors. Without hesitation, Aaron walked up the steps, down a lonely corridor to an inside room. It was dry and would stay that way. He removed his knapsack from his shoulder, folded the tattered plaid for a pillow, and fell into a deep sleep. The journey home had been long and arduous. But it was over.

For the next few days he had only to await his funeral.

• • •

Robert Mayfield's raucous laughter bounced off the stone walls.

"You, my friend, are most definitely not a sight for any eyes, much less sore ones! Blast it, but no one in London would believe me if I told them what a dirty old man you've turned out to be."

Aaron held out his hand for a hearty shake. "Believe me, they wouldn't be at all surprised! How was the funeral?"

"The same as most funerals I've ever attended. General platitudes of the great man everyone knew you weren't. If I hadn't known the Aaron Campbell of London fame, I would have almost believed it. You certainly had the preacher of Inveraray fooled! He actually called you a great man!"

Chastain walked in with Aaron's cousin and heir pretender, Ian. "I don't think Pastor MacGregor was very far off. It's been a while since you've had any close dealings with my employer, Mr. Mayfield."

Ian Campell, the heir impostor, stepped forward. "It's good to see you again, Aaron. That is you underneath that disguise, is it not?" His hazel eyes twinkled merrily.

"Of course. Actually, I'm quite comfortable. No baths. Never a need to change clothes. There's something to be said regarding an unfastidious lifestyle. I'm taking full advantage of the first of earthly blessings: independence."

Robert smirked. "It's the bachelor life taken to its natural conclusion."

Aaron clapped his cousin on the back. "So, Ian, how does it feel to be a duke?"

Ian shook his head with much doubt and drew a hand through the wavy brown hair. "Not good, cousin. It will be a relief when I can get back to Aberdeen and continue my research."

Ian was intensely interested in agricultural development. His enjoyment of research was equaled only by the many invitations he received to lecture at various schools and colleges. Due to their shared interest in farming, he and Colin had been especially close. Ian was only too happy to aid in the capture of his cousin's killer.

"Hopefully, you won't be inconvenienced for long. We intend to set this matter to rights long before autumn— right, Robert and Chastain?"

The two men nodded.

"Come with me back to the castle, m'lord," said Chastain to Ian, "before the rest of the mourners suspect something mysterious is afoot."

Ian agreed. "All right. Aaron, I'll check with you on my walks every so often. And I'll make sure food comes to you regularly. By the way, how do you stand that pompous butler of yours?"

"Don't worry about Jacobs, cousin. If he gives you any trouble, tie him up and put him in the pantry."

Chastain burst out in laughter. "Let us hasten. By the way," he handed Aaron a parcel, "here are the books you requested."

"Thank you," Aaron said as he walked them to the door.

Chastain gently grabbed his arm. "I must say, m'lord, I never expected to be involved in such subterfuge as this in the quietness of Inveraray Castle, but it does seem adventuresome, all the same. Although I am sure it could get dangerous, dealing with men the likes of Lucius Carlyle. You and your friends be careful now." He was an old man again.

The two men left, and Robert stayed behind. Reaching into his coat he pulled out a newspaper and threw it in Aaron's direction. The headline shouted noisily from the page: "CURSE OF THE TWINS: AARON CAMPBELL, THE DUKE OF ARGYLL, FOUND DEAD."

Aaron laughed, thinking what a piece of family memorabilia it would turn out to be. "This certainly isn't an experience most men get to have," he said, looking up at Robert. But he couldn't stop the shiver than ran up his spine at reading his own obituary. It saddened him to see what little they had to say about him. So different from the article about his brother. Breathing in deeply, Aaron resolved that once all this was over, he would step into Colin's shoes. Someday his true obituary was going to read volumes.

"Lucius swallowed the bait?"

Robert held his arms open wide. "Neither worm had a prayer. What's next?"

"I was hoping you had the answer. I suggest we lay low for another month. Give Lucius time. He must be settled back into his old ways. Until then, I'll communicate with you via Chastain."

"All right. Do you think you can stand it here for another month?"

"Stand it? This is heaven, laddie. No one bothers me, and I do nothing but read, write, and walk all day."

"Does anyone ever see you?"

"Occasionally."

Robert's brow wrinkled. "Do they bother you? Engage you in conversation?"

"Would you engage someone that looks like me in conversation?"

"Absolutely not!"

Aaron bowed. "There, you see? I am perfectly safe and profoundly hidden. You'd better get back before someone becomes suspicious."

· · ·

Hidden in the bundle of food lay a package. It was bound considerably and bore a familiar handwriting. With shaking fingers, Aaron removed his dirk from his stocking and cut the twine. Fine parchment lay upon a sheath of papers, and he looked down at his dirty hands. He spit upon them and wiped them with his plaid before lifting the precious letter written in Maria's delicate handwriting.

20 May 1844
Baltimore, Maryland

My Darling Aaron,

My name is Jane MacLeod.

Perhaps you don't recall the significance of it just yet, but you will.

Found underneath this letter, my dearest love, is research my father and your onetime professor William MacLeod wrote with his own hand. It concerns the matter at hand, namely the Brimstone Society. But before you read his words, I shall tell you who I really am.

I was born on the Isle of Skye on 15 February 1818. My mother died a year later, and Father, the grandson of the chief, took me with him to teach at the University of Edinburgh. Ten years later we left for Oxford, where he gained a post at Magdalen. During those years he became close friends with another professor of history, a Dr. Bartholomew St. John. In the spring of 1830 that same professor was murdered outside his home on Banbury Street. My father found him early in the morning, as they were accustomed to strolling together before beginning their tutelage sessions. Dr. St. John's throat was slit, and tucked inside was a playing card. The queen of spades. Some time before the murder, Father noticed the deep scar upon his friend's right palm. He inquired of him as to its nature, but St. John told him it was something he wouldn't want to know about. The murderer was finally found: a hired man. But before he was hung, my father bribed the prison guards to let him speak in confidence with the killer. He garnered enough information to begin an investigation, and what you see here is the end result. But the Society sees all. And you know the rest.

The morning before Father died, he called me into his study, placed this volume in my hands, along with his copy of the Scriptures and the remaining portion of his savings. He told me not to read it until I was 18, and he told me not to cry when I heard of his death. He was burned that night while I was on my way to Italy. I was 14 years old. An old student of his, a count, took me in for a while, but he would not keep me indefinitely. He found me employment with the contessa I told you about. The rest I told you. How could I fault you now for keeping secrets from me, when I was doing the very same to you? And all because of Brimstone.

As you know, you are in the greatest of dangers. The men in the higher offices of Brimstone (Father never found out their names) will stop at nothing to protect their secrets. They are called Misery's Guardians. The Guardians' power is far-reaching. But Brimstone must fall. I pray you will find a way to do this. Please, my darling, do not forget with whom you are dealing. These are dangerous men who rule England by violent dealings and threats. Yet, someone must challenge them, and there is no one better than you to do it. I have faith in your capabilities, my Aaron, because I know you realize the risks involved.

The lions are hungry, and you must be careful to emerge from their den with the breath of life still in you.

I love you, my darling. I am sorry we parted as we did, but when you pleaded with me that day at my hotel and I saw the scar so clearly on your palm and in such a terrible context, I realized then that you were in league with those who were responsible for my father's death. They destroyed the only human being I had on this earth, and I could not look beyond that fact just then. Bring them down. Fell their vile house. And when you do, I shall come home to your arms. For your arms are home, Aaron. My only home. I remain eternally,

Yours,

Maria

She must have heard news of his death since then, he realized with a painful twist of his heart. A battered trunk sat in the corner of Aaron's cell. Procuring a piece of paper, he wrote to Maria, explaining to her that he was indeed still alive.

After penning the letter, he sat back on his blanket-covered straw pallet and read the words of Dr. MacLeod. That afternoon two letters were on their way from Inveraray Castle. Robert Mayfield and George Lindsay showed up a week later.

• • •

According to Robert's latest letter, Lucius was back to his routine, none the wiser. Aaron could tell that Robert was enjoying his newfound role. Lucius owed him much, and to make sure Robert kept his silence, he was wined and dined repeatedly. Yet strangely enough, his messages had taken on a tone foreign to any Aaron had ever heard in their long friendship. He could tell Robert was thriving now that his life had some kind of purpose.

"Aaron!" Robert walked across the great hall and greeted him warmly. "It's good to see you, old man!"

Aaron greeted him in kind. "Is Lindsay waiting outside?"

"Yes. It took several acts of coercion to get him here without explaining fully, but I finally persuaded him, telling him that you were indeed alive. What's going on? What does Lindsay have to do with any of this?"

"It's Brimstone, Robert. You won't believe what I have to tell you. And although I'm going on a hunch, I feel certain that Lindsay will be able to back me up."

"Scotland Yard dropped by the other day," said Robert. "Sooner or later they would rule out your death as an accident. And I suppose they would come to your friends for questioning. Lucius, George, and Alex were visited as well."

"What kind of questions were they asking? Could you tell what they were getting at?"

"Inspector Glendenning said they're investigating to see if there is some connection between your murder and Colin's. The whole thing is really quite absurd. And the murders were so different. You and Colin were so different. Short of an eyewitness, I don't see how they can surmise anything."

"Well," interjected Aaron, "we do have a witness to Colin's murder."

Robert laughed. "I can hardly picture Jacob Beck coming forth with what he knows."

"Perhaps not, but I'm glad he's there if we need him. It must be done slowly. Lucius must suspect nothing."

Robert nodded. "I agree. I've been thinking about this night and day. And maybe the best way to go about it is to let him do it all by himself."

"Easier said than done. Let's call in George. I can't wait to see your face, Robert Mayfield, when you discover the true purpose of the Brotherhood."

• • •

George Lindsay, the Earl of Crawford, sat on the front steps leading up to the doorway of the keep. When Robert told him that Aaron was alive, his relief knew no boundaries. He should have warned Aaron of Robert's intentions. But he didn't, and the deep regret hadn't begun to subside. And he realized he was changed because of it. Next time—if there was one—he would not fail his friend, and because of this George grew twentyfold in moral fortitude and strength.

Upon arriving he had listened to every detail of Aaron's story, and now Dr. MacLeod's manuscript lay on his knee as he continued to turn page after page. His cigar sat in cold neglect beside him.

Finally, after 45 endless minutes, he looked up.

Aaron walked outside, having chosen to let George read the evidence in solitude. He sat down next to his friend. "Haven't we suspected this all along? Is it all true?"

"Most of it, yes."

Robert appeared. "Are you going to divulge these precious secrets to me?"

George held up a hand. "All in good time, Mayfield. How did you know I would be a member of the Guardians, Aaron?"

"You fit the description. Titled. Wealthy. And foolhardy at times."

"Yes, a perfect fit. Especially the foolhardy qualification."

"And what feat did you perform to gain such eminence?"

George looked Aaron in the eye and, without flinching, he responded. "They asked me to commit a murder."

CHAPTER
20

Robert raked a hand through his uproarious hair. "What are you saying?"

George retained his usual calm. "Sit down, old boy. It would be better if you didn't have to know any of this. The deeper secrets of Brimstone do not come cheaply. A price is always paid."

The June air moved softly in the trees above them as George began his careful explanation. There was no doubting the tone of relief in his voice. Someone else knew now. And for that he was almost glad.

"Brimstone is not what you know it to be. Alex was right when he conjectured its grand scale and sinister purposes. Let me tell you what hell is like. . . .

"After graduating from Oxford, I forsook Scotland for London and proceeded with life as we've known it for years. Brimstone was to me then what you believe it to be now. A collection of university men bound by secrecy and a promise. The club was nothing more than a place to gamble, drink, and make deals with other Brothers. After my father died and his fortune became my own, I received a visit from senior members of Brimstone. It was obviously an interview, and as time wore down they began to speak in innuendo, slowly revealing to me the real purposes of the Brimstone Society. A year of such engagements passed by before they decided to enlist me in what is known as Misery's Guardians. Misery's Guardians is for those with money and the probability of power. Naturally, I was interested. Introductions were made, alliances were formed, and I found my fortune steadily growing. So I agreed to the initiation. A slashed palm and a bloody queen got me into the Brotherhood to begin with, so I assumed blood would be involved in this initiation as well."

Aaron's beliefs were being confirmed. "The murder?"

"Yes. Only the blood of an innocent man would do. It was all arranged. There was a shipping magnate whom the Society wanted relieved of his business for some Brother's personal gain. Do you remember hearing of the murder of Mr. Dickenson last Christmas?"

"Good heavens!" Robert exclaimed. "That was you, Lindsay?"

"Yes, it was. But there's more to explain. Once the 'aspirant' agrees to enter the Guardians, he is warned that when he is assigned his task, there is no turning back. Certain death would follow. And as you can see by the large number of successful men at the club, not many fail to do what is required. So I received my assignment."

He got up to stretch his legs, agitation running rampant through him. "I sent a message to Dickenson, asking him to meet me down at one of the docks. I had told him I wanted to arrange some business. When he arrived..."

Robert leaned forward, waiting to hear it all.

"When he arrived, I explained briefly to him that powerful men desired him dead. That he would be murdered shortly. Having laid out a detailed plan beforehand, I gave him 10,000 pounds and told him the rest would follow with his family. Contacts in the States were arranged in advance, and he would be taken care of in Boston. A small boat picked him up to take him to Liverpool. In the boat was a change of clothes, a razor and shears, as well as a pair of clear glass spectacles. I never saw him again."

Aaron was more than a little intrigued and quite impressed with his friend's craftiness. "So you faked the murder."

George nodded. "I had him give me his coat. I drove back to my estates, tied up a pig, put the coat on top of the animal and stabbed it to death. Then I brought the coat to the Brothers that had given me the assignment and told them I had sailed my yacht out to sea and dumped the body."

"That's right. Do you remember, Aaron, first reading in the paper of Dickenson's disappearance?"

Aaron nodded. "Did his family make it to the States?"

"Yes. So you see, I never really committed the murder."

"So what happened next?"

"I received another messenger from Brimstone. This one made demands. Heavy financial demands."

"Blackmail," Aaron said.

"Yes. Blackmail. Although we prefer to call them *dues.*"

"So Dr. MacLeod was on the right trail."

"Absolutely. Anyway, I was assured that if I did not continue to pay handsomely, I would indeed be turned in to the authorities for what I had done."

"There must be a chief benefactor," Aaron stated.

"No one knows."

"What?"

"That's right. The Guardians are powerful in number and alliance. Quite frankly, most of them are happy to be where they are. The high dues pay even greater dividends in their business dealings. To them the crime they committed was worth far more than a guilty conscience. Not that most of them talk about it. However," George's eyebrows raised, "I suspect there are some who feel like I do."

"And how is that?" Robert asked.

"Well, I'd like nothing better than to take this noose from about my neck. The dues are considerably high."

"So it's about the dues?" asked Aaron.

"For me, yes. And the guilt by association."

"Does anyone ever talk about it?" Robert questioned.

"No. At least I've never said anything to anyone. One can never tell who is sympathetic to the Supreme Masters."

Robert's brows met in puzzlement. "The Supreme Masters? Who are they?"

"The extortioners. The Masters' identification is a mystery."

Aaron shifted his position a bit. "How do they collect their money?"

"The man I spoke of before, the initial bearer of ill tidings, collects my dues, and from there no one knows where they end up. I doubt if even he knows. So you see, gentlemen, they seem to have everything airtight. There are no cracks in the organization that I can see."

"I suppose not. Men who have sold their souls to gain the world want that sale to remain highly secretive. And yet..." Aaron wasn't convinced the Society was truly invincible. "There must be a way to get at the top. Maybe we don't have to get to the top at all. Take out the foundation, and the tower will come crumbling down into the wreckage. We must simply find out what the foundation is."

George looked Aaron in the eye and uttered a single word.

"Fear."

"What?"

"Fear," he repeated. "It's true. What is the one thing that holds us together, more than the blood ceremony, more than the oath?"

"Aye," Aaron's brain began to turn at a rapid pace, "it is the fear of being found out."

"So you've never voiced your opinions to anyone?"

"No. Whom can one trust in such an atmosphere, Aaron? These men have sold their eternal souls for temporary riches. To voice such an opinion could cost me my life."

"And yet you said you believe there are some who feel as you do."

"Perhaps. I've talked with men who seem honorable. And some, through increased charity and great philanthropy, seem to be seeking a redemption of some kind. Although I've never talked to them in such a manner, I'd be willing to try."

Robert drew in his breath. "That might prove to be suicide, Lindsay. You could be killed."

George nodded. "Yes, I could. Perhaps I'm in need of a little redemption myself. I'll risk it."

Aaron's admiration for his friend grew great. "Then that is where we start."

George looked puzzled. "Start what?"

"Gentlemen, we are going to raze the Brotherhood of the Brimstone."

• • •

Robert and George had left hours before. As soon as

George set foot in London, the seeds would be sown. And the three now-disgruntled Brothers were indeed looking forward to a most bountiful harvest. Would they reap life or death? They didn't know. They were just doing what should have been done long ago. Aaron remembered the brief conversation he'd had with Chastain only an hour before. The old man listened calmly. And Aaron wondered how he could be so stoic when a man's life was on the line.

"Sir," Chastain smiled slightly, "do you believe that the Savior is in control of your life?"

"Aye, old man."

"Then He is in control of George's life as well. If He has assigned to you the task of exposing this evil organization, He will provide the means to do so. George will only talk to those whom God sees fit."

And as the evening began to deepen, Aaron took comfort in that, wishing he could fall to his knees in supplication and thanksgiving. But he had one more appointment to keep that day. He donned the heavy wig.

The hour was late as he began to trudge through darkened woods. He was comforted by the familiar planes of the earth beneath his feet. In contrast, he would soon be traveling upon new ground and the way seemed ominous, somehow lit by the flames of hell itself.

It took Aaron a while to achieve his final destination. But when he finally made it to the village, every home had snuffed out its light for the evening. It was dark, quiet, yet so very much alive. He breathed in deeply, imagining the goings-on of the day that had just expired. Small children following their mothers through the yard to the washtubs, thrusting their chubby hands and arms into the sun-warmed water with a childish giggle. The sounds of pans and pottery clinking together as they were cleaned. Horses and wagons passing each other along the road, the drivers greeting one another above the din of everyday village life.

But now silence reigned. The little noisemakers, with angelic, freshly scrubbed faces, were sleeping on their wee cots. And those who had worked hard and faithfully for yet another day rested gratefully atop their straw-tick mattresses. Yet the very fact that they still lived and breathed and would rise to greet the sun tomorrow fed Aaron's soul. Life at the keep was lonely. Reaching into his knapsack, he pulled out his pocket watch. Its hands told that him that it was 11:00. He was right on time. The back pew, nailed in place against the rear wall of the sanctuary, took his weight with no complaint. As he waited for his appointment, Aaron reached around the side of the bench to feel the carvings as he had done countless Sundays as a child. His fingers traced the lines of a Gothic rosette circle. The inside filigree he caught with his fingernail, the design much like a crusader's cross. Up, over, back, up. Down, over, back, down. Up, over, back, up . . . so it continued until he had completed the design and his finger returned to its starting place.

A cloaked figure soundlessly slid beside him in the carved wooden pew.

"Angus MacBeth?" he whispered.

"Aye, Beck, it is I. Did you have any trouble finding me?"

"No. I took the train to Glasgow and hired a horse. Since there is only one church in Inveraray, that made it easy."

Jacob Beck, clad impeccably as usual, settled himself more comfortably. His voice came out in a genial fashion, but any human warmth therein was purely an act. "So how is everything coming along? Out there in the general public, it seems as if you have indeed been murdered. What of here?"

"The only person who is aware of the true situation is my secretary. And, of course, my cousin Ian who is pretending to inherit my title."

"Good," nodded Beck. "So what now?"

"Robert and George Lindsay—the Earl of Crawford, another close friend of mine, completely trustworthy—were here this morning. We came up with a plan."

"Tell me."

"There is more to this whole affair than delivering Lucius Carlyle to the gibbet. But concerning the Earl of Beresford, I have a few definite plans, and they are as much for your benefit as for mine. You shall be paid in the usual handsome manner."

He went into the tale of Brimstone. Even Jacob Beck had not quite heard the likes, not that he would admit it. He simply made a mental note in the "future ideas" category of his brain.

Beck's eyes glittered. "Sounds intriguing. What would you have me do?"

"Tell me, Beck, can you frighten a man?"

"That's the only thing I know how to do, your grace. No man is at peace when he is about to die. Or thinks he is."

• • •

London
A week later—mid-June

It had been an especially profitable month for Lucius.

The coal mines were doing splendidly, he had purchased a major amount of shares in a South African diamond mine, and the Lady Lenora Dartmoor had finally agreed that it was in her best interest to receive his calls. He had been working on that deal for months, and it was one in which even Brimstone had not been able to aid him.

He loved London before the heat of summer settled in, but he was sure the country house, Grey Walls, was even more beautiful. He would go there soon. In a matter of months it would be restored to its former grandeur. Father would have been proud of his son's rapid succession of achievements. A deeper, more personal pride was blooming more robustly than the damask roses in the garden he was passing during his walk home.

A man the size of a figurehead, carved of ebony and shining with a strength that could snap a man's neck with ease, sidled up behind the Earl of Beresford. Daylight was making its final bow. The normally busy street was hushed and quiet. Most of London's population had already left their places of business and were dining with their families as the gentle evening breeze swept through their dining rooms.

"Lucius Carlyle," he whispered in a husky, heavily accented voice.

Lucius wheeled around quickly, only to look directly into the face of his follower. He almost collided with the massive square chest. Disconcerted, he gasped.

"What do you want? Who are you?"

"I'm Thaddeus, brother of the night."

He held up his right palm for Lucius to see.

In the fading light, Lucius looked for the sign, but the roughened pink skin bore nothing but the creases of nature. Just as he expected.

"I bear a message." He lowered his hand. "'The same shall drink of the wine of the wrath of God, which is poured out without mixture into the cup of his indignation; and he shall be tormented with fire and brimstone in the presence of the holy angels, and in the presence of the lamb.'"

Before Lucius could respond, Thaddeus was gone, and the Earl of Beresford, with a slow dread dissipating from the small of his back through his limbs to the very ends of his fingers and toes, had not the faintest idea in which direction the man had fled.

· · ·

George Lindsay fell exhausted into his bed.

Three down, two to go, he calculated. So far, events had gone better than he dared to have hoped. Even so, he never went anywhere anymore without looking over his shoulder.

· · ·

Robert's palms were sweaty as he rode in a hackney cab toward Whitehall and the headquarters of the Metropolitan Police—fondly known as Scotland Yard. The official policing organization was relatively new in a city as old as London. Robert Peel, who twice had been prime minister, founded it in 1829 when he was the home secretary. The headquarters were housed in a building near the ruins of Henry VIII's Whitehall Palace, the northern end of which was reserved for the kings of Scotland on their visits to London. The short street between the palace and the river was named Great Scotland Yard.

Somewhat agitated, Robert waited in the lobby for the man he had come to see. Sooner than he had expected, a gentleman of slim proportions with salty blue eyes and a drastically thinning hairline approached.

"Mr. Mayfield?"

"Yes. I am Robert Mayfield."

They shook hands briefly.

"I am Inspector Glendenning. I am in charge of the case regarding the alleged murder of Aaron Campbell, the Duke of Argyll."

"Yes, I know. One of your men came around to question me quite a while ago."

He swept a hand toward a hallway behind him. "Come this way to my office. We'll be somewhat more comfortable. Not much more, mind you. We're already outgrowing these facilities, it seems. My quarters are small, but at least there is a chair for you there."

Robert followed him down the dim corridor into a room near the end. Glendenning had been right. The room was small and inelegantly furnished. One straight-back wooden chair sat in front of the cluttered desk.

"Can I offer you something to drink?"

"No, thank you."

Glendenning sat behind his desk, put on a pair of spectacles, and lifted up a sheet of paper. His eyes scanned the page for almost a minute before he spoke. "Now, what is it you came for?"

Robert leaned forward in his chair. "Inspector, what I'm about to tell you will seem unbelievable. I will probably be dead in a matter of days along with my colleagues. Answer me this one question before I begin: How far will you go to catch a murderer?"

"I'd crawl through fire and brimstone to see him brought to justice."

• • •

Inveraray
July 1844

Chastain set down the parcel of food.

Aaron had been sitting on the front steps and smoking a cigar. "Thank you, Chastain. I was just thinking how funny this all is. In a perverse way, of course."

"Perverse–you keep using that word to describe this." Chastain laughed and walked inside the keep with the duke. "Your grace, if Rosie is looking down, she's getting a better laugh than she ever had here on earth. And let me tell you, she could laugh with the best of them!"

"What do you think of all this?" asked Aaron as he gratefully took the day's victuals and sat down on the raised hearth of the great hall.

"It's intriguing. And definitely more exciting than the only adventure a simple man like me has ever had."

"What was that?"

"It was the time Rosie got stuck in the window of an old abbey ruin near the house we lived in when we were first married. She enjoyed her sweets a little too much, I must say," he related, wandering from the topic, "but it never bothered me. I always said, 'Rosie, there's just more of you to love.'" Chastain sighed.

Aaron nodded, understanding. "Maria might be the same way. The way she loves French cooking so much. But that's all right. She'll have many more imperfections to put up with concerning me than I'll ever have where she is concerned."

"I know it, m'lord. I know it. But even some of those imperfections become lovable, and if it came down to it, you wouldn't change a thing about her! You and Maria have a special love, your grace. Not everyone is blessed with it. Rosie and I had it. But there are many households where it just can't be found. If I know anything about true love, and believe me I feel as if I could write a book on it, I'd say you will be able to keep that woman happy for the rest of her life."

There was enough of the old arrogance still alive in Aaron to believe that Chastain was right.

Aaron pulled out one of Cathy's cinnamon buns. "I do believe that the servants are better fed than the master at Inveraray Castle. This simple fare a castle cook would deign to send to a madman has been quite refreshing."

"Cathy does things right, m'lord."

"I'm going to miss her cooking."

Chastain perked up. "What are you talking about, your grace?"

"I'm leaving for a while, Chastain. London calls."

"Does this have to do with the dispatch you received from the Earl of Crawford yesterday?"

"It does indeed."

"When do you leave?"

"Tomorrow morning. Unfortunately, that means you have double your normal amount of work to do. I'm going to need some henna, working men's clothing, and enough money to get me on a stagecoach to Glasgow, and then on a train bound for London."

"Where will you stay once you arrive? I should know that, sir."

"I'll be staying at an inn in the East End."

Chastain looked horrified. "The East End?"

"Believe it or not, I have an acquaintance there. The establishment is named the Apple and Serpent. If you need to find me—and it should only be in the direst of circumstances, I might add, old man—I will be with a man named Jacob Beck. Naturally, I'll be staying there under an assumed name."

"And what will that be, m'lord?" He couldn't wait to hear this one.

"Enoch."

"Enoch, your grace?"

"Aye, a man who didn't see death. I'm hoping for the same ... on this trip, anyway."

Chastain smiled appreciatively, but inside he became worried all over again. This employer of his made a peaceable old age totally out of the question.

"Can you gather the necessities before supper?" Aaron knew he could.

"Of course."

"Go then, old man. And do not worry. I see that fatherly look you're trying to hide from me. I will be more than careful."

CHAPTER
21

A large yellow moon was shining that night, wandering at its highest noon. It was a living thing, a dancing specter in the sky. George Lindsay had always had an affair with the moon, loving its gentle light, especially when it favored the land with a golden, rounded hue. The place he sought in solitude had an ancient permanence, though built just six years before. Purified in the sun by day, massaged by the moon at night, the cemetery was a living thing, though all its regular inhabitants would never again lift their faces to either of the reigning heavenly bodies. Or so he thought, for George wasn't a religious man.

He was an exhausted one.

The shallow semicircle drive that skimmed the Gothic arched gateway and the adjoining caretaker's home admitted him into the South Metropolitan Cemetery at Norwood. George walked beside the wrought-iron fence that surrounded the park, then passed underneath the arch. By day the cemetery, laid out as an English landscaped park, was pastoral. And even now he could smell the flowers and fresh-cut grass that perfumed the July darkness.

He paused by an Egyptian-style mausoleum and waited.

A voice whispered from just inside the recessed doorway. "Lindsay?"

"Aaron? Is it you?"

Even though George knew it was coming, it still gave him the shivers when Aaron materialized beside him.

"It's me," Aaron answered. "Are you ready to walk to the chapel?"

"Let's take the long route to the left. We'll come up from behind."

They began their trek through a copse of evergreen trees. In a clearing to their left, a stone cross was silhouetted, and obelisks pointed accusingly at the heavens.

"How many are coming?"

"Five. Each man present is loyally attached to another."

"Do they know of my predicament?"

"No."

"Will Robert be there?"

"No. You will be the only non-Guardian present. And you will only be there as proof, Aaron."

"So it remains quite exclusive?"

"It has to, for now."

By this time they had circled the hill and began to make their ascent. Before them stood a Gothic chapel, quite large, with two bell towers flanking the front of the main building. Long wings were attached perpendicularly from either side, leading to two mausoleums at the ends.

"Are they here yet?"

"No." He pushed open the green, heavy wooden door at the back of the building. "The remainder will come in separately in the space of the next hour."

Several sconces were lit near the door, the hallway fading down to a tunnellike blackness. George really looked at Aaron for the first time.

"Blast, man, but you look as though you've had a bad quarter of an hour. At least you're barely recognizable."

"Perhaps. But death is the greatest disguiser, Lindsay."

Indeed, it was true. In the past three months Aaron's hair had grown overlong and thick. It was temporarily dyed to match the red beard which had grown naturally from his face since he started living at the keep. Chastain had delivered well—he was clad in the clothes of a tinsmith. No sane man would believe the person they had just seen was the Duke of Argyll.

• • •

Four candles burned in iron holders on the communion table at the front of the chapel. A forgotten bouquet of flowers had been thrown on the front pew, its wrinkled black ribbon cascading angularly onto the floor. The restless Guardians sat at the table. Tension built as each eyed the other, looking for signs of betrayal, seeking to clear his own brow to put his companions at ease, rendering his intentions pure. Indeed, when all the looks had passed and a bit of trust had been parceled from each man to the other, a true sense of brotherhood permeated the atmosphere. Their lives were now in someone else's hands. They felt almost like gladiators entering the theater of death, but instead of fighting one another, they had agreed beforehand to kill the big man in the royal toga. "To those who are about to die, we salute you." Wouldn't the rest of the Society be surprised when the dust cleared if these men were left standing with bloody carnage about them?

George rose from his chair.

"Gentlemen, it's fitting we have met in a cemetery since we have all been involved in death for far too long."

"Here, here," someone said as he cleared his throat.

"Why have we waited so long?" muttered another.

"Brimstone has been in existence well over two centuries. But the bondage of fear is broken tonight. What more can Brimstone do than take our lives? And if they kill us, then so be it! No more shall we be chained by blackmail and our own cowardice."

Heads nodded. Brilliant minds moved in one accord. And George continued.

"I shall give only a brief history of what has brought me to the point of action. As you are all aware, this spring one of our Brothers was found burned to death in an old mill house out in the country. The verdict was murder."

Lindsay began to pace before the gathered few. "That murder came about because of this." He reached into his pocket. His own queen of spades he held high, the smear of blood still highly visible in the dimness.

Then George began to relate the tale of Colin Campbell's death, Aaron's involvement, Lucius' refusal to do as he promised at Stonehenge, and the revelation at the Apple and Serpent.

"When Aaron Campbell realized that Lucius had killed his brother with his own hand, it was clear that this confusing masquerade had gone far enough. Another Brother, Robert Mayfield, agreed to murder Campbell for Lucius' sake, fearing the secrets of the Brotherhood would be unveiled. He abducted Campbell and was about to pull the trigger. But years of friendship prevailed—and the fact that Aaron fought like a bear, allowing him to relate what had happened."

He went on to explain the prevaricated death, funeral, and Maria's manuscript.

"Dr. MacLeod was murdered, but he garnered a vast amount of secret information before he died. When Campbell read of this dark side of Brimstone we have come to despise firsthand, he knew there was more to be done than the simple avenging of his brother's murder. He feels, and we can all concur, that the Society of the Brimstone must be destroyed!"

"Yes! Yes!" They all agreed.

"So, we must find out who the Supreme Masters are. But before we do that, there's someone I'd like to introduce to you, so that you are witnesses that what I have spoken is truth."

Aaron Campbell, in his workingman's garb, walked up the aisle to stand beside George.

"Gentlemen, here is our fellow Brother, and the man who is responsible for this sudden change within us all, the Duke of Argyll."

Aaron threw off his hood.

He took out a cigar and chomped it between his teeth. "Is there a match to be found in this desolate place?"

The small congregation of Brothers erupted in laughter. A few rose to shake his hand. And one set out to light his cigar.

George continued. "So, you see it is true."

Aaron took a seat at the table next to a man to whom he had once lost 200 sovereigns.

"No hard feelings?" the man whispered.

Aaron chuckled with a negative nod of his head.

George got back down to business. "The Brothers you see seated here have taken it upon themselves to do all they can to aid us. As I was saying, before we can do anything else, we must find out who the Supreme Masters are. This is of the utmost importance, for without their demise, more recruits will be made and this hellish cycle may continue for yet another 200 years. Scotland Yard knows everything, men, and could easily start convicting individuals, but they're complying with us. They see the importance of stopping these secret crimes altogether."

"How is it proposed we do this?" a Mr. Boone asked.

"First, I wish you to write down on your calling card to whom you pay your dues. We will need several volunteers."

"What for?" someone asked.

"To allow a trail to be placed on you. When you meet to make your payment, the trail will follow the man to whom you have given the money. Where he takes it and to whom he gives it should aid us further in identifying the Supreme Masters."

Each man reached into his pocket for a calling card and wrote down the name of his recruiter. Boone passed his hat around to collect the scraps.

Horace Batterberry, a well-educated, successful wine merchant, stood to his feet after reading the cards. "There are three names found among all the cards: Inigo Reese, Jonathan Graystone, Augustus Hyde. Do we have any volunteers?"

Mr. Boone, dressed especially fine, stood to his feet. "I'll do it. I'd give anything to see Inigo's face when it all comes to light."

"Same here!" said another man. "Count on me for Augustus Hyde."

Within the space of a minute, the three needed volunteers were found.

George stood again. "Gentlemen, thank you for coming. We will be in touch further. Of course, the meeting place will be changed. Will those men who volunteered their services please stay after the others have left? We shall need to find out when and where you will be making your payment. That is all. Good night, Brothers."

Mr. Boone rose to go and turned to Aaron. "You must leave London, my lord. As much danger as we have placed ourselves in, yours is the greatest."

"Thank you, Boone. I'll hasten back to Scotland, but only because I know that if I am discovered, you'll all be in peril. I'm having a deuce of a time not being in the thick of things."

"You can count on us, Campbell," Horace Batterberry said earnestly. "After all, we're doing what is right."

Mr. Boone and George nodded solemnly. They all were in it together.

Whatever the outcome.

. . .

"A message, sir."

The footman shifted uncomfortably in his starched livery as he presented the envelope on a silver salver to Lucius. The handwriting caused his heart to hammer in his chest. This was the second note he had received that week. The first merely stated in the same jagged writing, *"I know a little tale 'bout a night at Covent Garden."*

He tore open the note, his curiosity as well as his fear overcoming his innate refinement.

"Twenty thousand pounds."

Lucius ran to the front door and pulled it open. "Where is he? Who was he?" He turned to the footman. "What did the messenger look like?"

"Why, sir, that's him there." The servant pointed to the thick, black wrought-iron lamppost across the street. Thaddeus waited, arms across his chest. He was a fearless ebony giant, and Lucius knew he must be handled with care. There had to have been, at least once, one lucky serpent who bested the mongoose. He pulled his dignity back on, straightened his shoulders, and walked across the street.

"What do you know?" he said quietly to Thaddeus.

"Your lordship, Scotland Yard would not be pleased to find out about your shoddy dealings with the Campbells."

Lucius' composure slipped. "You know?"

Thaddeus' smile was wide. "Everything. For now. But it's amazing how quickly I forget when I've got a little money to spend. I'll be back here at 5 A.M. tomorrow. The money should be in a duffel bag."

• • •

Inveraray

Through the blanket of the dark, Aaron ventured back to the keep. It was with a sense of regret that he quitted London the day after the meeting and left George to continue to implement the rest of the plan. Now that the waters of need had fully surrounded the Earl of Crawford, Aaron knew there was no better man for the job. Lindsay wanted Brimstone destroyed. Not for Aaron or Robert or because of Lucius. He wanted it for himself.

• • •

29 June 1844
New York, New York

Darling:

If I wasn't so relieved, I should hate you! If I wasn't so proud of what you are doing, I should never forgive the torment you have put me through. But I am relieved and I am proud. And so I wait to hear more. Yet I know that further communication is perilous, and I trust you will use sound judgment. Please be careful.

Further, I am relieved that the manuscript made its way safely into your hands. That Papa did not die in vain has been my heart's longing. I shall return to London at the end of July. From there I shall travel to Castle Lachlan once again. For, as you now know, I am only a simple Scottish lass, and the Highlands are truly my home. There I shall await your contact, for I know better than to seek you out. Know that I love you in complete and utter desperation. And if the flowers are not blooming by the time that this is put to rest, I do not care. I'd marry you in a snowstorm if it meant being yours sooner. Until then I am most thoroughly and irrevocably,

Yours

Aaron smiled upon reading the note. In two weeks Maria was coming home to him.

CHAPTER

22

The thick smell of oiled machinery and burning coal permeated the air. It was warm for June. And the great black behemoths steaming on the tracks nearby only accentuated the heat.

"Were you followed?" Inigo Reese seeped from the deep shadows of a darkened corner at Paddington Station.

"I'm not stupid."

"You say that every time."

Barclay Boone, the major shareholder of the London Cemetery Company, slipped a hand into his coat. He kept an iron control on his thickset fingers, willing them not to shake as he drew out the envelope.

"It's all here."

Inigo, a pasty-skinned gentleman with a shock of red hair, laughed spitefully as he took the envelope, opened it with a papery crackle, and did a rough count. "Why wouldn't it be? Now go, Mr. Boone. Who knows what sort of individual is loitering around this station at this time of night?"

"Gladly I'll go."

Boone looked at him hard, just like always. Inigo laughed with disdain at his wolfish expression and threw up his chin. "Next month you'll be back. Don't forget that,

Mr. Boone. Next month. You know, it's a shame you aren't as enthusiastic as the others."

Boone said nothing but walked away, aware of each hair under his hat, each knuckle on his hand, each bend of his knee trying desperately to appear normal. Inigo stayed a minute longer. And when he left, Thaddeus went to work in the shadows surrounding him.

• • •

Robert joined George at his townhouse on Hanover Square. George quickly ushered him into his study and closed the door with a brisk snap.

Robert's eyes danced. "Did you find out anything?"

George smiled wide. "We've further narrowed the scope."

"What happened?"

Lindsay reached forward and took a pipe out of the box on his desk. "Beck's man followed each of the three men in question. They all reported to one person."

"Who?"

"No one of seeming consequence, really. A man named Jasper Greeley. He works down at the port during the day." He struck a match and set it to the fragrant tobacco.

"Did they see where he took the money?"

"No. As far as they knew, he never took it out of his house. They trailed him the next day. From what we can surmise, someone must have come to his house and picked up the bag while he was working."

Robert poured himself a drink. "Do any others still need to make payment?"

"Of course."

"Then there will be someone watching his house this week?"

"Naturally."

"Did you question Jasper?"

"No. He's obviously a nobody out to make a little extra money. He's sure to know nothing. And we don't want him warning anyone."

"Right."

Lindsay reached over to his desk yet again and pulled out a deck of cards. "Now, old man, what do you say we try and forget about all of this for a bit?"

Robert chuckled and drank deeply from his whiskey. "You read my mind, Lindsay. Blast it, but you read my mind."

. . .

The air smelled of old hay and the river Thames. Thaddeus, gleaming with the ever-present sweat of a warm summer, walked through Beck's room and out onto the rickety porch that surrounded the back courtyard of the old inn. The assassin reclined in a straight-back chair, its two front legs suspended in the air, his feet resting on the wooden balustrade.

"I found him." Thaddeus dragged a chair outside, its legs scraping on the uneven wood.

"Who?"

He eased his large frame weightlessly onto the chair. "The man who collects the money. His name is Alister Granger, works down at Barringer's bank. Took the bag inside, and that was the last I saw of him. I waited about until the end of the day, and sure enough, out he comes, and home he goes to Soho."

"Good."

"When do we set sail?"

"As soon as this is put to rest."

"Is the Carlyle money still safe?"

"Yes, my friend. Don't worry about that. When Lucius Carlyle is taken into custody, this godforsaken city will be only a memory."

"And the Duke of Argyll will not find out about our extortion?"

"No," Beck chuckled darkly, "he trusts me. And I'm not a stupid man, Thaddeus. I may need his favor one day. Though I doubt it. We'll be on our way to South America by the end of the month."

Thaddeus sniffed with a face full of distaste. "Too bad this bit of fortune couldn't have come our way before summer."

Beck pulled long on his pipe. "I know. The smell gets worse every year, doesn't it?"

• • •

Alister Granger wasn't much to look at. His chin was weak. His clothes were a tad too tight, and he had the annoying habit of breathing in through closed lips after every sentence he spoke. When the Earl of Crawford called him to his coach, Alister's brow creased in anxiety.

"Mr. Alister Granger?" George Lindsay called from the recesses of an unadorned vehicle. Its blue-velvet curtains were closed against an incandescent, sanguine sunset.

Alister visored the sun with his hand, and squinted through his hazel eyes into the recesses of the coach. "Yes?"

"I wish to converse with you."

Alister leaned closer. "Pardon me, but who is inquiring of me?" He put one foot on the attached step and, before he could blink, he was pulled in by a pair of strong black arms.

• • •

The basement of George Lindsay's townhouse was a vast labyrinth of closets and rooms. Alister stared in fear as the Earl of Crawford paced before him, set to begin the interrogation. Thaddeus stood near the door, directly in front of the frightened man—a visible threat, a man who could deliver a world of pain to anyone.

One candle was all the light Lindsay afforded. And it was placed near Alister's face, not his own. He prowled back and forth like a cat ready to strike. But he knew before he even started that Alister was not at the top of this. Not nearly. The man before him in the serviceable brown wool suit and black necktie wasn't smart enough for workings of such a magnitude. Not that he was stupid, mind you.

Lindsay began the interrogation. "By the looks of you, I can safely say you are a reasonable man."

"Yes, m'lord. I try to be, sir." His fingers picked at the sharp crease of his pants.

"Not married?"

"No."

"No one will have you, eh?" Lindsay joked.

Alister's attempt at a chuckle came out like a high-pitched cough.

"Good. I'm glad you're not married. Tell me this, Alister Granger, how much do you make a year?"

"Ninety pounds, your grace."

"Do you especially like working for Barringer's?"

"It's a job, sir."

"Good." George pounced. This wasn't the time for pleasantries. Best to catch the man off guard. "Now tell me, where do you take the money you pick up every Thursday during your lunch hour?"

"Sir?"

"You heard me. Where do you deposit the money?"

"I don't know what you're talking about, sir."

Thaddeus stirred, but Lindsay only laughed and reached into his pocket. He pulled out 100 one-pound notes and threw them on the table beside Alister. "How much is here?"

The man counted it in a glance. "One hundred pounds, m'lord."

"Where do you take the money?"

Granger deliberated silently for several seconds. "Back to the bank, sir."

"I know that. Forgive me—I was not as specific in my questioning as I should have been. To whom do you give this money?"

"No one, sir."

Lindsay let out a frustrated sigh, bordering on anger. Thaddeus clenched his fists and took a step forward.

"No," Alister interrupted. "I really mean it, m'lord. I leave the money in my bottom desk drawer. When I return to work the next day, it is gone."

"Haven't you ever questioned where it goes and who it is for?"

"In my mind, yes, sir. But a man's got to make a living, do as he's told. There are more clerks in London than there are jobs, your grace."

"Thank you, Alister. Now there's another bit of business I wish to discuss with you. In return for your silence until next Thursday night, we are prepared to offer you 500 pounds and a one-way ticket to America. Do you agree to the terms?"

Alister's eyes bulged. He didn't have to think but for a moment. "Yes, m'lord. Most certainly."

"Fine then. After leaving from work next Thursday, the same carriage I was in today will be waiting for you. Do not pack anything. The money will be under the seat as well as the arrangements for your passage. And don't try to make this a bidding game by finding out who you are presently servicing. Because I assure you, Mr. Granger, once these people realize you know something is indeed afoot, you will die."

Granger nodded. He wasn't a stupid man. "Am I free to go, your grace?"

Lindsay waved his hand. "As you wish."

Alister rose from his chair and began to pick his way back toward the stairs, avoiding Thaddeus at all costs.

"Granger!"

He turned around. "Yes, m'lord?"

"Make sure you leave your office door unlocked!"

• • •

Five days later

In the business of crime it does a villain well to have keen night vision. Jacob Beck was proud of this. Yet even as he sat in the corner of Alister Granger's office, he was thankful for the silver swatch of moonlight which draped across the clerk's desk. He had found it extremely funny that the door was left unlocked. An unnecessary courtesy, to be sure. There was hardly a lock in London that would keep Beck out.

Beck had done his homework that afternoon as he walked unnoticed through the great lobby of the bank. Portraits of bank officials and even Sir Silas Barringer himself, the president and now head of the 250-year-old banking dynasty, hung high on the wall. The man had way too much hair, Beck had decided. It was white and grew out of his head at impossible angles, making him look like an aging urban lion. The expression he wore contested to the man he was—a man given everything too soon. A hunger was evident in the dark eyes—not a needful hunger, but a deserving hunger.

Jacob Beck had been in the room since 5:30. A small pendulum clock on the wall proclaimed mutely that it was already past 9:00. He hadn't heard a sound in the building for over two hours. And curse them all, if he wasn't getting thirsty. The flask he found easily in his pocket. Just one sip. And that was all he took. Beck had nothing if not self-control. *And night vision*, he reminded himself with a feral smile.

The door opened.

Beck flattened himself against the wall, well concealed in shadow. The moonlight skimmed the surface of the desk, and all he could see at first were the man's hands. Massive hands with rounded almond nails. Cuffs of an evening shirt, ruby cuff links. And the sleeves of a black evening coat.

He was bent over, opening the bottom drawer. It slid with a grind on its tracks and came to a stop with a thunk as it was pulled out to its end. The fabric of the bag snagged softly against the unfinished wood inside the drawer. And as the man stood up straight, his face passed through the light, and Beck grinned wickedly. He had recognized the man beyond a shadow of a doubt.

• • •

Two days later

Inspector Glendenning opened the front door to his modest, yet charming home just outside London. Lining the curved front path were several varieties of lilies and creeping phlox. The house was made of stone. A white front door was rounded at the top with a little window that sported diamond panes of glass. Many of the upper windows were framed by gables and green window boxes. More flowers bloomed in the sturdy containers. Two bow windows flanked either side of the front door, and presently on this Saturday afternoon, the side panels were flung open and white, lace-trimmed curtains, freshly laundered and ironed, fluttered into the small sitting room. Jonah Glendenning was a different man when at home with his wife and two children. He loved to garden, to play with his girls, and as the day waned, to smoke a pipe in the back garden.

Robert and George greeted him.

"Come in! Come in!" Glendenning said with a relaxed smile. "Eva!" he called to his wife, "I've got company. Will you be a love and bring us some tea round to the back garden?"

"I'll be there in a jiffy, Jonah!" she called from somewhere upstairs.

"Right this way." He led them past a center staircase, down the hall to a glass door at the back of the house. They stepped into a section of shade where the sun had not yet ventured above the stone wall which surrounded the small yard. "This, gentlemen, is my garden." He was proud. "Do either of you garden?"

"No," said George.

"Nor I," said Robert.

"Good. People who don't garden enjoy others' gardens more freely. No comparisons going on, no thinking, 'Nice plot of ground, but what I could have done with it!' "

The men laughed politely as Jonah Glendenning seated them at a grouping of wicker lawn furniture spread with yellow cushions. But he could see they were strung more tightly than a fine violin. "Eva should be right down with the tea. Thank you for meeting me out here. I take one Saturday off a month, but I certainly don't mind using it for official purposes every now and again."

George sat forward in his chair and spoke. "Inspector, the plan can now go forward. We've acquired the information we've been seeking."

"Who?"

A lady's heels clicked down the stone path. It was Eva with the tea tray. Jonah helped her set it on the small round table in their midst. And he could never remember his beautiful, raven-haired wife taking so long to pour. Finally, she was done, and the back door closed behind her.

"Barringer."

Glendenning sat back in his chair, hand over his eyes. He exhaled heavily. "Are you sure?"

"Our man saw him take the money himself. It wasn't some messenger boy or clerk; it was Sir Silas Barringer himself, nine o'clock at night, the only one left in the building."

The tea began to go cold.

"Anyone else?"

"Not that we know of. And we've had him watched for two days. It's a one-man, one-family operation."

"Do you have a plan we can work with?"

"Yes, but first we must get some promises from you, Inspector."

Glendenning nodded. He had expected as much.

• • •

Aaron was on his way back to London. Disguised this time as a merchant, he found his clothes to be sturdy and practical, but slightly too big and not cut from the fine cloth of a wealthy man. His hair was still red, though now cropped close to his head, and his beard was trimmed and neat. A pair of wire-rimmed spectacles sat on his nose and bothered him where the arms, a tad too short, came to rest behind his ears. He had one stop to make before London, however.

• • •

A decided spring accompanied Lucius Carlyle's gait as he negotiated the front steps of the club. He looked upon the pillared facade with a sense of ownership, and it was all because of a message he had received that morning:

> *You are summoned to appear before the Supreme Masters on Wednesday, 2 August, at midnight. Stonehenge. Ceremonial garments required.*

To appear before the Supreme Masters . . . it was a summons, most definitely. And as someone whose business acumen and mental superiority had further fortified the

Brotherhood, he knew he was to be rewarded. His father had been so distinguished years before.

"Lucius!"

It was Lindsay, hailing him with an upraised hand. "How about a little game of cards, old man?"

The Earl of Beresford smiled in George's direction, walked over, and sat down at the table. "Haven't seen you around here for a while, George."

"Lord, no." Lindsay waved his hand. "My estates in Scotland are too beautiful this time of year to be wasted. I'm trying to stay out of London as much as possible until autumn. You going to be doing much with the lords this session?"

"I hope to score a few political victories. What of you?"

"Probably not. I've been quite comfortable as a back-bencher. Yet then again, one never knows what can happen between now and November. By the way," he leaned forward and spoke softly, a confidentiality hushing his tones, "did you receive a mysterious message from the Society?"

"You mean regarding the meeting at Stonehenge?"

"Ah," George sat back in apparent relief, "so you received one as well. What is it all about, old boy?"

"I haven't a clue. I didn't realize other people had gotten one." He felt slightly disappointed. But surely, he bolstered himself up again, the Supreme Masters would want others there to witness the spectacle.

"I don't know who else has. But I should look forward to it, if I were you. You seem to be the Brimstone darling right now, Lucius. Why, everything you're touching has become gold, and gold is most definitely something the Society understands. It's probably just another ridiculous ceremony."

"Will you be leaving from London to go to Salisbury?"

"Yes. I am going to stay on until Wednesday. Say, why don't we ride out together?"

"Your offer is gracious, and I accept it with pleasure."

• • •

The giant ship sailed into port. Maria, inwardly scolding herself for her foolishness, scanned the waiting throng upon the wharf. No one was there to greet her. Disappointed, yet understanding that it had to be this way, she hailed a cabbie, who loaded the luggage and took her and Martha off to meet the train headed for Glasgow.

Martha settled comfortably next to Maria in the private compartment and brought out a basket of lunch she had just purchased at a restaurant near the station. The scenery rolled before her, the intense population of the city suddenly thinning out to nothingness like a pat of butter left to melt on warm bread.

Maria picked up the program that had been handed out in New York. Her face stared back at her, smiling beguilingly, ebony ringlets cascading over her shoulders. It wasn't enough anymore, Maria suddenly realized. She had become all she had dreamed she would ever be. Now all she wanted was to become Aaron's wife.

Maria had loved New York. The new buildings, the wide variety of people milling around, unflinchingly going about their day. *Maybe one day I'll take Aaron there*, she thought. But Scotland was truly home. And she was so glad to be going home.

As she slowly placed the program on the seat beside her, she sighed, relieved that the decision made in the

States had come so easily. On the shores of the Colonies, England's greatest soprano had performed her last opera.

• • •

"She certainly is a beautiful woman, Aaron," Robert Mayfield said from an armchair in the corner of the small room they had taken at the Three Jolly Farmers. "Definitely worth the risk, I might add."

"Isn't she?" Aaron asked, eyes shining. He had felt so old for so long. Being dead definitely had its disadvantages. And hiding away had taken its toll. But now the old boyish sparkle was back in the aqua eyes, and he looked no more than a man a few years out of university. Hopefully, it would all be over soon.

He had seen her! Hopeful. Her eyes scanning the crowd. The quick expression of disappointment passing through the gray eyes. And he knew. She had been looking for him. The slight smile, the quick shake of her head told him she thought herself foolish for even hoping he'd be there. But she had hoped! Never had he loved her more than at that moment. Maria. His Maria. Proud. Talented. Beautiful beyond his imaginings. Totally and unquestionably in love with him.

Robert's laughter brought him back to reality.

"You must think I'm a bit daft," Aaron smiled without apology.

"Not at all," Robert said somewhat wistfully. "Would that the world and all who dwell therein were just as insane. You're a lucky man, Aaron."

Aaron smiled. "I'm a blessed man, Mayfield. Blessed."

CHAPTER
23

How long ago were the ancient stones erected? Who designed the temple, fashioned the trilithon arches in the center of the ring? Who stacked one stone upon two, creating legend out of space and ahead of time? An ancient king? Druids? Some said that Merlin spirited them from Ireland because Uther Pendragon was unable to move them. Others said the devil himself erected the monument. And one local woman swore she saw the stones become living things, to dance about in a circle like great giants, only to petrify once again as the first ray of morning sun kissed their fleshy facades.

Throughout the ages many had believed the mysterious stones contained a healing power. Vainly they would wash the sarcens, pouring that same water into a bath or placing stone scrapings on a grievous wound. Some were healed of their infirmities; others died anyway. Not Merlin, giants, or even the devil could save them. Only the One who created the rock from which the stones were carved could deliver them from sickness of body and soul.

The young earls of Crawford and Beresford rode from the town of Salisbury where they had procured rooms at a local inn, the Lamb and Crown. Quietness except for a gentle wind folded them unto her starlit bosom as a crescent moon reclined in the heavens above. But Lucius didn't care about the moon or the breeze. His lack of speech was caused by the musings of his brain:

Thank you, Supreme Masters. It is a privilege to accept this honor that you have placed upon me. If I have been a dutiful son of the Society, it is because you have fostered a love for the Brotherhood. The oaths and vows so ordained by you knit us together as though we shared one womb.

Yes. It was so easy to imagine what he was going to say. Father would have been proud.

Three hundred yards from the formation they tethered their horses to the branches of a low sprung apple tree. George was quiet, Lucius realized, and the silence continued as they swung their black shrouds around their shoulders and skimmed the cowls up over the backs of their heads to conceal their faces.

George's words issued forth with humorous skepticism. "Are you ready to proceed to the lair of the Supreme Masters?"

Lucius slapped him on the back. "Of course, George, old boy."

George's blue eyes sparkled. "Let's go. I'm glad that at least one of us is taking this whole matter seriously."

They moved quickly toward the circle.

Within the ring of arches, five torches flamed, their pointed sticks invading the chalky soil. The breeze caught at the torches, sucking wisps of fire from each small inferno, to extinguish it with its humid breath. It picked at the long grass of the meadow surrounding the stones, each stalk slavishly dancing to its nocturnal rhythms.

By the altar stone three men in red shrouds congregated and, like the six men standing in black in a semicircle before them, their hoods concealed their identity. Lucius knew that he was finally in the very presence of the Supreme Masters. In total, 11 men were present for the ceremony. He and George joined the others at the right end of the crescent. *Well,* Lucius thought, *this must be quite an exclusive gathering*. He had expected a larger congregation.

When the Masters turned to face this small group of Guardians, they became cloaked in ceremonial anonymity. George and Lucius were the Earl of Crawford and the Earl of Beresford no longer. They were Brothers, and one day years ago on this very spot they had sold their souls to become members of Brimstone. At this place they ceased to be individuals and became part of a collective whole. London made that easy to forget. But not here.

Never here.

Both men shivered involuntarily. The solemnity of the gathering affected Lucius considerably, a heaviness pressing upon his chest. Its weight—the weight of tradition and time, death and dark commitment—were somehow exhilarating, and his limbs felt light and strong as adrenaline fed them its empowering draught.

On the altar stone behind the sacred three, several articles sat: an urn, a goblet, a basket, and a dirk. The Supreme Master, the Ceremonial Lord, stepped forward from the left side. And the ceremony commenced.

Without an utterance he reached forward. His hands were well-formed and strong. No hesitation was to be found in his purposeful movements as he turned and lifted the goblet. It was medieval, an ancient cup, with a large bowl and a squat, thick stem. The carvings were intricate and the workmanship fine. A snake wended its way seemingly through the gold and around the bowl to meet its tail. In both hands he offered the cup to the moon, the goddess of the hunters who had roamed these plains thousands of years before. The man at the right, the Ministering Lord, picked the dirk up off the stone and slid it slowly from its sheath, its blade ever parallel with the ground. As its silver handle caught the torchlight, the blade danced and became a living thing. He handed it to the Ceremonial Lord, who now set down the cup on the center of the stone.

Grasping the knife, the blade still parallel with the ground, he opened his index finger with the sharpened steel. And turning to the cup, he squeezed blood into the shining bowl. The other two Masters did the same. The Ministering Master walked to the far end of the black-shrouded semicircle and handed the dirk to the first man. It was George.

"Do likewise."

Without a sigh or a shudder, George Lindsay stepped up to the stone and, drawing the blade across his finger, he squeezed his own blood, watching for a brief second as the crimson droplets mingled with the contents. Lucius followed suit, as did the rest of the congregation of Brothers.

When all had finished, the Ceremonial Master lifted the cup again in offering to the moon. The handle of the lipped urn met his fingers, and he poured wine—a thick, bitter wine—into the goblet.

He drank. As did the other two.

"Drink likewise, Brothers of Brimstone."

And the cup was passed from man to man, the warm, sticky liquid cleaving to their soft palates like living glue. The Ministering Lord placed the cup back onto the stone. With his thin, roughened hands, he reached into the basket on the altar stone and removed a loaf of bread. Earthen bread. Made by peasant hands and peasant toil.

The Ceremonial Master took the bread and stepped forward. He raised it to the moon as well. Then, lifting the loaf to his mouth, he bit through the crust and passed it to the other Masters.

His words came forth as before. "Eat likewise, Brotherhood."

Again the offering was passed around from man to man, each biting directly from the loaf next to where his Brother had bitten. The remains were placed back into the basket.

"Display homage to Brimstone!" The central figure, the Officiating Master, spoke for the first time.

The Ministering Lord slipped away.

In unison the hands were raised. Each man displaying the scar on his right palm for all to see. And as they had done so many years before, they began to sway as the leader, his massive hand illumined by the moon, chanted in the same dead language they had all heard before. When he ceased his hellish singing, the group halted its bodily echoes of the rhythmic tones. Silence struck the ceremony with such abruptness that it rang in their ears.

The absent Master returned, a scroll now held in his hands. He handed it to the Officiating Master, who stepped forward. Two minutes passed as with head bowed he stood motionless. Not a man present moved even a hair's breadth as he waited. Tension screamed forth, electrically stringing each man to the one beside him. Lucius, as brightly aware of his surroundings as the others, was bursting inside with impatient anticipation. But his iron will prevailed as always, and he stood calmly as not even one muscle on his taut body twitched.

Finally, the Officiating Master took yet another step forward and raised his head.

"Lucius Aurelius Carlyle, come forward."

• • •

It was just the right night for a pork chop. And that was exactly what he ordered. Alone he sat in the hotel dining room. Alone he ate his meal. Alone he called for his carriage. He was tired, and he was old. And oh, so very rapacious.

Being alone was what he loved most. When his wife died eight years ago, he was happy. Yes, happy, joyful, out of his mind with glee. No more dresses to buy, no more parties to give, no more inane talk about people he deemed despicable.

The coach rolled up to the grand entryway, and the footman opened the door for him.

Without looking, he muttered to his driver who was bent over, reaching under his seat for something. "Just take me home, Matthew."

The carriage door shut. Onto his seat the driver settled comfortably and snapped the reins. And darkness ensconced London in a drippy heat. The old man dozed. And the carriage made its way slowly out of the city. Once in the country, the air changed and the man awoke.

"What?" he sat up quickly and looked out the window. He thumped with his cane on the roof and bellowed,

"Matthew! What is the meaning of this? I thought I told you to take me home! Where are we?"

Not a sound from Matthew.

"Stop this carriage. Now! I order you to stop this carriage!"

The man's eyes bulged in fury, and he stomped his foot. And the carriage came to a halt.

"Matthew, come right here. This instant!"

He felt the vehicle sway slightly from side to side as the driver climbed down. When the door opened, the old man opened his mouth to speak, but it sat formed in an *O*. A huge face, dark as the night around it, loomed into the coach. He felt his heart grind within him.

Thaddeus smiled as Beck, brandishing a dagger, leaped into the coach.

"Don't think about calling for help. For surely your throat will be slit before your mouth utters a word."

• • •

The other members shuffled slightly in their shrouds like leftover autumn leaves in a warm spring breeze. Lucius' heart exploded with pride, its muscular form seeming to beat itself against the walls of his chest cavity in a strange, ricocheting tattoo. The back of his neck tightened, its skin becoming strong fingers, hot and constricting.

"Take off your hood," the Master ordered.

With steady hands, Lucius did as he was bid.

The true reason for the gathering had begun.

"Every so often," the Officiating Master said, "a Brother of the Brimstone Society distinguishes himself most certainly, is set apart by his actions, his true commitment to the ideals of the Brotherhood. That, Guardians, is why we are here tonight. For Lucius Carlyle, the Earl of Beresford, is such a man."

I knew it! Lucius was ecstatic, although outwardly he appeared as circumspect as ever.

The Supreme Master continued. "But we should not be surprised by this. Lucius Carlyle comes from a long line of Brimstone faithfuls. The illustrious family has been loyal to the Brotherhood almost since its inception. They have been committed recruiters for the Society, bringing in Brothers who might otherwise have not found their way into our haven. Truly, the Brotherhood of the Brimstone would not be as powerful an organization, would not be able to infiltrate all levels of government, business, and religion, without the trustworthy commitment of Julian Marcus and now Lucius Aurelius Carlyle.

"Brothers here assembled," his voice raised, "we come tonight not simply to pay homage to the Carlyle family, but chiefly to the man who stands before you. It is due to his insight that the Society has increased greatly in wealth over the past year. Did he not see that coal was the wave of the future? And now all of us are benefiting from his vision, his prophetic wisdom. His foresight into the changes of modern times has brought great changes in the separate financial kingdoms of the Guardians, and the lesser members of Brimstone as well. The Society of the Brimstone owes Lucius Carlyle much."

Lucius' head rose higher and higher, as a peculiar pride infused each cell of his body. His ruthless acumen was not simply appreciated, it was honored, revered. And he, Lucius Carlyle, was the recipient. Well he deserved it. For hadn't the Society always climbed to the top of the pyramids of wealth and privilege on the backs of others? The vows, the promises. He had taken advantage of all that Brimstone afforded. He had worked hard, shared his success in hopes of future favors. And now he was being given exactly what he deserved.

"Nevertheless," the Officiating Master continued, and the air grew suddenly still, "the honor of your initiation rite into Brimstone has been compromised."

At first Lucius did not grasp the meaning. *Who has compromised me?* he thought, waiting for an accusation against another Brother to begin. But the Supreme Master's meaning became all too clear, biting, and real, when out of the sinus of his robe he pulled a playing card smeared with Lucius Aurelius Carlyle's own blood. Torn in two. Just as it had been the last time he laid eyes upon it. The last time he laid eyes on Aaron Campbell.

The voice behind the hood became harsh. "What do you say to these charges?"

Lucius' chin raised, and his mind began to churn. "Who accuses me?"

"The Supreme Masters of the Brotherhood of Brimstone."

"And who else? No one knows who you are, lords. Who has made these accusations? And what are they exactly?"

"That I shall answer presently."

The Master opened the scroll. He walked nearer to the torch on his right, unrolled the paper, cleared his throat with one strong exhalation, and began to read.

"Failure to let a Brother carry out his promise of honor.

"Failure to carry out your promise of honor, namely to Aaron Campbell.

"And finally, contracting the murder of a Brother by a Brother under your own authority, without consulting the Society of the Brimstone."

He walked back over to Lucius in the midst of the semicircle and handed him the paper. "What do you have to say regarding these charges?"

Lucius held up the scroll. "Do I have an honest chance to explain my actions which resulted in the charges set herein?"

"You may speak, Lucius Aurelius Carlyle. And you may speak the truth only. For we will know whether or not you lie."

"How?"

"There are those here who will testify to what is and what is not truth."

"Then I stand alone."

"As you say."

Lucius turned and stared at George, who seemed just another anonymous player in his sudden tragedy. "Lindsay," he grated, "if you stand as one of my accusers, be a man about it."

"As you wish."

George threw off his hood. And Lucius immediately regretted his request. For Lindsay, standing taller and stronger than he ever had before, did not impart strength to Lucius by seeming weak and apologetic. His blue eyes glowed with the passions of justice, and he looked directly into Lucius' brown eyes without the smallest dart of the eye or the merest blink of his lids. He squared his shoulders and planted his feet wider, in a battle stance.

Lucius turned back to the council. Perhaps a little humility would be in order. He bowed his head, rapidly formulating in his mind where to start.

"Supreme Masters, I shall give explanation to my action. Regarding the first charge," he looked down and read, " 'Failure to let a Brother carry out his promise of honor.' That is a just accusation, on its face. But turn it over, lords, and you will see a different story. Aaron Campbell, when presented with my queen of spades, agreed to arrange the murder of his brother, Colin Campbell. Having received a message the next day telling me it was all arranged, I was, naturally, very relieved. As you may know, my father, Julian Carlyle, was still alive at that time, although his consumption was so bad I knew he could not last much longer. He was relieved, knowing that Colin's ceased activities in the reform movement would help assure the safety of our family's fortune. That night, right before the time the murder was to take place, I received a second message from Aaron. 'I cannot do it' was written on the paper. Father was upstairs looking into the face of death, and I knew that if Colin Campbell was not killed, he would die even sooner. Loving my father as I did, I would not dishonor him by allowing him to die thinking his family, fortune, and power were left to blow away with time. So I carried out Aaron's original plan. I went to Covent Garden myself. There was not time to hire someone. And there I killed the Duke of Argyll. You have stated tonight that you have all profited from my family's foresight into the emerging industries and their dependency on coal. So, gentlemen, you see that the death of the Duke of Argyll was good for the Brotherhood and for England itself.

"And as to the second charge, this is where it gets a bit complex, lords. I never told Aaron that his hired assassin did not kill his brother. He appeared after his brother's funeral, and after my father's funeral as well, and led me to believe that he thought his assassin did it. 'I didn't make it in time,' he said to me. Almost two years later, when he came back carrying a load of religion and a guilty conscience as well, requesting that I turn myself in with him, I laughed. Even when he handed over his queen. For you see, lords, I knew that Colin's blood was completely upon my hands, and my hands only. I would hang. As surely as a common cutthroat, I would hang until I was just as dead."

The moon slipped behind a darkened cloud.

"That brings us to the third charge . . . arranging the murder of Aaron Campbell. I'm sure I don't have to go into the story completely for you to see why. Aaron had to die, and with him the possibility of the investigation of Colin's murder being opened once again. I knew that it had been a mistake to kill Colin with my own hands. And I knew that Aaron had to die. I called Robert Mayfield, Alex Fairly, and George Lindsay together and told them that Aaron was going to turn me in for the murder of his brother to take the blame off himself. When I tied it all in with Brimstone, saying he was planning to divulge the secrets of the Society . . ."

"A lie, mind you," the first member of the Supreme Masters finally spoke.

Lucius nodded. "Yes. A lie, but an expedient one. Robert Mayfield, whom we all know to be overfond of the idea of a Brotherhood, volunteered. As you all read, Aaron Campbell was found burned in an abandoned mill house. And I was safe from his future deed of conscience and the possibility of the Society coming to light."

The Officiating Master held up a hand. "Lucius Carlyle, come forward and meet your fate."

The Master's voice seemed to come through a long tunnel, attached to some faceless, merciless judge.

"Do you willingly admit that the Duke of Argyll, Colin Campbell, died at your hands?"

"Yes."

"And do you further admit that you arranged through Robert Mayfield the assassination of the next Duke of Argyll, Aaron Campbell?"

"Yes."

"And you killed Colin Campbell purely for the love you bore for an old man?" The contempt in the Master's voice was obvious.

Lucius realized he must be strong. Now was the time to prove he was a force to be reckoned with, a powerful addition to Brimstone. He didn't doubt that the Society was planning to carry out their threat. He had failed to honor his promise. The vow had been clear. And Brimstone hadn't wasted any time in punishing his disobedience.

"No. There were reasons other than my father. I wanted it done just as badly. The old man had managed the family fortune without sense. Our only hope was coal. So I killed Colin Campbell with pleasure. And I would do it again, given the chance. Until the day I die, I shall never regret the night that I murdered that self-righteous man! And the fact that Aaron Campbell is now dead is not something for which I should be placed on trial. It is something the Brotherhood should be thanking me for."

Silence.

An unearthly juxtaposition between past and future melted in the air around the group. And a familiar voice spoke softly from the recesses of a red shroud.

"You're absolutely right, Lucius Carlyle." The Ceremonial Master spoke. This time in a voice that was undisguised.

Horror registered on Lucius' face as, simultaneously, the hoods were drawn down. There before him stood Aaron Campbell. Grinning, face shining empyrean in the moonlight. Next to him stood the Officiating Master, Professor Luther Eliot, scarred palm outstretched. The third Master kept his face concealed. Robert stepped forward from the ranks of the Guardians, as did Lindsay, to join the others.

For the first time in his life, Lucius was dumbfounded. "Who would have thought that you would prove so formidable an adversary, Aaron Campbell? But tell me, what does this masquerade prove, gentlemen? Why the Greek tragedy? Unsheathe your dagger and be done with it."

"No, it won't be that easy, Lucius. We are turning you over to the authorities."

"It will be your word against mine."

"Not quite. Lucius Carlyle," Aaron said, "I'd like you to meet Inspector Glendenning of Scotland Yard. Inspector," he said, putting his hand on the man's arm as the red cowl was pushed back to reveal his face, "here is Lucius Carlyle, the instigator of my murder, and the murderer of my brother, Colin."

"Bind him, Harvey," Glendenning said officiously, as another officer appeared from behind a black hood. "We heard enough to stretch this man's neck a mile and a half."

"I'll fight you to the end," Lucius promised. But he was led off just the same.

The rest of the congregation began to disrobe. Including the five who had originally met in the cemetery. Mr. Boone beamed with broad satisfaction, and they all shook hands, congratulating Aaron, George, and each other.

Aaron held out a hand. "Thank you, Inspector. For all your help."

"Think nothing of it, your grace. I only wish it could bring your brother back."

Aaron bowed his head slightly, knowing now he had done all he could. "I know it could never do that. But it's good to know that from now on the man who took such a light out of the world will be snuffed out himself. Colin is avenged, and I am glad."

It was enough. It had to be.

Professor Eliot laid a bony hand on Aaron's arm. "Justice has been served. And justice is never wrong. You've emerged from this whole episode a man of honor, which is more than most can say."

"Here, here!" said Robert. "What do you say we head into Salisbury to the Lamb and Crown, get a bite to eat, and a good night's sleep? I know I could use it after all of this. I can't tell you how glad I am that it is over!"

"Sounds like a good idea to me," agreed the professor. "How about you, m'lord?"

No one had noticed that the once-again Duke of Argyll had slipped away and was halfway to his horse. "Aaron, old man, where are you going?" Robert yelled.

"To London and the next train to Glasgow!" he yelled over his shoulder. No explanation was necessary.

"Wait for me!" George yelled. "I'll go with you!" He whipped off his shroud and began running. He couldn't wait to get back home to Scotland.

Glendenning sighed as the rest of the Brothers began to assemble near him. They each handed him a sheet of paper. "I've got to finish this job in London. With these signed confessions and the information you've already given us, we should have more than enough evidence to implicate Barringer and many of the Guardians. The work has just begun. We will start with the press, tell them everything."

"That which has thriven in darkness will be brought into the light of day," Eliot said.

Each man present felt a profound relief.

Glendenning finished up. "All right, sirs! Go home and get a good night's sleep. You will need it. We are beginning the arrests tomorrow. I'd advise you to quit London for the next month or so. We've already begun to work with the courts, and you will be notified when it is safe to return. For I assure you, some will escape before we can find them, and you will not be safe if they should find you!"

The inspector bowed and turned to go. George's compatriots followed.

"So," said Robert to the professor, remembering him from Oxford, "it looks as if only you and I are left to one another's company. Shall we be off?"

"Certainly, lad."

"You were Colin's mentor, I believe Aaron told me?" Hope sprang from his voice.

"Yes, Robert, I was."

"Would you be of a mind for some conversation in front of the fire at the Lamb and Crown?" Robert asked.

"Being in an inn so named, I'm confident our conversation will be quite beneficial."

And in the small hours of the morning, Professor Eliot once again was able to bring a young man to the Savior. His love for ancient history could not be compared to the joy he felt at ushering someone into the kingdom of heaven. In paying for his terrible deed of long ago, he had been blessed by the Lord beyond all expectation.

· · ·

"I'll have an answer from you," Silas Barringer said through clenched teeth.

"Aye, you will," Beck answered. "We're taking you back to the bank, and I'll tell you, Mr. Barringer, if you want answers you'll have to pay."

An hour later Silas Barringer stood by the great safe. "How much? Ten thousand? Twenty thousand?"

Beck kept the knife near the old man's neck. "Fifty thousand pounds."

"You jest!"

"Oh no, surely we don't jest, sir." Beck was enjoying it all immensely, although his exterior was as stoic as ever.

The great chin lifted in a last-ditch effort at defiance. "And if I don't agree?"

Beck shrugged loosely. "You'll die." He spoke the news as one telling the time.

"You'll never get away with it."

Thaddeus laughed, his great shoulders shaking. "Mr. Barringer, we know about getting away with things as much as you do."

Beck pricked the side of Barringer's neck. "Being a Supreme Master can be an expensive proposition, Mr. Barringer. It's hard to keep something like that a secret once someone knows. Of course, if we're rich and gone from Britain, there will be no one the wiser."

"All right." His voice was agitated, aggravated. And he reached in and counted out the money. "Here. Now off you go. And don't say a word of this to anyone."

Beck moved lithely toward the window. "We won't have to. Somebody's already done that for us."

"What?"

Beck slipped out onto the sill, and Thaddeus followed with surprising ease. Jacob Beck leaned back in. "They're on their way up the stairs now. In fact, they should be opening the door just about . . . now."

The door opened, and Jacob Beck and Thaddeus disappeared into the dark world they would never leave.

The old man shook his fist and shouted. "You double-crossing . . ."

Jonah Glendenning spoke with an iron voice. "Silas Barringer, you are under arrest."

And the old man was taken away in shackles, bearing the load of his sins and those of his father before him.

CHAPTER
24

Martha ran as fast as she could. The pins worked their way out of her black bun, and her heels dug into the turf as she made her way to the shore of the loch. Maria sat in quiet contemplation, the waiting growing harder each day. True, she hadn't been back to Scotland long, but not being able to see Aaron right away made it seem as if she had been waiting forever.

No word yet. But she knew it was only a matter of time. Aaron was the man she loved, and he would be back if it took years to bring down Brimstone. And knowing he would bring that about was worth the wait.

"Mrs. Rosetti!" Martha puffed as she achieved her destination.

"What is it, Martha?"

"A carriage has come. You're summoned to Inveraray, and the matter is urgent."

"Did they say what it is about?"

"No, ma'am. Here is the note." She held it forward.

Maria pulled it open and read an unfamiliar handwriting, presumably Chastain's. It told her nothing more than Martha had already.

• • •

The turret room was freshened and ready for her arrival. All during the carriage ride, Maria was torn. Was the news good or bad? She didn't know. But she prayed intensely that today would be the day she would behold the face of her beloved again.

The doubts and fears were quickly removed when she saw what lay on the bed.

"Oh, Mrs. Rosetti!" Martha gasped. "It's beautiful."

"And it can mean only one thing!" Maria rejoiced, picking up the white gown and hugging it to her chest. "Today is my wedding day!"

• • •

Sometimes the most simple things are the most beautiful.

Maria let Martha help her into the plain gown with haste. It was comprised of a flowing shift of soft white linen with full sleeves. Over that she put on a white velvet bodice that laced up the front. The bottom of it was embroidered with a thin, delicate row of twining leaves. And for her hair there was a wreath of ivy with pink rosebuds mingled at variance through the greenery. Two long strands of ribbon fell down the back to her waist.

"You look like a medieval lady," Martha remarked, the simple nature of the costume right in line with her own ideals. "It suits you well, ma'am."

She was right. Maria had never looked lovelier. All the silks, satins, laces, and jewels she had worn with an almost religious regularity had been serving all these years to mask her natural beauty. After a quick glance in the mirror, she picked up the small bouquet of fragrant pink roses and proceeded carefully down the steps.

• • •

Aaron waited impatiently in the garden for his beloved's arrival. The gown he had provided had been purposely simple. He wanted her down by his side as quickly as possible. He himself had been ready for hours, and the wait was excruciating. The pleats in his kilt were pressed perfectly, and over a black jacket his plaid in the Campbell tartan fell from an ancient pin worn by his ancestors. His white shirt shone in the sunshine, and the blondness of his hair glistened as the summer breeze blew it across his forehead. More brightly the aqua eyes had never shone.

She was there. On the arm of Chastain. And Aaron inhaled quickly at the sight of her. His life had been turned upside down, and for so long he didn't know whether he would wind up on his head or his feet. But standing there now, his feet firmly planted on the ground, he knew the path before him was bright with promise. Maria was there, his own Scottish lassie, to walk beside him through sun, rain, and storm.

They vowed then to one another and their God that it would always be that way. It was sealed with a precious kiss, long missed, eagerly awaited.

Life wasn't going to be easy. He was learning to fight a good fight, and it was true that the past year had helped to prepare him for future battles in Britain's rough terrain of political warfare. *Fight a good fight.* Aaron knew God would aid him. And though he would be tempted to ease up on his newfound commitments, to live a life of separation from the trials of grueling service, he took comfort in the words of the apostle Paul: "God will not allow you to be tempted above that which ye are able to bear." And Aaron knew it was so.

Epilogue

The Duke of Argyll was shown into the Earl of Crawford's bedchamber. It was a day common to the Highlands, a light rain diffusing itself through the atmosphere. And the way to his friend's ancestral home in Kincardine had been taxing.

George Lindsay smiled weakly, the tartan coverlet tucked around his waist. "You've come."

Aaron Campbell sat down with a groan and put his cane across his knees.

"Well, Lindsay, I figured it was urgent."

George closed his eyes. "Aye, my friend. The time has come."

Aaron placed a hand on George's bony one, not knowing what to say.

Through the years George had been with him through each celebration. And there had been many. Seven children. All grown now and living in various parts of the world. His eldest son, Colin, was still at Inveraray, handling with certain capability the estates of the Campbells.

The two men had shared political victories as well, continuing to help the children of the mines and gaining the title "Sons of Thunder" from other members of Parliament. And George had shared in all of the trials Aaron faced during the 40 years since Brimstone fell. Robert, divorced by his wife, died 5 years after Stonehenge, killed by the hostile tribe in Africa he was so desperately trying to reach for the Savior. Chastain lived to the ripe old age of 88, gone now for almost 20 years. Mother returned eventually and lived out her life for her grandchildren. And then Maria's death three years ago was the sorest time Aaron's soul had yet to bear. But George was always there, extending his sympathy and the hand of a brother.

"I believe I am finally ready to go, Aaron, my friend."

Aaron looked sharply into Lindsay's eyes. The only thing they hadn't shared during their turbulent lives was a love for the Savior. Aaron had never stopped praying, though. "What are you saying, old friend? Can it be true?"

George nodded, that boyish sparkle still evident in his pale-blue eyes. "Aye, old boy. As I lay here, knowing death was coming soon, I realized that nothing could be worse than going to a place described as fire and brimstone and spending eternity with the likes of Barringer and Lucius Carlyle."

Aaron chuckled with a bit of a wheeze.

George continued. "I've wasted my life and now, I am sad to say, I have waited until the end of my life to believe."

Aaron's soul soared. "But you *have* believed. And that is all that is required."

"And so I can finally go. God was merciful to me, Aaron. He was truly merciful."

"To die is gain, George."

"Aye . . ." the eyes closed, "to die is gain."

Four hours later George Lindsay traveled from a world of care to a joy-filled heaven.

So I am the only one left, Aaron thought two days later as he stood by the grave of his dear friend. Everyone had gone on before him, and although he should have felt alone, he didn't. They were waiting for him above. Obviously, God still had plans for Aaron Campbell here on earth.

As the death bell tolled and the mourners began to leave, Aaron followed suit, tamping his hat down upon his shocking white hair. He was an old man, and though he leaned heavily upon his cane to ease the pain in his right hip, he walked as a dignified statesman. He had lived a full life and had loved with a full heart.

The road before him was as mysterious as it ever was, but he knew the Savior was still beside him, still had a hold of the hand Aaron had placed in His so many years before. And as he did each morning when he arose, Aaron thought afresh, *This is only the beginning.* Life with the Father never ceased to be an adventure.

About the Author

Lisa Samson has always had a keen interest in history. During a time of study at Oxford University, she fell in love with British history, and out of that love grew *The Highlander and His Lady*, her first novel, and *The Legend of Robin Brodie*, her second novel in this Highlander Series. A graduate of Liberty University with a degree in telecommunications, Lisa lives in Virginia with her husband, Will, daughter, Tyler, and son, Jake.

The Highlanders—

a striking series set in eighteenth-century Scotland,
where love is tested, passions run deep, and
an abiding faith in God moves
men and women to action.

by **Lisa Samson**

The Highlander and His Lady

A man of quiet strength and unwavering loyalty, Kyle Mac-
Lachlan is bound by honor to stand with his clansmen in their war
with the British. Destined to rule his people, nothing stirs his soul
like his zeal for clan and country... until Jenny.

Raised under mysterious circumstances, Jenny Matheson led a
simple, sheltered life... until Kyle. In him she finds a kindred
spirit, a man whose heart beats as her own.

> *Two people whose lives meet at the crossroads.*
> *He follows a call to duty.*
> *She yearns for a new beginning.*
> *Have they fallen in love only to lose everything?*

The Legend of Robin Brodie

In the woods of Scotland he was a legend–a guardian of the ancient ways, an unseen protector of the innocent. With bow in hand,
a wolf at his side, and a refusal to give up his kilt and plaid, Robin
Brodie carves out a solitary existence as a guardsman against the
enemies of Scotland. Only in one woman–Alix Maclachlan–does
he find a loving soul who touches the depths of his troubled heart.

> *His love knew no end,*
> *though she could never be his.*
> *What will he sacrifice to protect her?*

Other Good
Harvest House Fiction

LORI WICK

Sophie's Heart

A Place Called Home

A Place Called Home
A Song for Silas
The Long Road Home
A Gathering of Memories

The Californians

Whatever Tomorrow Brings
As Time Goes By
Sean Donovan
Donovan's Daughter

The Kensington Chronicles

The Hawk and the Jewel
Wings of the Morning
Who Brings Forth the Wind
The Knight and the Dove

MARYANN MINATRA
The Alcott Legacy

The Tapestry
The Masterpiece
The Heirloom

ELLEN TRAYLOR

Esther
Joseph
Moses
Joshua
Samson
Jerusalem